BOOK OF THE DEAD

A ZOMBIE ANTHOLOGY

OTHER LIVING DEAD PRESS BOOKS

THE ZOMBIE IN THE BASEMENT (YOUNG ADULT)
FAMILY OF THE DEAD
DEAD WORLDS: UNDEAD STORIES VOLUME 1, 2 & 3
END OF DAYS: AN APOCALYPTIC ANTHOLOGY 1
REVOLUTION OF THE DEAD
KINGDOM OF THE DEAD
THE MONSTER UNDER THE BED
DEAD TALES: SHORT STORIES TO DIE FOR
ROAD KILL: A ZOMBIE TALE
DEAD MOURNING: A ZOMBIE HORROR STORY
DEADFREEZE
DEADFALL
SOUL-EATER
THE DARK
RISE OF THE DEAD
DARK PLACES
VISIONS OF THE DEAD: A ZOMBIE STORY
THE LAZARUS CULTURE: A ZOMBIE NOVEL
RANY AND WALTER: PORTRAIT OF TWO KILLERS
THE DEADWATER SERIES
DEADWATER
DEADWATER: Expanded Edition
DEADRAIN
DEADCITY
DEADWAVE
DEAD HARVEST
DEAD UNION
DEAD VALLEY
DEAD TOWN
DEAD SALVATION
DEAD ARMY

COMING SOON

BOOK OF THE DEAD VOLUME 2
BLOOD RAGE by Anthony Giangregorio
DEAD WORLDS: UNDEAD STORIES 4, 5
DEAD CHRISTMAS: A Zombie Anthology

BOOK OF THE DEAD

A ZOMBIE ANTHOLOGY

EDITED BY
ANTHONY GIANGREGORIO

BOOK OF THE DEAD: A ZOMBIE ANTHOLOGY

For more info on obtaining additional copies of this book, contact:
www.livingdeadpress.com
2nd Edition Revised

Table of Contents

FOREWORD

The book you hold in your hands is more than just a book to me. It's a homage to the past.

I, as a person, am very nostalgic. I have a 1970 Harley Davidson and a 1969 Chevrolet Camaro, and when I drive them, they are not just vehicles, but a window into the past. When I think about the day they rolled off the showroom floor, back in the 70's, and how life was back then...well, like always, I digress.

Imagine this; the *internet* wasn't a word anyone knew back then.

It didn't exist.

Hard for the young ones to understand, but if you're in your forties like me, it will always bring a chuckle to each of us my age or older.

A time without the internet seems like a barbaric way to live.

How did people communicate? How did you find out what your favorite stars were thinking a minute after they thought it?

Well, we did have the telephone and television, though cable didn't exist. There were maybe seven or eight channels on the television, 2, 4, 5, 7, 25, 38, and 56.

That was it.

After 7:30 pm, and *Zoom* and *The Electric Company* were over on PBS, there were no longer any children's shows on. There were no cartoons to watch and the TV shows that were on were all geared toward adults; though Saturday mornings were killer.

So you say what the hell does any of this have to do with this book?

Well, everything.

I love the past and one of the things I truly enjoyed was the Book of the Dead. The publisher got together a bunch of zombie stories in the 1990's when zombie stories weren't cool. And they did it all for the simple love of the genre.

But, though the book is filled with great stories, many of the tales are *not* classic-type zombie stories.

And the reason for this is simple.

As an editor, if you go to the great names of the time and ask them to write you a zombie tale, you don't turn it down if it's not exactly what you wanted. So, though the book is wonderful, as a homage to what a zombie truly is, it falls vastly short.

And this, too, for almost every zombie anthology I have ever read, past and present. There is always that one or two stories that don't fit, either by having talking zombies, or ones that use firearms. Or the worst, the zombie love story.

And as I have dabbled in the zombie universe, I decided it was time to do it right.

So every single tale in this book is faithful to what a zombie should truly be.

Each story has to portray a certain tone that couldn't be explained to the writers, but had to be felt by the reader.

The stories herein are the best of the lot. There are no killer viruses, fast running zombies, no zombies that think or want to have coffee with you. There are no stories that go on and on and at the end you find out the character is a zombie; and the entire time not one gut-munching moment.

So, if I did my job right, then each of these stories could be dropped into a universe where slow moving zombies rule the land.

Of course, you may not agree with all my choices, but at the risk of sounding selfish, this book was made for me alone, though I also made it for fellow fans of the genre.

And so, to wrap this up. This is the go to book for what the true zombie is; a walking, flesh-eating, animated corpse that for some unknown reason has risen from the dead and now wants to eat the flesh of the living.

It's a simple formula; one that I love, and I believe there are many others out there in the world that feel the same way.

So welcome to the *Book the Dead*, and remember, enjoy life now, because no matter whom you are or how far you run, in the end, Death will find you.

Anthony Giangregorio
July 2009

KELLY M. HUDSON

CASEY'S LAST STAND

All around the world, the recently dead were coming back to life and killing any living human they ran across. Casey Davender didn't know about this because Casey was a man consumed by a desire for revenge and justice. He'd driven his truck down to Hound Holler with one mission in mind: kill Barry White.

Casey jammed on the gas and crashed through the gate of Barry's farm, snapping the rusty chain and lock that held it shut. The chain flew off and landed with a thunk out in the bumpy grass as the lock tumbled off in the opposite direction. The gate banged open, swung out, and slammed against the fence.

Casey had to slow down once he was through because the road was full of potholes. He didn't go too slowly, however, because his fury towards Barry White was burning too hot in his chest.

Barry White, a man Casey had known and loathed his entire life. Barry, despite the color of his namesake's skin, was as ivory as his last name, the polar opposite of Casey, who was as black as a chunk of coal and proud of it.

Casey and Barry had gone to school together and hated each other every step of the way. Barry despised blacks and tried in vain to resurrect the Klan, with him as the leader. When that didn't work, Barry dropped out of high school and started cooking up Crystal Meth, his sole purpose to crush the blacks the way they did it in the big cities up north: he'd sell them drugs.

Casey had gone on to college and was on his summer break from studying English at the University. He wore a fat afro and normally dressed in traditional African garb. Tonight, however, he was decked out in all black, his leather jacket and beret a throwback to the Black Panthers.

Casey was tall and thin but had the body of a boxer. He ran five miles every morning and swam at the University when the weather was too inclement for him to go jogging. He had fierce, focused eyes and was handsome in his own way, if a little too hillbilly for most of the girls at school. He was smart and studious and had a bad temper, much to his detriment.

Casey rolled his window down and felt the warm summer wind against his cheek as he stared into the blackness of the night. Clouds covered the sky, blocking out the stars and moon, which was nearly full, making the gloomy night darker still. Up ahead, in the spill of his truck lights, stood Barry's house and out behind it, the barn where Barry cooked the meth, the drug that had nearly killed Casey's younger brother, Chester.

That was why Casey was on a tear. He'd come back home for the summer to help his mother work the small farm she owned and found Chester hooked on meth, now just a shivering, sad mess of a kid. Casey had asked around and found that Barry was still in charge of the drugs, and in fact was poisoning lots of poor folks, black and white. Casey's bad temper took over and he grabbed his shotgun, some shells, and jumped into his truck.

The farmhouse loomed up ahead. It was a squat, fat building with shutters that hung on like a suicide jumper who'd changed his mind at the last second. A long porch dotted with chairs ran along the front of the house, and had at one end a busted swing hanging on two chains. One end of it scraped the floor every time a slight breeze came along. Barry's mother lived in the house, but she was senile and slow and wasn't involved in the drug business.

Casey drove around the house and to the barn, where he slammed on his brakes. His truck skidded to a stop just short of three dead bodies that were lying on the ground in front of the open barn door. He turned his truck off, grabbed his shotgun, and got out. Casey checked behind him and up ahead but didn't see anybody.

A single light, hanging above the barn doors, illuminated the ground in front of Casey. He bent down and looked at the body closest to him. It was a man, about Casey's age, lying on his stomach, and he was certainly dead because he wasn't breathing and when Casey checked his pulse he got nothing. The second body was that of a woman lying on her back, staring straight up into the sky. Her eyes didn't blink. Her ample chest didn't move, either, and Casey didn't bother with her pulse. She was as dead as a pile of road kill.

The last body was another woman that lay on her side, and Casey recognized her. It was Rhonda, a girl he'd gone to school with, the Valedictorian who'd had the brightest future ahead of her. He hardly recognized her because she was so skinny, like a skeleton, and her eyes were sunken in like something had stuck a vacuum cleaner inside her head, pointed it at the front of her skull, and turned it on. But he was sure it was her, and he was also sure she was dead.

So were the eight other bodies inside the barn, all lying in different positions around tables full of whatever it was that they used to make the Crystal Meth. Casey had walked inside and carefully worked his way through the big, open space, the florescent overhead lights brightening the room so Casey could see the entire scene in all its surreal glory. The door to the back of the barn was open and a few scattered dead bodies were lying out there, too. Casey looked them over and his nose wrinkled from the smell inside the barn. It was faint but pungent and Casey reckoned if he spent any more time in the barn, he might get sick. He also figured whatever was in the air was what had killed those people. He walked out the back of the barn, careful not to step on anyone or anything.

Once outside, Casey glanced up and saw a big machine, one of those backhoes, suddenly surge to life. Black smoke vomited from its exhaust and it ran around what looked to be a big pit dug into the ground. Riding the backhoe, fat and pale as Moby Dick, was Barry White. He looked just like Casey remembered him, chubby and stupid, with brown, beady eyes, tufts of wispy hair on his head, and wearing the same pair of overalls he'd worn in high school. Barry sported layers of gold chains around his throat like some kind of redneck Mr. T.

Barry shifted some gears and the backhoe dug out a hunk of earth and dumped it on a mound of soil dirt to the pit. Casey crept closer to check it out and Barry, concentrating on his work, didn't notice him at all. The pit was a good eight feet deep and about twenty yards square. Casey shook his head, raised his shotgun into the air, and fired off both barrels.

Barry's head jerked and when he laid eyes on Casey, he gave him an awkward smile. Barry turned the machine off and slowly climbed out; weighed down by his fat ass, all those gold chains, and what looked to be, from the expression on his face, a guilty conscience.

"Howdy," Barry said. He wiped his hands on the sides of his overalls and waved meekly at Casey.

"You kill them people?" Casey asked. He normally had better diction, but when he got riled, the country boy in him came out. And right then, Casey was riled.

"What? Oh, hell no, son. They was in there working when something went wrong," Barry said. He glanced at the shotgun Casey was brandishing at him, something he hadn't really noted up to that point. "Such is the nature of the business. Say, why you got the gun?"

"I've come here to kill your cracker ass," Casey said. He held the gun up and aimed it at Barry's chest.

"Now why would you do that? I ain't done nothin' to you," Barry said. He'd stopped walking and stood next to the backhoe. His eyes flicked over and settled on the .357 stashed under the seat.

"You got my brother high and now he's hooked," Casey said.

"That's on him. He chose to sample the goods. I didn't tie him down and make him do anything," Barry said. He edged back a little more.

"And now you done killed those folks inside. What were you planning on doing with them? Burying them and pretending nothing happened?" Casey said, his finger tightened on the trigger.

"Something like that," Barry said. "I was gonna bury 'em and then recruit some new folks to work the barn. Can't fault me for that. They signed up to work knowing the risks. Hell, they're lucky they didn't get blowed up."

"You're lucky I don't cut you in half right now," Casey said. "And don't think about going for that pistol, either."

Barry's hand froze and he withdrew it back from the seat. He looked up at Casey and then his face fell. His color went whiter than white, if that was even possible. He stared past Casey and shook his head slowly.

"I guess they didn't die," Barry said. He pointed at the barn behind Casey.

"I ain't that stupid," Casey said. He held the gun firmly on Barry. But he couldn't figure out how Barry was faking it so well because the dumb son of a bitch sure looked shocked.

A piece of glass crunched behind Casey and he whirled around, afraid that maybe some of Barry's business partners had come over and were about to jump him. Instead, what he saw nearly made him go as white as Barry had.

The dead people, poisoned by the meth gasses, were standing upright and shuffling towards him, a low moan coming from some of their mouths. They didn't look right, their skin blotchy purple in some spots and dull and almost translucent in others. Casey's first thought was that they hadn't died, just like Barry had said, but he could feel in his guts that something wasn't right about them.

They shambled forward, stumbling like their legs were made of limp noodles, casting long, dark shadows across the ground from the barn light behind them.

Casey took a step back and nearly screamed when he bumped into Barry, who'd run over behind him. Barry stared at the risen dead, the .357 filling his fat hand, and Casey stared at him, fascinated for a moment by the trickle of tobacco juice running from the left corner of his mouth and down his chin. It pooled in the rolls of fat on his neck and then dripped over and stained the top of his gold chains.

"I'll be damned," Barry said. His breath smelled sweet and tangy from the tobacco in his mouth. He worked the wad back and forth, from one cheek to the next, like a nervous habit on steroids.

Up above, the clouds parted as if by some miracle and the moon, full and bright, cast its radiance down on the countryside, throwing the lurching dead into bright relief. Casey and Barry could see them much better now, and it was clear that something wasn't right with them.

"What in the hell is going on out here?" Barry's Momma shouted, stumbling through the barn. She was a sight to see, standing just four feet tall, with peppered gray hair fluffing on the top of her head in patches just like her son's. She limped, a metal brace that ran from the middle of her left thigh and down into a big boot that flopped around—obviously too large for her foot— squeaking like a gerbil running on one of those spinning wheels. She wore a flower print dress that she'd hiked up and held in both hands as she stormed over towards Casey and Barry, her thick glasses glinting in the light from the barn.

"I was watching my programs," she said. "And all this racket's getting on my nerves."

"Go back inside, Momma," Barry said.

"Boy, I squirted you out between my legs, bathed and fed you. Don't you tell me what to do," Momma said. "Honor thy mother."

Barry turned to Casey. "Momma's got a bit of a temper."

Momma walked amongst the dead, pushing one dead girl out her way, causing the girl's feet to tangle with a boy next to her. They both tripped and fell in a heap.

"And who're these morons?" Momma asked, wrinkling her nose up in disgust. "They stink to high heaven."

A dead woman, the left half of her face one big bruise from lay- ing on it as the blood pooled inside of her, tilted her head and buried her teeth into Momma's neck and yanked back, tearing a chunk of skin out that glistened wet in the glowing moonlight. Blood arced out of the gash and suddenly the dead surrounding Momma all groaned and turned, as if some light switch was turned on in their decaying brains. They fell on the old woman, their teeth clacking together, searching for soft, warm flesh.

Momma screamed and dropped the dress she was holding up and started throwing punches. She was a tough old bag and wasn't going down without a fight. Unfortunately for her, there were too many of the dead. They bit her arms and legs and stabbed at her with their greedy fingers, gouging flesh and tearing holes in her that weren't the least bit natural. Her fists found yielding bones but unyielding resolve. For every punch she landed, one of the dead ripped her skin open and more of her blood poured out and splat- tered on the ground.

Momma staggered a couple of steps and then fell down, the metal brace on her leg cracking and snapping.

Casey didn't move, completely stunned by what was happening before his very eyes. He held his shotgun out in front of him and watched as Barry's mother was torn apart. The dead dug in, tearing her to pieces. One girl dug her fingers in at the top of her scalp and ripped back, pulling off the top flap of skin. Tufts of hair were torn from her head and then the dead woman pressed her fingers down, pushing in and cracking Momma's skull.

Barry screamed his mother's name and charged into the dead, firing his gun wildly, with only a couple of bullets striking one of the ghouls. The rounds thumped the creature in its back and knocked it on its face. The thing got right back up, congealed blood and pieces of its intestines dripping from the hole the bullets tore out of its stomach, as it lunged forward and bit Momma's leg.

Casey started walking backwards, scared and out of sorts. He didn't know what was going on, but he knew he wanted far, far away from this horrible place. He turned to run when his feet found open and air Casey looked down, feeling very much like the Roadrunner from those old cartoons, as he saw he'd run out over the opening of the pit Barry had dug. Casey dropped into it, hitting the ground and rolling.

He stood up and looked into the sky, wanting to scream. Casey ran over to the far end of the pit, his feet slipping in soft, wet mud, and tried to jump up and out. His hands found the top of the hole but the ground was too damp and it came out in clumps as he fell back on his ass. He slid a couple of feet and hit something metal. It was his shotgun. Casey realized he'd dropped it when he fell in and was glad to find it so quickly. He stood and slipped again, nearly falling. It was treacherous inside that pit and would be hard going, but he'd have to do it. He'd have to climb out somehow and get to safety.

Up out of the hole he heard Barry scream and then heard him cuss such a blue streak as to make Satan blush. Then it all went quiet up there and Casey wished he could see what was going on. He listened hard, standing his ground, and heard the whispering of naked feet brushing over the grass and the continuous moan coming from the mouths of the dead.

This quiet was suddenly interrupted by the cranking of an engine and then the belching roar of the backhoe. Casey walked backwards so that his back was against the wall of the hole and he went to his toes, straining to see what was going on out there.

"Yahoo!" he heard Barry yelp and then all at once, he saw the arm of the backhoe, sweeping six of the walking dead over to the edge of the pit to dump them down into it. They fell on their faces and then stood up, awkwardly trying to maintain their balance in the slick mud.

Of the six, two were woman and four were men. Casey didn't recognize any of them except for one of the girls. It was Rhonda, the Valedictorian. Her face was smeared with blood and a long string of flesh hung from the corner of her mouth. Upon closer inspection, Casey reckoned it was a ligament, or a tendon of some sort. Rhonda opened her mouth and groaned and Casey could see that the ligament was jammed between two of her teeth, stuck there and hanging like a whipped puppy dog's tail.

The dead moved towards Casey, intent on making a meal of him.

Barry let out another whoop and Casey saw the arm of the backhoe again and this time it swept four more of the dead into the pit. These bodies landed on those that had just gotten to their feet, knocking them down again.

One of the newly arrived dead, a man with a big hat that was pulled down so tight over his head that his ears bulged out, stood up. In doing so, Big Hat stepped on the ligament hanging from Rhonda's mouth as she lay on the ground. Rhonda, oblivious to what was happening, leaned back and sat up on her haunches. The ligament ripped from her mouth, jerking out four teeth with it. The teeth tumbled across the dark mud like someone throwing dice and gleamed white in the moonlight.

Ten dead people got to their feet and shambled towards Casey, their eyes dull of intent but their mouths open and dripping with saliva.

Casey checked his shotgun. He had two shells in it, full of buckshot. He felt in his pockets and quickly counted how much ammo he'd brought with him and reckoned it would be enough. He'd grabbed a couple of handfuls when he left the house, hasty with anger, and if he remembered correctly, most of them had been buckshot, but a few had been slugs. It didn't matter, though.

Whatever these people were, if they were hopped up on meth or something else entirely, he had enough to deal with them.

He aimed his shotgun at Big Hat's legs and let go with both barrels. Big Hat's knees shattered, shredded by the buzzing buckshot, and he fell forward, landing full on his face. Casey smiled and reloaded.

Big Hat, his eyes still dull and showing no pain, looked up at Casey and reached out, clawing the mud in front of him. Big Hat dragged his body towards Casey as the dead behind him shuffled forward.

Casey looked down at Big Hat. His legs were severed at the knees and goopy, congealed blood, black as a witch's hat, dribbled from the stumps. How Big Hat was still moving let alone coming after him was something Casey couldn't figure.

Up above, the backhoe rumbled and farted out dark smoke and shook the ground as Barry rode it around. He whooped and hollered and Casey looked up as the arm swung around again and four more dead people fell into the pit. They got to their feet, stared at Casey, and shambled towards him.

Big Hat was only two feet away now, moaning low and reaching for Casey's feet. Casey put the barrels of the shotgun to the front of Big Hat's face and pulled the trigger. The hat flew off and up into the air, landing on the head of one of the dead stumbling towards Casey while Big Hat's head exploded, bone, brains and black blood flying out in every direction. Big Hat stopped moving. Casey grinned to himself. Shoot them in the head, he reckoned, was the only way to put them down for good.

The dead pressed themselves towards Casey, five feet away and closing. He brought the gun up, reloaded, and shot the dead man who was wearing Big Hat's hat in the head. This time the hat flopped off and fell into the mud, joined by the body of its host, his head sheared in half by the buckshot.

Casey reloaded, aimed for Rhonda's head, and blew the back of her skull out. Rhonda's body slipped in the mud from the force of the blast, flew up into the air, and landed on its back. Two dead people behind her tripped over her prone body and fell to the side.

The walking dead were three feet away now, their arms outstretched like some kind of Frankenstein monster, their fingers ripping at the air in front of them, eager to tear his tender flesh.

Casey reloaded.

One dead person, this one wearing a flannel shirt and blue jeans, had a face purple from death and dotted with bits of black blood and pieces of Rhonda's head. It lurched at Casey, who stepped back, brought the shotgun around, and clocked Flannel Shirt upside his head. Teeth rained like broken glass but Flannel Shirt simply turned his head back towards Casey and reached for him, unphased by the blow.

Casey brought the shotgun up, pushed it under Flannel Shirt's jaw, and pulled the trigger. Flannel Shirt's jawbone burst from his head and flew to the left; spinning like a boomerang, then became jammed into the right eye of a dead woman wearing a plaid dress behind him. The jawbone slammed into the brain of Plaid Dress and she slumped over and crumpled into a ball. The rest of Flannel Shirt's head splashed into hundreds of pieces, flying into the air and washing down on the other dead people, now only two feet away.

They were too close and there was still too many of them for Casey to defend himself. He'd been cocky just moments before, thinking that they being so slow and he being so loaded with shotgun shells that they'd be easy pickings, but now he knew how wrong he'd been.

Casey took a step back and his butt hit the solid wall of mud behind him and he had nowhere else to run. The dead reached for him, fingers scraping the air just inches from his face.

In a moment of inspired genius, Casey dropped to his haunches and threw himself forward, rolling into a ball and ramming the dead all around him. He pictured himself as a bowling ball and the dead as the pins at the end of the alley. He would bowl a strike or he was dead.

The move worked, for the most part. The dead tripped and fell over each other as Casey kept rolling. He came through on the other side of them and stood up, feeling triumphant until he got dizzy and the ground pitched to his left and he thought he might fall. Casey shook his head clear just in time to see the dead recover, turn, and stalk towards him once again.

He backed up, firing his shotgun and reloading. He killed two more of them, leaving eight of them and him. Casey took a deep breath, cracked open his shotgun, and reloaded. A wad of tobacco juice hit him in his left eye, blinding him for a moment and nearly causing him to drop his gun. Something cold and hard whacked him upside his head, then slapped his hands and knocked the shotgun to the ground. Casey staggered and fell against the wall of the pit.

"How ya doing down there?" Barry asked.

He was standing at the lip of the hole, holding a long metal pole and chewing his wad of tobacco. Casey glared up at him and saw that he wasn't looking so good. Blood poured from several torn holes in his arms where it looked like he'd been bitten on and chewed. Barry had another one of those gouges in his neck and it was bleeding worse than his arms, pouring down and staining his overalls black. He looked like a guy that worked in a factory slaughtering hogs returning home from a hard day's work.

"Help me," Casey said, wiping the tobacco spit from his eye.

"Boy, you are one crazy negro," Barry laughed. His voice was hoarse and his eyes were bloodshot. "You know what that is down there with you? Them's the dead, and they come to eat ya."

"It's us against them," Casey said.

"Boy, there's only one thing worse than the walking dead," Barry said. "And that's a nigger."

Casey leapt and grabbed the pole Barry had swung at him, snatching it from his hands. He used the end of it to jab Barry in the stomach.

"Cracker!" Casey said.

Behind him, the dead closed in.

Casey swung the pole and popped Barry on the side of his head and the man fell down and disappeared from Casey's view. Casey stumbled back and laughed out loud.

A dead man, shirtless with buckteeth, chomped on Casey's right hand. His teeth raked the skin off of the back of Casey's hand and Casey jerked it away, dropping the pole in the process. Buckteeth gobbled down the flap of flesh and lurched forward as another of the dead, this one a woman with a tall, beehive hairdo, grabbed Casey's shoulder and pinched a piece of skin off under his shirt. Casey punched Beehive in her nose, shattering it. Thick black blood burbled from Beehive's nostrils but she kept coming, like they all did.

The dead had Casey pinned to the wall and were inches away from their feast when Casey dropped and tried his bowling ball roll again. This time, though, he failed. The dead fell on him, pinning him beneath their weight.

Their bodies pressed down on him and Casey couldn't see the moon or the stars anymore. All he saw was darkness and the occasional flash of skin and clothing. They stunk, these walking dead, of the chemicals that killed them and the shit they'd crapped on themselves when they died.

Casey fought hard, twisting in the mud, constantly moving, trying to keep them from getting hold of him. One of them bit his calf and Casey screamed but he kept fighting, knowing that if he quit, it was curtains for sure. He punched and writhed and felt another pair of teeth bite his ass. His pants were too thick for the teeth to go through, but they still tore his skin and it hurt like hell.

Casey kept struggling, pushing back against the dead, but their weight was too much and he was growing tired.

His hands fell on something steel and hard and he realized it was his shotgun. Casey pulled it to him as a pair of teeth found his chin and bit. He screamed, pulling back as white light filled his vision, feeling his skin tear as warm blood poured down his neck. Casey squeezed the trigger, the shotgun exploding, and suddenly Casey could see the moon again. He pulled the gun to him, grabbed shells from his pocket, reloaded, and shot the creature on top of him in the face. The dead body, a young woman with long, straight hair, sat up, black blood burbling from the jagged top of her head. Casey looked at her, drawn to the piece of metal tangled in her hair, horrified to see it was a piece of the brace that had been on Momma's leg. The woman fell over backwards, freeing Casey from the waist up.

Casey squirmed free of the dead and crawled a few feet away from the tangle of bodies still writhing like a mass of worms, unaware he wasn't among them anymore.

Blood spilled down his chest and Casey rubbed his chin, finding only smooth bone and slick blood. They'd bitten his chin clean off.

The dead came out of their huddle, sliding off of each other and turning to face Casey again. He sat on his butt, one cheek still smarting from being bit, and reloaded his shotgun.

"Die for real, you sons-a-bitches," Casey growled.

He pointed his shotgun and shot Buckteeth in the face. He aimed and blasted Beehive in the throat. Her head flew up into the air, severed from her body, her teeth chomping open and shut. The head fell into the mud four feet away and rolled into a corner, nose against the wall.

He got to his feet.

The world spun again and he fell down. Casey gathered himself, got back up and walked over to Beehive's head. He knocked it over and jammed the barrels of his shotgun into the stump of the neck. He pulled the trigger and showered the side of the pit with brain, bone, and thick, black blood.

Casey fell on his ass and sat for a long while. He bled all over and his body hurt something fierce. He felt like rolling over and taking a nap, but knew he'd have to get out of the hole and get to a doctor. There was no telling what nasty infections those dead people had.

He got up and walked to the wall of the pit, slogging through the dozen dead bodies at his feet. He was in the same spot he was in before the dead got dumped in there with him, only now he had that pole that Barry had whacked him with.

What had happened to Barry?

Casey hadn't heard a peep from him once he got to really killing all those dead folks, and he wondered if Barry had taken off or if he was laying up there, knocked out. Casey hoped he was up there, 'cause he was going to kill his ass and dump him in with all of the other dead.

Using the pole, Casey was eventually able to climb out. It took him a couple of tries, but he slid up it and rolled over onto the cool, damp ground. He stared up at the sky and saw the prettiest moon he'd ever seen. It was full and bright and seemed to be winking down at him as if to say everything would all be all right.

He was exhausted from his battle and loss of blood and his stomach didn't feel right. His head hurt. There was a buzzing in his ears, like a fly got stuck down there and was trying to find its way out. Casey couldn't do much about any of it and after a little bit, his head rolled to the side and he wasn't looking at the moon anymore.

He stared at Barry, laying over to his right, dead as a polecat run over by a car. It was too bad because Casey had really wanted to kill that cracker.

A movement flickered in the corner of his eye, and Casey, unable to move, unable to feel anything in his body anymore except for that buzz in his head, moved his eyes to see what it was. It would be the last thing his living eyes would set upon.

Momma's head, nothing left of her body but a pile of mushy red skin and foaming bodily juices, wriggled across the grass towards him. One eye was gone and half the skin from her face was peeled back and flapping in the cool, slight breeze. Her spine, still attached to the back of her head, wiggled back and forth, twisting and writhing; pushing her head forward. Her jaws snapped open and shut and a low moan whistled from between her teeth.

Casey closed his eyes and wished the horror away.

*   *   *

About half an hour later, Barry's dead body moved slightly, then he sat up and looked around. He got to his feet, swaying slightly, his skin a blotchy, dark purple that dripped with half-clotted blood.

Five minutes later, Casey sat up, his nose eaten away by Momma and the bone of his chin gleaming in the moonlight. Momma's head, teeth still chewing on Casey's nose, fell away and rolled over.

Barry glanced over at Casey who looked back at him, and then Casey shuffled over next to Barry.

They walked off together, shambling towards the smell of fresh flesh a couple of farms over, united in death.

JOHN GOODRICH

DEATH ON THE AMERICAN FARM

George Orne was drinking his morning cup of coffee and listening to his father's old AM radio when he got the first inkling of what was coming. The radio was a worn, maroon Bakelite monstrosity nearly as old as George. Like everything on the farm, it was a bit run down, but hadn't given up the ghost yet. The radio newsman was reporting that a New York City gang, high on some cocktail of drugs, was rampaging through the city. Chaos, panic, and blood were streaming through the city streets, and nobody knew what was going on.

George shook his head.

Damn city people weren't good for anything, he thought and shut the radio off.

"I was listening to that." Martha held a cup of steaming tea to warm her hands. She'd given up coffee nine years ago on account of her stomach. George suspected that she snuck a bit of his when he left to do the morning chores. He wasn't about to say anything. They were both in their sixties, and had precious few pleasures left. What harm in a little coffee?

"Just wait until I've gone out before you turn it back on. I want a little peace this morning." It wasn't long before George went out into the chill October morning to milk the cows.

George forgot about the news over the day. Most news didn't much affect him. East Harrow was too small for even a traffic light, a small, dying farm community in the remote hills of Vermont. Whatever happened in New York City or Boston was their problem. His taxes were killing him, the state dairy subsidy had expired last year, and some developer was pressuring him to sell his best field to build McMansions on. George had enough troubles without borrowing New York's.

The next morning their usual radio station was out. George cranked the needle up and down the dial, and found nothing but a few automated beep stations. He turned the power off in disgust. Clearly, the ancient vacuum tubes had finally packed it in. Well, that was just great.

That afternoon, he took a moment to talk with Bob Ford, who kept the farm next to him. At seventy, Bob was no longer the thick trunk of a man he had been. Neither of them was getting any younger, and farming wasn't getting any easier.

"You have a problem with your radio this morning?"

Bob flipped off his battered John Deere baseball cap, rubbed a calloused hand over his brown, hairless pate, then pulled the cap back into place.

"You should watch more television, George."

"There hasn't been a newsman worth watching since Cronkite went off the air." George felt his lips compress in distaste. Bob ran a thick hand under his cap again.

"Boston's a big mess, and New York is, too. People are just going crazy." Bob brought his weathered, moon-round face conspiratorially close. "They say they're eating each other in dark alleys, George."

Bob Ford was a good man. He was steady, and didn't spread gossip. If Bob Ford said it, you could rely on it. And either he had lost his marbles, or the rest of the world had.

"Damn city people. What the hell's wrong with them?"

"Dunno." Bob's face was set in a perturbed scowl. "The TV announcer looked pretty scared. Then there wasn't anyone on the air this morning."

"Probably some Halloween prank. Television people got too much time on their hands."

Bob peered at him. "You think so, George?"

There was an uncomfortable silence, and George looked back over his fields.

"I really hope so."

Above them, a swift-moving line of geese stretched from horizon to horizon. It took a moment for George to realize they were flying north, the wrong way for migration. He wondered what they were fleeing.

That afternoon, the phone came up dead, and George decided not to share Bob's fears with Martha. He saw no sense in upsetting her. But the thought of cannibalism in the cities kept him awake long into the night. What was going on? He didn't realize he'd fallen asleep until the frightened lowing of cows woke him.

In the dark, he pulled his winter coat and muck boots over his flannel pajamas. Probably some damn fox had come in from the cold. On his way out, George picked up his old shotgun, loading it with deer slugs.

The cows were in a frenzy now, he could hear them kicking at their stalls. George broke into a trot when he smelled blood. The stars were remote pinpoints, the moon not yet up, the barn dark as a coal cellar.

The door opened easily.

Shotgun at the ready, face set in a grim frown, George flicked on the light.

A stick-skinny girl in a torn and filthy evening dress was crouched over the prone form of his best milch cow, who'd collapsed in her stall. The air stank of blood and the urine-drenched panic of cows. The woman didn't react to the lights. Instead, she wrenched a mouthful of red, bloody muscle out of Daisy's neck and bolted it down like a starving dog. Most things didn't rattle George like they used to but this sent a shock of electricity from his groin to his neck. He stared at the skinny girl, trying to figure out what she thought she was doing. She swallowed the raw gobbet she'd been chewing, the blood running down her chin, and dove in for another bite.

"Get your damn self out of that stall right now, missy!" George bellowed.

She turned her head toward him. The cow's blood was smeared from her neck up into her hair. Below the fresh crimson layer her face was painted with a cracked black that might have been week-old blood. Dark clotted chunks matted her hair and dress.

Goddamn kid was playing at being a zombie. What the hell was wrong with people? And why did she have to come here?

She moaned something unintelligible, and started toward him. If she'd run, he would have just shot her right then. Instead, she stumbled towards him, as if she needed leg braces, or her knees didn't work right.

"I'm not kidding here." His voice came out shrill.

She was out of Daisy's stall now, less than ten feet away, twitching fingers reaching for him. She was almost close enough to touch the shotgun's barrel when he let her have it in the gut. The discharge was deafening in the enclosed barn, and the slug smashed through her abdomen. She didn't fall. She didn't even hesitate. George fell back, eyeing the thumb-sized hole he'd blasted clear through her torso.

Only someone hopped up on serious drugs could ignore that. George fired again, this time in her chest. Black, gooey blood and chunks of bone spattered over the stalls, and the girl went down in the scattered hay on the floor of the barn.

She wasn't done yet. She couldn't move her legs, but her arms scrabbled around until they found purchase. Then she crawled painfully toward him.

The barn door slammed open, and Martha stood in the doorframe, her shotgun at the ready.

"Stay back," he warned her.

"What the hell, George?" came Martha's voice from the door.

The dead woman's head whipped around at the voice, the jaw snapping hungrily.

Martha moved up next to George. Together, they watched the determined torso drag itself across the packed dirt of the barn.

"What's going on?" Martha demanded again, but he still had no answer. He'd only just noticed that the front of the intruder's dress had come open, and her pale and rubbery breasts were in full view. He stared at them for a moment before he figured out what was wrong.

"She's not breathing."

Martha didn't contradict him, bent down for a look, and realized her foolishness when a hand clawed at her.

George fired again, the deer slug slamming a fist-sized chunk of putrescent brains out of the crawling thing's skull. That seemed to do the trick. The woman collapsed, her arms twitching without purpose. After a moment, she lay entirely still.

"I think she was dead," he said. George felt stupid, but what could he say?

Martha rested her shotgun's butt stock on her hip.

"That's pretty certain. You took off most of her head, George."

"No, I mean before. She was dead before." His voice softened. "And I think we should have gone to church a little more."

There wasn't any more sleep for them that night. Between deciding what to do with the dead girl, dragging Daisy's dead bulk out of the barn, and hosing the sticky mess out of Daisy's stall, it was dawn before they were done. The shattered, bird-boned corpse of the woman didn't have any sort of pocketbook or identification and they couldn't call the sheriff with the phones out. Martha took some pictures of the girl in her tattered dress, as well as the mess she'd made in Daisy's stall in case someone came inquiring. They buried her in an unmarked grave in an unused corner of the property.

Martha read a few words from the Bible about her sending her soul to peace.

Since they wouldn't be getting any milk from the cows that morning, George and Martha sat down at the dinner table and had a discussion. Both were of the opinion that the dead girl and the general disaster in the city were related, and that it might take a couple of months before everything was back to normal. The first thing they needed to do, Martha argued, was to get to town and be with other people. See what was going on; see what other people were doing. George said they should sit tight. Going into town would leave the farm unprotected. What if more dead people wandered onto their land? Who knew how much livestock those things could eat, and how quickly? While he allowed it was unlikely that they'd be able to catch chickens, he worried about the cows. It hadn't taken the skinny woman much time to do in poor old Daisy. They did agree not to head off in different directions. They were going to stay together, whatever decision they made.

Eventually, George wore Martha down, they way he usually did, by being more stubborn than her. They'd stay on the farm; keep within earshot of each other, shotguns close at hand.

He was glad he'd replaced Martha's old double-barreled shotgun, which she'd inherited from her mother, with a newer pump-action model. He'd bought it for her just after they'd seen Terminator 2.

"Just like an action hero," he'd said. And while she'd flushed with a mix of embarrassment and frustration at his absurdity, she never told him to take it back.

The next few days were quiet.

George was figuring out how to work the farm without electricity or gas, planning for the worst case scenario. It wouldn't be easy, stepping back a hundred years; not at their age. They had a wood stove, but how much chopping would they be able to do? On the positive side, George figured he could safely skip this quarter's tax bill.

Three days after they'd buried the zombie and Daisy, Bob Ford pulled into their driveway. Martha had her shotgun at the ready, even though George argued that zombies couldn't drive cars.

"George, Martha? You there?" Bob called out in his querulous voice from next to the suburban, ready to jump back in at any sign of trouble.

"We're here, Bob," George replied.

"We were afraid they'd gotten you," Martha added.

"Nope, I'm fine. I thought the same about you two," Bob said as he stepped towards the house.

"Not yet, at least. Come on in," George said.

The electricity was still on, so they treated Bob to a hot cup of tea.

"They got the Wolfes in their beds, near as I can tell. Tore them apart," Bob told them.

George's heart sank. Howard and Judy Wolfe made the best pies in East Harrow. Not the most polite neighbors he'd ever had, but who deserved to get eaten?

"That's a real shame. Anyone else?" George asked.

"We think they got Annie Harwood. Nobody's seen her for two days," Bob said and took a sip of his tea.

Annie had been just sixteen. She was a smart kid, well-behaved, got good grades, and spent a lot of nights with a telescope. She usually won a prize for her astronomy notes at the County Fair. Probably, that was how they'd gotten her, when she was out alone at night, gazing up at the stars.

"Anybody selling ammunition or anything?" Martha wanted to know.

"There was a bit of a run on it a couple of days ago," Bob said, "but there's still some left. Andy Tritter's got five AK-47s that he's brought out of his barn, and he's charging people an arm and a leg for bullets and guns."

"Andy's been twitchy since he got back from Iraq. He's not causing trouble, is he?" Martha asked. There was motherly concern in her eyes.

"He might, once he figures out he can't eat his guns. Bob Keeler's keeping an eye on him."

Martha nodded.

"Do we have any idea how many of those things are out there?" George asked.

Bob just shook his head. "There's a lot. And we don't know how many more are coming. You'd be safer if you came into town."

George looked at Martha, then back at Bob.

"We're not leaving the farm."

Bob nodded. "There's a couple of people that're stubborn like you two. The gas station's dry, so you'd better hang on to what fuel you've got left."

Bob got up.

"Thanks for the tea."

"We going to see you again, Bob?" George asked.

"Don't know. I'm seeing who's still around."

George nodded.

"Well, thanks for coming out."

"You sure you won't reconsider coming into town?" Bob pleaded. "We could use your help."

"I'm not going to leave my cows," George said firmly.

Bob turned to Martha.

"You staying with this stubborn old fool?"

Martha's smile was sad.

"I won't leave George, no matter how pig-headed he's being."

George put his hand over hers and smiled.

"All right then." There was something in Bob's voice that sounded frightened, and that got to George. Bob had served in Korea. He never talked about it, but nothing seemed to shake him after he came back.

George stood and shook Bob's rough, honest hand.

"You two take care, then," Bob said as he turned to leave.

"You too, Bob."

Bob climbed back into his Suburban. It wasn't long before the sound of the car was lost in the distance. George felt alone, then. He went back to the porch and put his arm around Martha, and the two of them watched the vast empty expanse of sky above them.

*   *   *

The army of the dead came for them the next day.

The first one showed up around the middle of the afternoon. George noticed it shuffling along in the dead, stripped corn stalks, heading for the barn. He wondered if it was the heat or the lowing of the cows that attracted the dead things. He retrieved his shotgun, and warned Martha. Side by side, they headed for the stranger.

From a distance, he could have been anybody, but the jerky, unnatural walk made it clear he was dead. He'd been a businessman. Now his expensive suit was torn, and only one loafer remained on his shuffling feet. Like the skinny girl, his face was caked with a black, flaky layer of blood where he'd buried his head in something.

He smelled pretty bad, too.

George slammed a deer slug through his face, shattering it like an overripe pumpkin. The black, tarry substance was like nothing George had ever seen in a body before. Martha tugged at his sleeve. George turned, and saw more than a dozen dark figures shuffling out of the corn. One was a big guy in a leather jacket, another a middle-aged woman in mourning black, her torn and ruined face filled with metal piercings. He could see a naked couple with terrible wounds on their bodies, who looked like they'd been in the shower. Many wore business suits; others dragged the straggling remains of what they'd been wearing. None of them looked like Annie Harwood, and for that George thanked God.

He missed the head-shot on the guy in the leather jacket, but his follow-up took the lid right off the man's skull, showering the woman in black with a filthy goo that smelled worse than a chicken coop on a hot day.

After the first five went down, their bodies lying in pools of tarry black glop, he stopped thinking of them as people. The jerky walk and the putrescent liquid they had instead of organs made it clear these were no longer human beings.

It was easier to do the work after that.

They all walked with an eerie, jerky gait that made him think of a half-squashed spider. And they were deceptively fast, like a toddler when you weren't watching. While he was reloading, one popped up close to him. He should have seen it, but the zombie had been quiet, and his peripheral vision wasn't so good. He froze, shells dropping from his nerveless fingers.

The zombie's head vanished in a geyser of black, sticky tar that landed on his face. The bitter taste overwhelmed the metallic fear that was flooding his mouth. Martha just looked at him, nodded, then swiveled to take out another shambling, reaching form. He spat, trying not to retch, and wiped at his face. There was an itchy tingle where the evil-smelling fluid had landed on his skin. He hoped nothing bad would come of it.

Martha fired twice more, and then the yard was silent.

George fumbled a couple more shells into his shotgun, noting the way little red tubes were scattered over the yard, small satellites of the ugly pools of black sludge the dead left behind. Martha stood, strong like an oak tree, and racked another shell into the chamber.

More forms emerged from the corn. Six, then a dozen, then more. A flood of the shaking, twitching zombies attracted by the sound of gunfire.

"Back to the house." Martha said it low, but insistent.

They headed for the house as best they could, the dead too slow to follow closely. After slamming the solid oak door closed, he fumbled with the box of shells on the dining room table. After they had reloaded, he took the luxury of a moment to gaze at her. She was, and always had been, his rock. He took her hand and squeezed it. She squeezed his back. No words were necessary.

He took a deep breath and opened the front door. Jerky, slow-moving forms were pouring out of the tall, dead corn.

"We don't have enough ammunition." Martha let it out as a breath rather than words.

What would they do now? They could board up the house, and that might keep them off for a little while. The hundred and fifty year-old farmhouse had solid, sturdy doors, but what were they going to do about the cows? He turned toward Martha, about to ask her a question, when she came up with one herself.

"Is there diesel in the combine?" she asked.

George felt a smile spread over his face.

"Fill your pocket with shells. We'll have to run for it," he said.

The longer they delayed, the harder it would be to get to the barn. Martha dumped shells into her coat pocket, spilling most of them on the floor. She knelt to pick them up, but he took her by the arm.

"We'll clean up when we get back." He didn't say if.

More than a hundred forms had emerged from the corn, making their slow way towards the barn. A couple of the leaders had come across their fallen companions, and nausea roiled up in his gut when he realized they were worrying the rotting corpses like dogs at a bone.

Still, it slowed them down enough that George and Martha made it to the barn, stopping only once to blow a hole in a blubbery man with a squashed face. Then Martha was watching his back as he opened the wide doors.

The combine still had the corn head on – eight long, wide prongs designed to channel the cornstalk and pop the ears off. Chains pushed the stripped ears into the feed throat. He didn't know if it would work on zombies, but it was sure as hell going to be a mess.

The combine roared to life like God clearing His throat. He sat in the enclosed cabin, and Martha took up a station outside the protective glass. He didn't like her being exposed like that, but there wasn't anywhere for a passenger to sit in the tiny cabin.

The combine groaned and lurched into gear. Once clear of the barn, he swung it toward the corn field and the mass of the shuffling dead. From the cabin's height, he could see hundreds of forms moving through the ragged cornstalks. He raised the corn head to about five feet, and pushed down on the accelerator.

The smooth, round prongs neatly channeled the zombies like cornstalks waiting for harvest, and the chains ripped through rotten necks like they were made of wheat. A quick glance behind showed the combine vomiting chunky, black slurry onto the ground.

He imagined this was how guys in tanks felt, on top of the world, nearly invincible. He turned toward another cluster of the jerky forms, aiming straight for one that looked like a banker. Beside him, above the roar of the combine, he heard the explosion of Martha's shotgun going off. He'd missed a dead man in jeans and a black t-shirt over to the right, and she'd taken care of him.

The combine ground away, greedily stuffing more heads into the feed throat. He was sure he'd never want to eat food harvested by the machine again.

Over the racket, he heard Martha swear. He turned and saw a clawed hand tearing at the cuff of Martha's pants. One of them had gotten on the combine, and was climbing up the large farm machine, its snapping teeth ready to rend and tear. He stared at the struggle helplessly. The zombie was about to dig its teeth into Martha's leg when she wrenched away. A solid smash with the butt of the shotgun snapped the wrist at an unnatural angle. With a smooth efficiency, she reversed the shotgun, laying the muzzle directly on the thing's forehead. It looked up the barrel, apparently curious in the moment before the deer slug turned its head into sludge and bone shard soup.

The combine scythed through the massed dead. Heads snapped off, bodies were crushed under its wheels, and reeking sludge poured out the back. The ride and George's heady sense of invulnerability lasted almost until sunset, when the combine choked, and expired. By that time there wasn't anything else moving in the dim sunset.

They walked back to the house together, hand in hand, each cradling a shotgun in the other arm.

*　　*　　*

In the spring, East Harrow mourned their dead, burning them out of fear. Toby Monroe brought a pair of oxen to the Orne's farm and ploughed five acres on the promise of part of the yield.

As the green corn started to come up, George noticed a strange, crazily wandering trail where the crops didn't grow. He stared at it for a couple of minutes before realizing it ended at the dead hulk of the combine. The zombies' fetid bodies must have poisoned the ground where the black sludge had soaked in.

"Damn city-folk," he groused to Martha over dinner. "Not even good for fertilizer."

ALISON SEAY

DELIVERY

The impact left Serena panting and the contractions came hard and fast. They were already on their way to the hospital when the asshole in the ancient black Nova rear-ended them.

Josh had jumped out of the car after fighting back the Saturn's air bag, and had gone after the guy who'd hit them. For whatever reason, the Nova driver had wandered off into the woods on the edge of the road. If the contractions weren't killing her, Serena might have actually been concerned for him, but she was a little occupied at the moment.

Josh had only given chase for a few moments before he returned to her. Serena and the baby were more important than anything else.

With nothing to be done about the driver of the Nova and no time to wait for police, he had jumped back into the car and headed for the hospital again.

Now, in the delivery room, he paced and cussed and ran his big hands through his short dark hair.

Another contraction yanked hard at her core and Serena bit her tongue, torn between the pain of her delivery and worry for Josh.

"It's okay, Josh. It really is. He barely tapped us. Just enough to set off that damn air bag." She broke off, panting, trying not to scream because that would only freak him out. But the pain was twisting, twisting, twisting inside of her. It was more painful than a tooth in need of a root canal. More painful than a broken bone. This pain rivaled any pain she had ever felt.

Josh turned his face to her. It was bone white and pale, creased with concern for her

"I know that," he said.

"So stop fretting. The baby's fine. He's so fine he's kicking my ass," she laughed and then the laugh made the pain worse and she flinched.

Josh was beside her in a flash, holding her hand.

"It was just so weird." He shrugged and then brushed the hair off her sweaty forehead with the fingers of his right hand. "That guy just left the scene of an accident. Maybe he was sick or something. I wanted to kick his ass, but also call the cops. He could be delusional or something, Rena."

She was breathing in and out like she'd learned, trying to control the pain, but she still managed to focus on Josh's words

"We'll figure it out. Let's get your son here first. Then we'll worry about the guy in the Nova," she breathed heavily.

When she brought up the baby-to-be, Nicholas Joshua (Nick for short) Josh's face lit up as usual. Which made her laugh. Which triggered the pain. Which made her bend like a thin tree in a high wind.

"Should I go find the nurse?"

She nodded.

Josh pressed his warm soft lips to her forehead and Serena could only nod. "Right back, baby. You hang tight."

Serena closed her eyes and listened to the heavy door hiss shut on its hydraulic hinges. In her mind's eye, she pictured the unstable, off-balance gait of the Nova driver as the man had gone off into the woods. She did hope he was okay. Even if he was jerk enough to leave a hit and run.

Then another contraction struck, coiling up her insides, turning her thoughts red like fire and she forgot all about the mystery driver.

*　　*　　*

She was smiling when Josh came back with a nurse, but only for a moment. Two nurses to be exact. One of them had blood splattered over the pristine white bib of her dress. The other had tie-dyed splatters artfully arced across her pale blue scrubs. The women were wide-eyed but calm. Josh was more rattled. His hands shook and his teeth chattered even as he took an IV stand from behind the door and slid it through the door's horseshoe shaped handle. The IV pole effectively stopped the door from being pulled open.

It was then that Serena's stomach dipped hollowly. Not a painful feeling. A fearful feeling. The tickle of panic that buzzed in her like a faulty neon sign.

"Josh?"

He waved his hand at her and she caught the fine tremor so unusual for her husband. "It's okay, baby. It's all going to be okay," he said.

Something heavy hit the pale wooden door and everyone in the room jumped. Another contraction struck and Serena pulled in on herself, making a comma of her legs and torso. She tried to breathe, tried not to be afraid, but she could feel panic welling up inside her.

The smaller nurse in the traditional white uniform stepped forward and smiled. It looked more like the smile on a corpse right before they close the coffin than a woman about to bring a life into the world.

"Let's see how you're doing there...Serena's your name, right?

Serena nodded.

"Okay then, I'm Sally, one of your nurses. Let's see about that baby. Can you let your legs fall open for me?" She said the words as if by rote and her voice was one of parched terror. A voice full of sand and dry wind. The nurse was trying to hold it together, but the question was; what was she so terrified of?

Serena turned, surrendering to the sharp stab of pain in her gut. She let her legs fall open froggy style as she had about a zillion times since conceiving Nick. No longer embarrassed or modest about her body, Serena patiently waited to be checked.

"The baby's crowning, dammit," the small nurse said, muttering it almost to herself. The taller nurse covered in blood stepped forward and looked over her shoulder.

"She should be pushing soon. She's ready to pop," the tall nurse said.

It scared Serena that they talked as if she wasn't there. It scared her more that Josh still hovered by the room's only entrance instead of being by her side. His eyes stayed glued to the windowless door and she opened her mouth to call to him when another resounding thud shook the heavy door in its frame.

"Jesus Christ, Mother Mary, God help us," the taller nurse said. Her nametag read **Pat** and her eyes were red like she'd been crying. She had a ragged wound on her arm that looked nasty and she absently touched it and winced.

"What is it? What?" Serena said nervously. "Something's wrong. Is it the baby?" Serena felt the anxiety muddy her head and jackrabbit her pulse. She needed everyone to be calm and no one was. She needed this to be about her and the baby. But for some reason it wasn't. She needed Josh but when she looked to him his back was to her, his attention only for the closed door.

A contraction doubled her up and the nurses clustered close, watching her monitor she was connected to for her heart, smoothing her hair.

"We'll be done soon enough. Let's get your feet in the stirrups," Sally said.

The door was hit again and this time Josh cried out. He staggered two steps back because there was a very faint cracking sound now coming from the doorway. "Josh?" Serena asked.

"It's okay, baby." But when he turned to her his face said he was lying. And not a white lie. A huge, huge lie that meant big trouble.

"What is it? What's going on?" she asked again.

"Some people are sick," he said.

Sally was putting her feet in the cold stirrups and no one had brought her the socks that were promised and her feet became cold. She heard moaning from the hallway as if a hoard of people were all suffering a similar pain.

"Of course they are; this is a hospital!" She tried too hard to laugh, because the laughter would sound good to her, but what came out was more of a sob. They were scaring her, damn them!

Josh tapped his temple and tried a smile. It was ghastly. "Sick in the head. Maybe it's a full moon tonight."

For some reason his attempt at a joke made her think of their vehicular assault and the shambling gait of the man who was lost somewhere in the New Jersey woods. She shivered with cold sweat. Nurse Pat looked a bit green around the gills. Serena hoped she wouldn't be a problem. Maybe she wasn't normally on the maternity ward.

Sally peeked again. "This baby is coming one way or the other. I suggest you get over here, dad, and help. Pat can watch the door."

Serena wanted to know why someone needed to watch the door but the staggering urge to push consumed the question and it was gone. Her body made the decision for her even as the tall nurse and her husband swapped positions. Josh took her hand and for just an instant, he looked happy.

"Here he comes, babe. He's on his way." He bent in and kissed her. "We'll be fine. I promise you. Whatever happens, focus on you and Nick. That's your job. I have all the rest covered."

Serena didn't know what he meant by that, but she couldn't think about it now. She was being turned inside out.

"Epidural?" She spit it out, desperate to quell the pain.

Sally shook her head. Made a shushing sound. "No, no. I'm sorry, honey. You were too far gone when you got here. He's nearly here. I promise you." The nurse actually stopped as the door let loose with another faint cracking sound and the moans in the hall torqued up a notch, sounding like an off key chorus

Sally made the Girl Scout sign. "I promise you, on my honor, this will be over pretty fast if you just focus and push with all your might. Can you do that?"

Serena didn't see a choice, so she nodded, trying her best to be brave. Apparently they were under siege from a bunch of mentally ill people. Maybe the psych ward had had a security breach.

Whatever the problem was, she was having Nicholas.

Now, not later.

*   *   *

It was on her third push that Nurse Pat's face seemed to go blank and she slumped in her chair as she guarded the door. But seconds later, her head raised up and eyes looked around the room.

Spotting the IV, she went to it and tried to pull the IV rack from the door. By doing this she would be allowing the door to be opened during the delivery; to whatever lunatics were desperately trying to gain access to Birthing Suite 213.

Nurse Sally abandoned her post between Serena's legs and yelled as she ran at Pat to stop her.

"Pat! Don't do that!" Nurse Sally screamed, grabbing the woman by the arm and halting her. "We don't know what the problem is out there! We're not sure of contagion. Help me with the birth!"

Serena was doing her recuperative breathing, gaining her strength before the next round of pushing, when Nurse Pat sank her teeth into Nurse Sally's shoulder. The sound of blunt human teeth forcing through white bleached cotton, flesh, and tendon was as audible as if she had bitten into a ripe tomato in August. Nurse Sally threw back her head and screamed at the fluorescents above her as blood arced from Nurse Pat's mouth.

Pat was shaking her head back and forth, moaning and growling the way a dog will when it snags a rabbit. Then Serena was screaming and bearing down at the same time, trying to process the nightmare in the room and simultaneously, inadvertently really, birthing her son into said nightmare.

Nurse Pat continued to gnaw and shake her head and Sally was losing color fast as blood shot from the wound.

"Focus, Serena," Nurse Sally managed even as Pat tossed back her blood-painted face and found a new place to bite.

The entire time Pat attacked Sally; Josh was rooted to the spot, too shocked to do anything but stare.

Then he gave one startled cry that sounded much like a sea gull at the boardwalk. He hefted another IV stand sitting unused in the corner of the room and planted the hooked end through Nurse Pat's neck. Her head rocked back and the sound of bone and flesh surrendering to metal was nauseating.

With the spine severed, the brain was separated from the body and Pat dropped to the floor, spasming. Nurse Sally stumbled away, her hand on her wound as blood seeped from between white fingers.

"Josh! What is...?" That was as far as Serena got when lightning-white pain surged through her pelvis. Her hearing dimmed to a dull roar and her sight narrowed to a shady pinpoint. Serena could only hear one thing, the command of her body to push.

"I don't know what's wrong! I don't know, baby, Just focus!" Josh's voice was high and tight and his face was a floury color that made her worry. His eyes rolled round in his sockets like a frightened horse. When Nurse Sally staggered forward and lifted the sheet covering Serena's upper body, he yelled, "Don't touch her! Get away, now!"

"There's time," Sally assured him in a whisper, her color gone, her neck leaking a steady scarlet ribbon. The coppery smell of blood filled Serena's head even as she pushed and pushed and pushed to bring Nick into the world, though she wished now he could stay safely inside her, not coming out just yet.

"How long before you..." Josh broke off. Instead he wiped Serena's forehead and lied to her. "It's fine baby. It's probably some kind of rabies or something out there. They'll figure it out. Some new strain, maybe. Something really bad but fixable. Everything's fixable, yeah?"

Serena nodded in agreement, then gave a third push. But what he was saying was bullshit and they both knew it.

"A few more should do it," Nurse Sally said, her voice weak, her eyes cloudy from loss of blood.

But the baby was being stubborn. He got hung up and didn't want to come out. Maybe he sensed the horror waiting for him in the hospital. He stayed stuck in the birth canal and the tiny monitor by the bed gave green blips to show his heartbeat. Sally watched them, frowning. A light sweat had bloomed on her upper lip. Small diamonds of moisture. Her skin had tinted a grayish color that frightened Serena. Having no one who knew how to birth a baby with her frightened her even more.

The minutes ticked by and a small crack appeared in the big hospital door as fists pounded on it repeatedly. More minutes passed and something hit the reinforced window facing the street. A rock, a brick, a bird? Serena wasn't sure what it could be. It was when Sally gave a low moan that called to mind the mental patients in the hall, and also the man who had struck their car. These images made Serena panic.

Nurse Sally went and sat down for a moment, mumbling about needing a second to rest, but no sooner did she sit, then her head slumped forward like she was asleep. Seconds past and she raised her head, opened her eyes and stood on shaky legs, then she went back to Serena to help with the birth.

"She's one of them! She's one of them!" Serena screamed and Josh moved toward the nurse, their only lifeline to hospital personal even as the baby slid from her body with a wet, pulling sound. Nurse Sally caught the precious baby and cradled him in her now gray mottled hands. Her eyes, the color of old linens turned up to meet Serena's.

Milky and foreign, inside them still swam some kind of human nature.

The nurse raised Serena's son in her hands, smacked him until he gave a hearty complaint and then, dipping her head almost delicately, Nurse Sally bit the umbilical chord with her clean white teeth. Her now twisted fingers, reminiscent of ancient branches, tossed the baby to Serena and went back to devouring the blood rich cord she clutched.

"Jesus Christ!" Josh shouted. He bent to check the baby who now screamed full-on with the rage of being born, or possibly at being severed from his mother in such a barbaric way.

Serena wept tears of joy, the new tears commingling with tears of terror as the nurse devoured the rest of the umbilical cord.

The afterbirth slipped free of her body and Serena felt the sudden and profound emptiness that Doctor Amora had tried to describe to her. He hadn't wanted her to be afraid when she felt it.

Serena cradled Nick to her bosom and wondered about Dr. Amora. Was he outside feasting on an orderly or possibly a candy striper? The tears came faster now, but milk appeared at her breast for the baby who continued to cry so copiously.

There was a shuffling grunt as Nurse Sally dove for the afterbirth. The wet, sloshing sounds were not easy for Serena to block out. Josh smashed a chair against the wall, prying off the leg so that he had a makeshift stake.

"Brain or neck?" he muttered as if the question made all the sense in the world.

Sadly, to some degree with the maternal thing already kicking in, it did make sense.

"Be careful, baby," Serena said even as she latched Nicholas to her breast the way they had taught her in the pre-birth classes. "Be careful, daddy, you have a son, now." She nodded to herself, liking the sound of her words. "Be careful, Josh, you have a beautiful son." She said it over and over again like a mantra as he advanced on Nurse Sally.

He made a good first lunge, but with her new-found strength, Sally managed to hit him right above the knee on the inside of his thigh. There was a crunch and a pop like a chicken leg being snapped at a Sunday picnic. Josh didn't scream, though. He clenched his jaw tight and brought the impromptu steak down over and over again on the back of her head and neck while Nurse Sally chewed at his leg like a bear.

"Die, bitch, die, bitch, die, die, die!" he chanted.

Blood, gristle, and bone matter speckled him as he pulled the splintered wood free only to drive it in again and again. Some of it was hers, some of it was his.

Serena wept a she watched and Josh made some soundless cry with his mouth. It gaped open in a silent scream like a fish on dry land as he finally, mercifully, landed the final blow that drove deep into Nurse Sally's remaining blue eye. The sound when it punctured her brain was a high brief *pop* like something exploding in the microwave.

"Hurry," Serena said, knowing what was going to happen next after seeing both nurses succumb. She was no fool. She knew by now that their time was limited. For all of them probably, but definitely for her husband of nine years.

He shuffled forward, his mutilated leg dragging under the flapping gray material of his shorts. The weather was warm, the cicadas were singing.

Nicholas would be a summer baby, his birthday falling just three days after the birthday of our nation. "Hurry. See him, kiss him, say goodbye." Her voice broke and so did her heart.

Joshua kissed his son. "Daddy loves you. Daddy loves you. Daddy's sorry. So, so, so damn sorry."

Nicholas nursed and nursed and nursed like there would never be enough. The pain in her nipple was greater than expected the way he nursed. He watched his father with fervent, alert eyes like he understood. They were dark gray eyes like a stormy sky. Just like his father's.

Josh felt faint and he leaned against the wall and slumped to the floor. As he closed his eyes he had a smile on his face, a large, wide smile even death could never wipe clean.

Seconds later he opened his eyes and the smile vanished as he slowly clawed his way to his feet. But his eyes still has something left of who he was before returning.

When the very first moan escaped his lips, when the very first speck of milky covering glossed his normally bright eyes, he broke the small vanity mirror on the wall and drove the shard deep into his right socket. Serena heard that moist explosive sound again, but swallowed her scream. She had to watch out for the baby now.

A small sliver of wood popped free from the door as a fresh assault was mounted from the hallway. An opaque eye that maybe once was brown pressed to the opening. When they spotted her and little Nick, fresh meat, so to speak, their melancholy clamor grew even louder.

"Hush, little baby, don't say a word. Mamma's gonna buy you a mocking bird." Serena sang it because it was all she could think of to sing. She hated the song, though, and watched her son nurse. She felt the harsh biting pain of his strong little mouth on her flesh. Should it hurt that much, she wondered?

Another chink in the pale wood of the thick hospital door fell in. She refused to be afraid; even with three dead bodies around her, and more dead trying to enter.

She needed to be strong for Nicholas of for no other reason.

One of the people in the hall got his head through. He examined the IV pole in an oddly atavistic way, like he was working a math problem in his head. Serena glanced down at her son when a sharp pain shot through her breast, making her wince. His once clear gray eyes now shone milky white in the low light.

"Oh, no."

But her exhausted, frazzled mind put it together. The bite-severed umbilical cord. Whatever it was had gone straight to

Nicholas. And now it was done. She had lost Josh, and that she could handle if the Universe saw fit to be such a raging bitch as to take him. But not her son.

The man in the hole with dead eyes, the *thing* in the hole, forced its body slowly, inch by inch, through the doorway.

In a weird way it was like its own slow, awkward delivery into the room; some kind of cursed backwards birth.

She had a choice. She could die by that thing and the others behind it, or by her own son. Serena dipped her head, kissed Nicholas on the forehead, smelling the bloody but sweet baby smell of him and said, "Mommy loves you."

Then she tipped her head back on the pillow, giving over to the pain in her tender body and let her son nurse.

JENNIFER HUDOCK

TWO WEEKS

There was a moment when I thought her glazed and watery stare held recognition, and my father's handgun trembled in my hand. She was still my mommy. The nurturer who had picked me up fall after fall from the moment I started stumbling through life and set me back on my feet again.

Jagged bone tore through the skin where her ankle snapped when she fell down the stairs, and every dragged step toward me was an effort. Driven, determined to reach me, she didn't recognize me. She was hungry.

I aimed, squeezed my eyes shut and pulled the trigger. Warm bits of bloodied bone and brain matter splattered against my face and arms. She should have fallen backward, but she staggered on unsure footing and fell against me. I had been taller than her since the seventh grade, but she was solid and her weight knocked me backwards. I slammed into the refrigerator and spasms of pain rushed like fire up my spine. The sticky warmth leaked out onto my faded jeans from the hole in her forehead and puddled beside me on the cream and green checked linoleum. She hated that pattern. Said it was too damn hard to keep clean.

The hideous design her insides left across the front of my white t-shirt was a slap of awareness. My vomit mixed with her blood, turning the pool beside me putrid shades of pink and orange. The colors horrified me, reminded me of sickness, infection and death.

I wanted to wash away the contamination, but struggled to push her off of me. If I didn't wash it off, would I become infected too? Hot tears slipped down my face and clung like beads to the burgundy strands of my chin-length hair. I struggled underneath her dead weight, whining and grunting until a half-strangled scream of frustration empowered my escape.

My scream signaled a guttural complaint from the living room, and I scanned the floor for the gun. It had slid across the kitchen and the barrel lodged under the stove. I stretched through vomit and blood, but couldn't reach the handle because my mother's body blocked me. A moaning shadow breeched the doorway and I pushed her over onto her back so I could get around her. Dead eyes stared upward, free from the milky haze of disease. She looked almost human again.

It all reminded me of a movie I'd watched as a little girl, *Old Yeller*. When the dog turned rabid, the oldest brother had no choice but to shoot the family pet, but what if it had been his mother or father? What if he'd had to put down his little brother? Could he do it, or would he turn the gun on himself?

I scrambled toward the stove and reached the gun. The grip stuck to the sweaty palm of my hand, but I couldn't let myself think about why. I grabbed for the edge of the countertop and pulled myself to stand, ignoring the fiery pain wracking my entire body.

I leaned on the counter for support and looked down at the gun in my hand. Would it hurt to die? Would I escape the viral reanimation that had taken over my infected family and turned them into hideous, nightmare creatures? Then it hit me. Death meant leaving my own corpse behind to nourish the sickly appetite of my loved ones. Vomit lurched into my esophagus again, but I kept it down.

I had no choice. I aimed toward the doorway as my father's crippled form staggered into the room.

"Daddy?" My tone rasped with sorrow, and yet I still hoped for some kind of recognition. Nothing.

A glaze of tears distorted his image. I didn't close my eyes when I squeezed the trigger, and when the bullet erupted from the barrel, I heard only my own ragged scream ringing in my ears.

Two weeks later.

"Gates?"

Radio static wrapped around the sound of my name. Acidic vomit burned the back of my tongue and my empty stomach lurched. I swallowed hard against the lump of reality lodged in my throat and pushed my back against the wall. I scanned my sur-roundings carefully, guilt-ridden that I had actually dozed off during my watch.

"Gates, you copy?"

I dug into the deep pocket of my coat and brought out the two way radio. "Affirmative, go ahead."

"We're on our way back now, so round them up," Johns said. "We'll be there in fifteen. Over."

Either my voice or the tweet of the two-way stirred the body in the bed by the door. "Give us twenty."

"Say again?"

"Twenty minutes," I said. "Copy that?"

"Affirmative," he responded. "Time to soldier on."

Soldier on was Johns' favorite phrase. It was always time to soldier on. When we lost Martinez the week before, he said we'd find a way to soldier on. In the face of our enemies, what more could we do, but soldier on? But we weren't soldiers. Just lucky survivors in a world gone three steps beyond mad.

"Over," Johns added.

"Over and out."

My jaw clenched against tension and cold. I pushed off the floor and scanned the dimly lit motel room. With the wooden dresser pushed up against the door, I'd positioned myself across the room just in case I needed to fire. Thick golden-orange curtains cast an eerie hue across the room, like broken daylight.

Midwestern November without heat and I could see my breath mist out in small puffs. We were headed even further north to Doug Marshall's family's cabin in Minnesota. He said we'd be able to stick out the winter there, but I worried that heading into brutal winter would be the death of us.

"Doug?"

He sat up and reached for his glasses on the bedside table.

"We're moving out."

Doug groaned and edged his long legs toward the floor.

"You sleep?"

"I tried not to."

He stood in front of me and less than an inch of space sepa-rated us. The closeness meant I had to tilt my face to look up into his eyes. The corner of his mouth twitched slightly left before he brought his hand up to my shoulder. He squeezed and slid his palm down the back of my arm to grip my elbow. "You can sleep on the ride."

I didn't want to sleep on the drive. Every day I woke from that same nightmare, and I never wanted to sleep again. Those dreams burned a hole in my memory and left an aching pit in my stomach. Or maybe it was an ulcer, possibly even malnutrition. None of us had eaten right in more than a week, breeding constant, underlying hunger. I ignored the pangs out of fear that being hungry would somehow lead me down the cannibalistic path the world had taken on.

Even in the half-dark light Doug Marshall's eyes were intense. Behind the lenses of his black-framed glasses, dark steel flecked against cobalt blue—they were amazing in sunlight, but in the dark those eyes were serious. Doug reminded me a little of Christopher Reeves as Clark Kent, or maybe it was just the glasses. But he was serious and sexy, intelligent and confident.

And he wanted me. Two weeks earlier, I would not have even looked twice at a man his age, but the lingering conventions of society no longer seemed important, and the twelve year gap in our ages was obsolete. Emotionally tangled between fear and longing, I wanted him more than I could remember ever wanting anything before. It was like he reminded me that I was still alive.

Fingertips fluttered against the back of my arm. "Andrea," he started. "You need to sleep."

"I can sleep when I'm dead." My quirky meets tough with a dash of humor didn't amuse him. Suddenly that gap in our ages made me feel immature and unreasonable.

"If you don't sleep, you'll wind up dead."

I dropped my head back onto my shoulders. Eyes squeezed tight, the tingling sensation that preceded tears slithered up the length of my spine. I hadn't cried in over a week, and I didn't want to start again.

"What if that's not enough, Doug?" The gloss of tears washed over my lenses. "What if we rest and hide and do everything right, but we die anyway?"

His fingertips dug into my flesh and thwarted my sluggish hesitation to look away again. "That's a very real possibility, but you can't just lie down for them."

"What if it's the only outcome?"

"You're just tired."

"I'm just realistic."

"No," he shook his head in refusal. "You're letting nightmares cloud your judgment."

"They're not just nightmares, Doug. They're memories."

"We all have things in our past that we'd rather forget."

"But that's just it. I can't forget. I can't even get it out of my head, and every day we just run and I... I don't even know if it's really worth it. This isn't living."

"Yes," he jarred me forward and lowered his face so close to mine that I couldn't look away. "You're alive, Andrea, and every second we have left to fight for our lives is worth it. Do you hear me?"

His lower lip quivered against the straight row of his bottom teeth. I wanted him to kiss me. Crush my body close and show me what it really felt like to be alive. In the course of my short existence I couldn't recall ever wanting to be so close to another human being.

Doug relaxed his grip and lifted my chin before resting the palm of his hand along my cheek.

"I'm sorry," I pressed my face into his touch. "I'm so tired, Doug. I never imagined..."

"None of us did." He leaned his forehead against mine, and for a long time we said nothing. He blinked the heavy lids of his eyes slowly. "We will make it through this, Andrea."

In a half-nod, my closed eyes sent the proper signal. His dry lips brushed against mine. He seemed to savor the moment for several seconds, and then we opened our mouths together in eager acceptance. Like mouth to mouth, Doug's kiss sparked life in me, rekindled my will to carry on. His arms slid over my sides and tightened around my waist.

"I need you," the coarse stubble on his chin felt delicious against my neck.

"What about the boy?"

He glanced over his shoulder, "He's asleep. The doors barricaded."

"But there's not much time."

His right eyebrow arched in accompaniment to an irresistible grin. Fingers wrapped around my wrist and tugged me forward. "Let's make time."

The windowless bathroom was so dark I could have easily pretended he was anyone, but even with my eyes closed his face was all I saw. His body collided with mine against the cold door. Eager fingers fumbled with unseen buttons and zippers in a frantic quest for liberation.

Two weeks earlier I would not have been caught dead having sex with a man I barely knew in a motel bathroom—not even with a condom.

Gasping breath worked against the silence. He moved slowly inside me, or maybe that was my quest to commemorate what might be our only chance to make love. I didn't think about the white skin that circled his left ring-finger, the obvious remains of a wedding band, or the fact that before him I had only been with one other guy. In those few stolen moments, Doug Marshall and I were one being, one soul, alive.

I feared the connection would falter once we let the light in, but it lingered in his expression when he hovered close and tucked my hair behind my ear. He kissed me again. I wanted to tell him I loved him, but was afraid it might sound juvenile. Even if it was true.

*   *   *

The springs creaked under my weight, but the boy didn't stir when I sat on the edge of the bed. Undisturbed, and for the moment completely at peace, I watched him sleep. He had been with us for days, but my connection to him felt stronger. It was like I'd known him my whole life, at least the most important parts of it anyway.

We had found him stumbling down a back road outside of Scranton, Pennsylvania. He couldn't have been more than eight years old, and how he managed to escape was a mystery because he hadn't said a single word since we'd picked him up. Dazed and covered in blood, the moment he realized we hadn't gone all wrong like the rest of the world, he threw his arms around my legs and howled in agony.

Our travel companion, Kyle Simpkin, was the only one who protested. A kid would slow us down. He was right, but I couldn't leave an eight-year-old boy to fend for himself. That would be inhuman.

"Fine then," I crossed my arms and stared Simpkin down. "You go. We'll find our own way."

"No!" Doug and Johns protested within seconds of each other.

"Are you fucking crazy, Gates?" Johns looked between the boy and me. "You won't last a day on your own, especially with a kid."

"Well, I am not leaving him."

"Of course we're not leaving him," Doug said. "And anyone who doesn't like it is welcome to stay behind."

That was when I knew I loved Doug.

Simpkin tried to play it tough, but by nightfall the boy had become a part of our survival routine, and all of us were glad we'd found him. He was a distraction, a reminder of the way things were supposed to be, and we went out of our way to keep him happy.

"It's time to go, kiddo," my hand jarred him from sleep.

Upright and alert, his wide brown eyes darted through the dusk-hued motel room in search of Doug. He relaxed when Doug emerged from the bathroom. Then he offered me an almost appreciative smile for the brush of my hand into the hair across his forehead.

"You can go back to sleep in the car, but you should brush your teeth before we leave."

He nodded and stretched himself out of the bed. While he rifled through his knapsack for a toothbrush, Doug searched through packets of coffee and powdered creamer in a basket beside the battery-powered coffee pot. He used bottled water from his knapsack to make coffee, and within seconds the machine began to rumble and hiss.

"How far do you think we'll get today?" I asked.

"Hard to tell," Doug slid into the sleeves of his flannel shirt and buttoned up the front. "Depending on road blockage and weather, we have a pretty good chance of getting to Minneapolis by early afternoon. We could make the cabin by nightfall."

"That might be a good place to stock up on major necessities."

"I thought so too," he agreed. "But it'll be really dangerous if we get too close to the city."

"Do you have a plan to get around it?"

"There are a couple of routes we could take," he nodded. "There's no way to tell how backed up they'll be though unless we try them."

"Simpkin won't like it," I noted.

"Simpkin can kiss my ass," he said. "I'd give my left arm for a hot shower right about now."

I groaned at the thought, and drew the fur-lined weight of my coat closer. The last time we'd encountered hot water had been a Pennsylvania campground we'd stayed in just hours after encountering the little one. Even then, the public shower hadn't exactly been a delight. The aftermath of seasonal campers had left the grounds an autumnal mess, and maintenance was obviously sluggish. The shower floor was muddy and clogged with leaves. To make matters even more uncomfortable, I was the only woman among three men. Johns had stood guard to watch for trouble while I'd cleaned up, but no matter how long I stood under the water I didn't feel clean.

"My family usually keeps the cabin well stocked for the winter," Doug said. "We saw a lot of long snow storms, drifts so high not even snowshoes would get you to the nearest town."

"You really think we'll be safe there?"

"Safe enough until we can figure out what else to do," he said. "We can hole up there for the winter and make plans. Maybe we can trek up into Canada in the spring, see if whatever's going on here has hit there too."

"The news said they were shutting down borders in an attempt to isolate and control whatever's happening."

"Yeah, well," he turned back toward the coffee pot. "There hasn't been news for more than a week now."

"I know."

"We can talk more about Canada once we've reached the cabin."

"I have this sudden urge to sing *Oh, Canada*," the laugh that followed felt as nervous in my chest as a panic attack. Two weeks earlier I had never even experienced a panic attack. Now the world seemed to fall down around me in heavy chunks on a regular basis; panic was a muse inspiring survival.

"We'll all sing it in the car," Doug winked and squeezed my shoulder.

The boy came out of the bathroom and methodically returned his toothbrush and toothpaste to the front pocket of his knapsack. Maybe making him brush his teeth seemed stupid in the face of it all, but I'd learned in one of my psychology courses at the university about the familiarity of routines. Maybe if I continued to put normal tasks before him every day, he'd start to feel comfortable and human again. Maybe he'd tell us his name.

Doug poured coffee into insulated travel mugs, and with our few belongings packed into individual knapsacks we formed a line at the door. Doug ducked out to survey the staircase and the distance to the car. A small hand gripped the fabric of my coat, and I reached my arm back in silent gesture, a double pat of reassurance that also drew him closer.

The motel itself had been far enough off the highway and just outside of a small town. The only living dead we encountered had been the motel manager and two leftover tenants. Johns found the remains of a family in the end room just under the stairs, their bodies nearly picked clean. The manager hovered in the shadows and waited for the next impulse to peak his senses. He'd caught the scent of fresh prey and might have caught them off guard if it hadn't been for the foul smell and winded, guttural moan that preceded him.

From the crack in the door, I watched exhaust fumes putter gray clouds against a bleak dawn. It looked like snow, and the further north we traveled, the more likely we would be to encounter it. Johns and Simpkin hurried around the opened back of the Hummer, situating supplies foraged in the night.

"Clear," Doug pushed the door open for us to follow and held his hand out to the kid. We hurried down the metal staircase, our booted footsteps ringing out like a homing beacon.

Waist high mist cut through the fabric of my jeans, and I drew my coat in even tighter. The boy climbed into the backseat beside Johns, and Simpkin isolated himself in the furthest seat from the front. Before I broke from the back end of the Hummer, Doug reached for my hand and held me in place.

"Look, Andrea," his hand curled around my forearm, "I wanted you to know..."

"Doug," I said. "I have no regrets."

"Neither do I," Through the shadow of stubble two dimples accompanied his slow grin.

I almost looked away and let things go unsaid, but knew I would be sorry later. We lived in a world now where later wasn't always an option, but more often a regret. "Look, Doug, I don't want to think about where I'd be now if we hadn't found each other."

"Me either," the back of his finger glided down my cheek. Nervous laughter puffed into the curtain of my hair, and then we broke contact.

I climbed up into the passenger seat and strapped myself in and looked into the back. The new car smell that had pervaded the interior just five days earlier smelled like a combination of diesel fumes and old elevator. Simpkin had already ducked down and checked out. The little one had drawn a blanket up under his neck, but I could tell from the strained marks beside his eyes he wasn't asleep yet.

Johns leaned forward and in between the front seats. "That was thirty," he noted.

"Thirty what?" Doug checked the rearview mirror before backing up.

"Thirty minutes," he said. "Gates said twenty."

"Sorry," I turned forward in the seat, my face flushed with heat.

Doug's sidelong gaze darted toward me and a smile peaked at the corner of his mouth. Johns rustled in the backseat, nylon on leather for several minutes as we traveled along the deserted road until finally the only sound was tires on pavement.

The Hummer was the most ridiculous vehicle I had ever been inside of or driven, but it had saved our lives at least a dozen times since Johns had stolen it off the lot in Rhode Island. Large enough to push through a small mob of the walking dead, the diesel powered engine also gave us hours of uninterrupted daylight travel.

I lifted my knapsack against the window and nestled my head into it like a pillow. I didn't want to sleep, but the continual hum of the road beneath the tires hypnotized me. Soon my mind replayed our stolen moment. Doug's unshaven skin against my neck, his whisper in the dark.

He'd saved my life, and was keeper of the only secret I couldn't face. Doug knew I had killed my mother, and if he hadn't showed up I might not have gotten away from my father either.

Two weeks ago.

The sound of my screaming seemed so much louder than the bullet erupting from the barrel. I shook so hard that the bullet struck the left side of my father's neck. The close range of the shot had knocked him backward, but he quickly regained his balance and hunched forward.

"Shit!" In a frantic state I pulled the trigger again, but it only clicked against an empty shell, not once, not twice, but three times. "Shit! Shit! Shit!"

His reanimated corpse staggered onward. The confrontation with my mother had cornered me in the kitchen, and the granite-top island bar was the only obstacle to my freedom. I hadn't jumped hurdles since high school track, hadn't run for competition in more than five years, but I had it in my mind that if I could just get over the bar I would be free, and I could run until every muscle in my body was on fire.

I stepped tentatively in that direction, but slipped a little in the puddle of vomit on the floor. I gripped the counter top and heaved myself up onto the shelf in one of the opened, lower cupboards. On top of the island, and about to leap over the opposite side, Dad's powerful arms swung around to reach for me and caught me off guard. I tumbled backward to the sound of metallic thunder as dad's head exploded, and then white pain exploded as my head cracked against the opposite countertop.

Fireworks erupted behind my eyes as I blinked them open and tried to sit up.

A flashlight preceded a voice in the darkness, "Don't sit up."

Throbbing pain pulsed to the beat of my heart. "Who're you?"

He knelt down beside the sofa and tilted his head as he studied me. "Doug," he said. "Doug Marshall." He brushed the hair away from my face and asked, "How's your head? You took a pretty nasty spill."

My raw throat prompted memories of screaming, and images of what had happened returned in rushing waves of agony and nausea. "I shot my mom."

"You're in shock, just lie back."

I hung over the edge of the couch, "I think I'm going to be sick."

Doug hunched beside the couch while I threw up into a bowl of popcorn kernels someone had left on the coffee table. The thick fake butter smell mixed with bile and made me feel sicker, and I wretched even after there was nothing left in my stomach. Dry heaves wracked my body until finally the sobs took over. He covered me with the knitted afghan from the back of my mother's chair. It smelled like lilac and hand cream. I started to cry.

"She wasn't your mother," Doug reached over and lowered a hand onto my forearm. "Not anymore."

*   *   *

Sunlight glinted off the drifting snow and made Doug squint behind his sunglasses. The Hummer cruised effortlessly along the side of the road to avoid coming up on major off-ramp back-ups. Black smoke painted the horizon of the town below and throngs of the dead huddled and staggered against the twisted line of abandoned vehicles. They moved like flies, sporadic and strange against the collapsed vein of humanity that lined the road for miles.

"That's a lot of cars," I noted.

"Yeah, it is," he agreed.

While we pushed through the unsatisfied mob, the interior design of the Hummer made it impossible to hear their bewildered moans of hunger and outraged cries.

Doug maneuvered the hummer off-road, the rough transition jostling our backseat passengers enough to evoke a curse from Simpkin. I glanced back at the wide-eyed child. He scanned the roadside for only a few seconds and then pulled his blanket up over his head. I wanted to mimic him, and hide away under a barrier of fabric until the nightmare monsters went away, but they lived on inside my head.

"What's going on?" Johns asked.

"Just a little creative driving," Doug said.

"What are we doing on such a major stretch of highway?"

"We're heading toward Minneapolis for supplies."

Simpkin's protest rang in my ears, "Are you trying to get us killed, Marshall?"

"He's trying to keep us alive," I narrowed my eyes over Simpkin. "We need supplies, especially ammo if we're going to stick it out for an entire winter."

"So what, we're driving right into the Mall of America?"

"I'm not an idiot, Simpkin."

"I'm not so sure about that. The last place we need to be heading into right now is a zombie fucking war zone."

"I hate to say this, but maybe Simpkin is right," Johns said. "Maybe driving into such a big city is a bad idea."

"We're not going into the city," Doug promised. "We're heading toward it, into the suburbs to find a hardware or sporting goods store. Besides, we're going to need to fill the gas tank. It's another three hundred miles to Waskish."

"All right," Johns patted Doug on the shoulder and sat back. "I trust you, man."

"You trust everyone," I didn't have to look back at Simpkin to see his eyes roll.

"We could drop you off here, Simpkin," I reminded him. "Stop trying to start a fight over every decision that's made without your stamp of approval."

"This is my fucking life," I could hear that his teeth were clenched. "What's the point of even trying to get to this cabin if we're stepping into every death trap we can find along the way?"

I turned in my seat again, this time just enough to narrow my eyes like scimitar-sharp slits. "If you have a problem with the plan..."

"Why am I the only one that ever has a problem with Marshall's plans? You're obviously fucking him, Gates, so I get that, but Johns..."

"Shut up!"

"What are you gonna do if I don't?"

My hand closed over the seatbelt, finger poised over the release button. I envisioned myself scurrying over the seat dividers in a flash of red coat and flying fists, but the last thing I wanted to do was cause Doug to crash.

"I'm gonna open the door and push you out at eighty miles per hour, how's that sound?"

"Don't think for a minute I won't take you with me," he promised.

The wickedness of his grin made me sick inside, like some part of him actually enjoyed the tension and the fighting.

"Simpkin," Doug didn't take his eyes from the road. "I understand that it's hard to deal with not having control, none of us has control anymore. But if you want to remain welcome on this ride, I suggest you check yourself."

The little boy beside Johns hadn't made a sound, but his gaze darted around the interior of the Hummer nervously.

Tension gripped the air until finally Johns said, "There're dozens of suburbs around Minneapolis and St. Paul. I'm sure one of them will have what we need."

Doug looked back at him in the rearview mirror, a silent gesture of thanks. "That's what I'm hoping for."

"Do you still think we'll make it to your cabin before nightfall?" I asked.

"Not likely, but we can navigate the road into Waskish in the dark."

When the boy made eye contact with me, I offered a reassuring wink that made the corners of his mouth twitch toward a tentative smile. While Doug drove on, maneuvering around the long trail of abandoned cars and occasional hordes of living dead that gathered at the sound of our motor, I closed my eyes and tried to remember how to meditate.

My deep breathing techniques relaxed me, but instead of meditation I fell into a dream state. Images of Doug and I breathless as we ran through the woods after leaving my house. I could hear gunshots in the distance. Though there seemed to be few survivors, those who hadn't been eaten alive had turned to looting. We did everything we could to stay invisible, and over a period of four days, the two of us managed to walk from Plymouth, New Hampshire down into Massachusetts. We had packed light, taken whatever food we could find in my house and searched for supplies wherever we could along the way.

That first twenty-four hours we hardly spoke, taking turns watching out for each other while we rested, and fighting back to back whenever we came up against the walking dead. Sometimes we ran until we couldn't run anymore, but mostly we walked in silence.

It ate at me, though. My mother's face haunted my every moment and made me wish I'd taken the job I'd been offered two months earlier in New York City. Inside I knew I'd have a completely new set of regrets, but at least her blood wouldn't be on my hands.

"Why did you help me?" I didn't look at Doug when I asked for fear that I'd find signs of regret in his eyes. "I mean, you risked your life to help me. Why?"

"Are you kidding? What kind of person would I be if I'd just walked away?"

"I don't know," the fabric of my coat swished with a shrug. "Maybe you'd be further along by now."

"Or maybe I'd be dead," he noted. "You saved my life a few times too these last couple days."

"I guess," The wind felt sharp as tiny knives against my chapped face, and made my stinging eyes water. "Wouldn't it be easier to be alone?"

"I don't understand."

"This might sound crazy, but I could easily live out the rest of my life, be it two hours or two weeks, without having to kill another person I know."

"So you'd be happier if I left you alone?"

Alone? The prospect made my chest feel so hollow my heartbeat thrummed inside my ears. "No," I shook my head. "I'm saying

I'll be happier if I never have to use the blunt end of a crowbar on you."

It was the first time either of us had laughed. He stumbled forward deliberately and lowered an arm onto my shoulder. "Here's hoping it never comes to that," he squeezed just a little, and it felt good. For a moment we were just two people enjoying a human experience in a world that had become suddenly devoid of humanity.

"If it does though," Doug leaned outward, his gaze serious and grave.

"It won't."

"We don't know that," he said. "We don't even know what's causing it, or if it'll stop. Look, I need to know I can count on you to do me in if it comes down to it."

I shrugged his arm off of my shoulders and marched forward like a pouty teenager. "How can you ask me to kill you after you saved my life? That's just wrong. I mean, you might even be the last person on Earth."

"Andrea," three quick steps and he'd caught up with me. He grabbed onto my coat sleeve and spun me around. "You can't think of me as someone you know if that happens."

We had come up on our share of zombies in the days since we'd left my house, and though most instances had allowed us to run, there had been a few close calls. I had done what needed to be done, but that was different. They weren't people I could identify with, so killing them was easier. I had only known Doug a few days, but he'd risked his life to save mine, and that made him undeniably human in my eyes.

"Promise me you won't let that happen to me," he said. As his eyes pleaded with mine, I noticed their intensity, the silver flecks that shone against the blue. "Seriously, I don't want to go out like that."

I wanted to look away and make some hollow promise that didn't need to be kept, but I couldn't. "Fine," I shrugged out of his grasp. "You promise me the same."

"I promise," he said.

Richard Johns came up on us in a pick-up truck just moments after our sworn pact to kill each other and asked, "You two headed my way?"

The Hummer hit a bump in the road, jarring me awake.

When I opened my eyes, the sun had disappeared behind a thick cover of black clouds. Muffled blips and beeps sounded from the backseat, and when I turned to look behind me our young charge's face was hidden behind the dual screen of a Game Boy we'd picked up to entertain him during a supply run. Johns watched buildings pass by out the window and Simpkin scowled out the left-side window.

"Where are we?" I sat up and reached for the cold cup of coffee I'd left sitting in the cup holder on the dashboard.

"**Oak Grove**," Doug said, turning into the parking lot of a huge white building with a broken green marquis sign that said Oak Grove in white letters. "I saw a hardware store a few streets back. I say we fill up the gas tank here and turn around to see if we can find a back-up generator to take with us."

"Sounds good to me," Johns agreed.

"We're already here," Simpkin whined. "What good does it do to protest now?"

The parking lot was all but empty, save for an abandoned eighteen wheeler with the driver's side door left open, and a green jeep. The sight sent chills up my spine, and I wondered where all of the town residents had migrated to.

"We're still pretty close to Minneapolis, aren't we?"

"It's about thirty miles south," Doug parked the Hummer and turned off the ignition. He left the keys dangle and moved to unbuckle his seatbelt. "Johns, you want to help me pour fuel into the tank?"

"I can do it," I said. "I need to stretch my legs anyway."

"We could all probably use a good stretch," Johns noted, and the metallic un-clicking of seatbelts circulated through the interior.

I hopped down from the passenger seat and the boy slid out behind Johns. I grabbed onto his jacket sleeve and said, "Stay close, okay?"

He nodded and followed Johns around to the back where Doug unloaded five gallon cans of diesel. I stretched my cramped and aching legs and bent down to touch my toes, feeling the delectable tug on every muscle in my back as I came back upright. Cold air scorched my lungs as I drew in a deep breath and then released a gray stream of steam.

No matter where we went, it was difficult to get used to how quiet everything was. No cars running along distant highways, no factory machines. The simple sound of conversation on a busy street was the stuff the children of tomorrow would hear stories about, but never be able to quite wrap their minds around. The world had grown so silent that even the slightest whisper might carry for miles.

Simpkin's attempt to be sly failed miserably, and his tightlipped tirade against Doug echoed across the parking lot. I bent down to look through the windows. Johns stood with his arms crossed and shaking his head just behind Doug as Simpkin raved on.

How were we going to be able to live through the winter with him in a remote cabin? Doug insisted more than once that just because Simpkin was an asshole, didn't mean we should leave him to fend for himself, but I wasn't so sure. Eventually one of his tirades was going to get someone killed.

I came around the opposite end of the car just in time to catch the end of Doug's threat, "...before you find yourself out on your ass."

"You know what, that's fine! That's just fine. I'd rather make it on my own anyway." Simpkin backed away, his head cocked arrogantly to the left.

"If that's what you really want, I won't stand in your way," Doug shifted his attention to the gas can tilted into the tank.

Simpkin took several steps backwards with his hands in his pockets and his expression curdled. "You aren't gonna make it anyway," he said. "I'd be better off on my own."

"Don't be an idiot," Johns started toward him.

I stood beside Doug and scanned the area quickly for the little one. He huddled in Johns' shadow, hands stuffed into his coat pockets with the dark hood hugged tight to his face. "Why don't you come over here with me?"

The child responded without acknowledgement, hovering in between Doug and me, but still distracted by the commotion between Simpkin and Johns.

Doug's expression was strained, as if it took all of his strength to remain calm. Out of everyone Doug seemed to be the only one who could keep his head. He had to be on fire on the inside. A part of him must have silently screamed against the shackles of leadership that put him in this role again and again.

"Do you want me to drive?"

The sound of my voice softened his features, "You feeling up to it?"

I nodded, "I've got the directions to the cabin memorized."

He chuckled softly, "Then you should have no trouble finding it in the dark."

"You can navigate from the passenger's seat."

"Absolutely."

Johns had stopped Simpkin near the middle of the parking lot. So much open space combined with heated voices made me nervous. I swore to myself that if anything happened I would never forgive Simpkin. I walked around the back and hoisted another five gallon can of diesel out. Lugging it over, I lowered it onto the ground beside Doug and watched the commotion from a distance.

"He's so worried about getting killed, yet here he is sending out voice flares to anyone or anything within a fifty mile radius."

Doug smirked, "Well, we've all seen first hand that he's not exactly the sharpest tool in the shed."

"No," I shook my head. "He's just a tool."

I glanced back just in time to catch Johns throwing up his arms in defeat. He stalked back to the Hummer and opened the back door. He took out Simpkin's knapsack and marched like a madman back across the parking lot. Johns' body language begged for a fight, but Simpkin was a coward.

The boy had turned his attention away and was watching Doug pour the diesel. "You know," I reached out and laid my hand on top of the boy's hood, "there was a part of me that didn't think we'd make it even this far, but now I have this little ray of hope."

"I promised you I'd do whatever I could to get us someplace safe," Doug said.

"Thank you," I pressed my back into the cold metal of the hummer and withdrew my hand.

"Thank you for believing in me."

I shrugged. "You saved my life, who wouldn't believe in that?"

Johns threw Simpkin's knapsack at him before he turned back toward us, hollering over his shoulder, "Remember, this was your choice."

Simpkin slung the sack over his shoulder and began to walk in the direction we had come from. At his side swung the aluminum baseball bat he'd carried with him everywhere since we'd met him.

The silence and the emptiness made him look weak and vulnerable. I shuddered at the thought of him alone, afraid and I knew internally that it was fear that made him such a jerk. His life had been so controlled before, but now no matter how hard he tried to grasp at control it was always just out of reach. The biggest part of me hated him, but more than that I felt sorry for him.

"Doug," I should have just bitten my tongue. "I know he's an asshole, but we can't just let him wander off on his own like this."

"No?" He withdrew the emptied gas can from the tank and laid it on the cement beside the full one.

I shook my head.

"Do you want me to talk to him?"

"If something happened to him, I would never forgive myself."

A sarcastic snort escaped Johns, "If something happens to him, we'll never know about it."

"I won't be able to stop wondering," I admitted. "Maybe I can talk to him?"

Doug was shaking his head no before I'd even finished my sentence. "I'll go, but if he still wants to go off, there's nothing else we can do."

"I know."

"I'll do what I can."

"Thank you." I stretched up onto the tips of my toes and kissed his mouth.

The act seemed to leave him breathless, at first, but then he welcomed it by drawing me closer with his free arm against the small of my back.

"I'll be right back," he winked at me, ruffled the boy's hood and started after Simpkin.

"Hey, Johns, you want to help me out with this?" I gestured toward the gas can on the ground.

Later on I would blame myself for sending Doug after Simpkin, for not watching them as they walked dangerously away from where were parked. There had been too much commotion already, and we were bound to attract attention. It was the boy who saw it happen. The horde moved in from behind and caught them off guard. The child tugged frantically at the hem of my coat, but by the time Johns and I realized what was going on Doug and Simpkin were overwhelmed by a mob of at least thirty bodies.

There was gunfire, and Johns ran in that direction with his own hand gun flashing silver against dying daylight. I didn't even throw the empty gas can into the back. I just ran for the driver's side.

"Get in!" I cried out to the boy, who was already halfway into the back seat.

I started up the engine and whipped the vehicle around in the direction of the attack. I honked the horn at Johns who fired two shots into the mob and then staggered backward toward the Hummer.

He wasn't even all the way inside when he commanded, "Drive!"

"We can't leave them here!"

"Gates, drive!"

"I won't leave him, Johns."

"It's too late," he slammed the door and locked it behind him. "They're both already gone."

"No!" I pressed down so hard on the brake pedal that my calf muscle ached. "I heard Doug fire his gun."

"Andrea, Doug is dead!" His bellow shook through me, waves of terror that made my entire body feel like it was made from rubber. "Drive, now!"

I shut down and drove. Later I would barely remember leaving the parking lot, or Johns barking out directions while quiet sobs hiccoughed from the backseat. There was just the blur of the road unraveling before us until finally Johns told me to pull over.

He drove the last leg of our journey. I crawled into the backseat and curled into a ball. Small arms encircled my body, and as the two of us wept, I replayed those final minutes with Doug over and over again. I had tasted coffee on his lips as the smell of diesel wafted between us. His kind eyes said *yes*, he would do whatever I asked, and I had asked him to go after Simpkin. It was my fault he was dead.

*   *   *

Besides writing it down, Doug had made each of us memorize the route to his family's cabin in case we got separated. Just as he'd promised, it was the perfect stronghold. Situated on a hilltop overlooking the lake, we could see for miles in all directions. It was a long hike to the neighboring resort, and we didn't encounter a single soul until Johns and I began scavenging the resort's cabins for the supplies we'd never picked up.

During our raids we came face to face with four zombies. As we destroyed them, vengeance burned inside me. Even though I knew they had nothing to do with what happened to my family and Doug, it was the principle.

None of us talked about what happened to Doug and Simpkin. We just soldiered on.

Two weeks in the cabin without a single zombie sighting wasn't enough to provide even a false sense of security. Johns and I began to show the boy how to defend himself, first with Johns' handgun, and then the rifle. If anything happened to us, I wanted him to at least have a fighting chance.

As winter layered over us, the three of us tucked ourselves away in the cabin and did all we could to entertain each other. We told stories, read books and played games while the snow packed us in so tightly it inspired a sense of claustrophobia which both lulled and terrified me.

Every night I dreamed about Doug; listless, decaying and torn apart by rabid mouths. He dragged himself toward me with one hand always reaching, and instead of the identifying moan that seemed to escape the ghastly throats of the walking dead, it was my name on his lips. "Andrea, kill me."

As the months of winter unraveled, our safe haven began to feel like a trap. The winds of March swept another blizzard in, and I was restless. I sat awake in the den listening to the wind howl through barren branches while Johns and the boy slept in front of the fireplace.

My hand slid over the fluttering in my belly only I could feel, but the visual evidence of my fifteen minutes with Doug grew more obvious every day. I told myself routinely that if Doug had lived, I would not have conceived during that one frantic act to feel human and alive.

I paced the floor while they slept, on watch even though we hadn't seen a single threat all winter. When the weeping set in, I bundled up in blankets, jammed my feet into my boots and stepped out onto the porch to watch the clouds paw at the face of the silver moon. Even though it wasn't full, its light was enough to reflect off the snow, making it bright as dusk.

The wind was subtle, but frigid as it cut through the layers of quilt wrapped around my shoulders. It tickled through a patch of dry leaves clinging desperately to the oak tree behind the cabin. I closed my eyes and listened to the crispness, like paper teeth chattering against the cold.

The occasional mild day told of coming spring, and Johns had been talking about heading west in search of other survivors once it started to thaw. Every time he mentioned it, I thought of Canada and Doug's plans to head further north in search of refuge. All I knew was that we couldn't stay in the cabin forever. Being there all winter had been a constant reminder of Doug, and while I relished the closeness, it was time to move on.

"Is that stupid?" I asked Johns. "That I want to both stay to be near him, but leave to get away?"

Johns looked down at my belly and shook his head, "He'll be with you no matter where you go."

I squeezed my eyes tight against my tears. It was cold enough they'd probably freeze to the corners of my eyes if I actually let them fall. Drawing in a deep breath, I caught the hint of a strange odor on the breeze. It was like a boarded up basement that hadn't circulated fresh air in years had been opened nearby.

The wind died down, and the leaves grew still, but in the distance the crunch and scuff of something hard against the frozen snow moved closer. At first I wrote it off as a small herd of deer coming down to the nearby lake in search of water, but when the air current shifted again, it carried a low moan in my direction that froze the blood inside my veins.

I squinted and scanned the miles of white for some hint of movement. I was just about to give up and head back inside when I saw it. It was far enough away that I couldn't gauge the size, but I could tell by the awkward crawl that it was one of the undead.

Suddenly I felt vulnerable, as though we'd taken advantage of our safety when at any time one of them could have come up on us.

I pulled the edges of the blanket up off the porch and hurried into the cabin to grab the rifle. Once inside I shrugged out of the blanket, grabbed the gun and the binoculars, and headed back out into the night.

Holding the rifle in one hand, I lifted the night-vision binoculars and peered out into the darkness. It took me almost a minute to relocate the staggering figure, but when I did, my lungs tightened with a horrified gasp against the cold.

Black-rimmed glasses hung askew against a marred and empty face. There was little left of the army green parka he'd been wearing, pieces of it now in tatters, and the polyester stuffing hung out in dirty, white clumps.

The binoculars trembled in my unsteady hands. All of those dreams, and I knew what he wanted from me. I'd promised him I would, even though I'd crossed my fingers and prayed to God I'd die long before him and never have to worry about fulfilling that promise.

His voice rang clear through my memory, *"You can't think of me as someone you know if that happens."*

But Doug was wrong.

There was a part of him inside still aware of who he was, otherwise, how would he have known exactly where to find us?

The sound of my whimper carried on the wind, only to be answered by a long, howling moan.

"Promise me you won't let that happen to me."

I lowered the binoculars and lifted the rifle.

I stared through the scope and blinked through several tears burning my wind-chapped cheeks as he staggered closer.

"You're not Doug," I lied.

My finger squeezed the trigger.

SCOTT MICHAEL KESSMAN

TRAVELING COMPANIONS

When the small boy emerged from the alleyway, appearing dirty and disheveled but otherwise fine, Samantha wondered how the child had managed to survive on his own.

But when the boy stepped away from the shadows and into the revealing moonlight, the former schoolteacher's heart sank, and despair overtook her optimism.

The dead child ambled forward at a slow, lumbering pace. Sam aimed the muzzle of her revolver at the patch of pale flesh above the boy's cloudy, empty gaze and fired, plastering his brains across the brick wall.

That was the moment she said goodbye to her old life forever. The gunshot still rang hollow in her ears, and as the sound slowly faded, so too did all her hopes that things might ever be normal again.

She watched the corpse of the child slump to the ground, blood pooling on the cement and seeping into the cracks. The boy was perhaps only nine or ten, the same age as her students. She wondered now if the children in her class were also all dead, or whether some were still safely hidden and protected with their families.

The army had come through her small hometown of Beaumont a short while ago, offering to escort residents to defensible shelters. Sam's neighbors had pleaded with her to join them, but she had declined. The idea of relying upon the army to protect her from the increasing numbers of walking corpses didn't appeal to her. She figured that it was probably some sort of army radiation test that had spread the strange contagion across the Earth anyways.

After the army rolled through, recruiting many men to join a local militia in the process, the town was nearly deserted. Sam had quickly realized the folly of staying put when the walking dead began wandering down her street on a daily basis.

So she packed some food and water and, under cover of night, left the home she had grown up in. The once familiar street had absorbed many memories over the years; Samantha learning to ride a bike, playing with friends, being picked up and dropped off on dates, and raising a family. But the night she left town, the street seemed as empty and lifeless as the horrid creatures that had risen from the earth in the local cemetery just a few miles away.

She had quietly but quickly made her way across a few fields and farms, until she reached Tom Davis' place. Tom bred horses, and Sam had figured a horse would be a more ideal means of travel. She planned on sticking mainly to the country rather than the highway, figuring it would be easier to avoid the zombies that way.

She panicked when she arrived at the homestead and found it deserted of all livestock, save for a few chickens that had the run of the place. Tom and his family had obviously left some time ago, and Tom had apparently freed all the animals as well, including the horses.

Undeterred, Samantha decided that a search of the premises might still be prudent. She had found the front door unlocked, and though she felt a little funny to be entering Tom's home without invitation, survival was of more importance than her conscience.

It had turned out to be a wise decision, because Sam found a nice cache of weapons that had served her well thus far. And upon leaving the house, she also found that one horse did not leave for greener pastures after all. It must have come from around the side of the house, and glanced at Sam nonchalantly as though it had been waiting for her all along.

Samantha had led the horse to the barn and saddled it. Then she left Beaumont forever.

The good horse served her well, but only for a week. It fell prey to an unseen hole in the ground and snapped its leg. Samantha had spent a moment wondering whether she should save her bullets, or if she should be kind and put an end to the horse's misery. She cried uncontrollably then, not so much for the horse alone, but for all that had been lost. It was the first time she had allowed herself to seriously feel the weight of the heavy blanket of dread that stretched over the earth.

With her emotions released at last, she composed herself and then shot the horse.

* * *

One rifle and one revolver.

That's all that remained of her small arsenal now, and her ammunition was quickly deteriorating. The revolver was loaded for the last time, and when it was empty, when its bullets had shattered one last skull, it would be thrown away, just a useless piece of metal left to rust and ruin.

The shotgun ammunition was the first of the ammo to be depleted, most of it all in one night, in which they had made a grisly mess of more than a few zombies.

It was the night she learned that lingering in one place too long was never a good idea. The dead always managed to show up at some point, as if they had some way of sniffing out the living.

She had been asleep in an abandoned barn when they came, but was awakened by their odd moans and shrieks before they could descend upon her. The barn had been a stupid place to seek rest, but she was exhausted to a point beyond caring. She'd closed the door, of course, but there was no way to secure it.

Somehow, the zombies sensed her presence in the barn. They pushed the door open and spilled through like a tide of vermin, hungrily seeking her flesh. Samantha had built a rudimentary barricade out of wood and materials found in the barn, but it was no match for the sheer strength of the zombie's numbers and determination. They poured into the barn and kept coming as she fired away at each one of them in turn with the shotgun, splattering their heads into bloody pieces and chunks.

The first line of the loathsome things met their ghastly end and fell to the ground, impeding the progress of those behind them. Sam rapidly and repeatedly reloaded the shotgun. A large number of corpses already littered the floor of the barn. They were trampled upon. Zombies cared little for their fallen comrades; their only desire was for a fresh meal of ripe flesh and wet, warm organs.

They did not fear the shotgun. They did not cringe at the sound of the blast. They simply walked forward undaunted, undeterred.

Sam fired the shotgun twice more, and two more nearly headless zombies dropped like rag dolls. At last she spied a break in the tide. She managed to grab the remainder of her guns and a small supply of food. Running for the hole, she knocked the shuffling, moaning creatures aside, and fled into the night.

*   *   *

Finding the entrance to the old bomb shelter amidst the scattered debris and severely overgrown lawn was lucky. It would provide a suitable location to rest and regain some strength before continuing her journey across what was once a thriving suburb, but now little more than a barren wasteland.

The small confines of the bomb shelter made her nervous. She checked the locks on the heavy steel door a third time. She paced the tiny room and repeatedly scanned the empty shelves as if a fresh supply of water and canned goods might suddenly appear.

She had been careful to avoid detection as she crept silently through the neighborhood, keeping to the shadows as much as she could. Still, you could never be too sure. The zombies could be sneaky bastards sometimes. They were slow, but they were also usually quiet, and in the darkness, you might be standing right next to one and not know it until it grabs you and tears away a chunk of your flesh with its rotted teeth.

But Sam had been careful.

She sat upon the cot. The mattress was comfortable. She looked worriedly at the door. Though it was locked, she was still nervous.

The door was the only way out. If any of the dead had seen her enter, then even now they could be falling down the concrete steps, piling their bulk against the door as they sought to gain entry. More would come during the night, following the others without really knowing why.

She imagined them wandering out there in the dark, shrouded in fog, hungering for her flesh, seeking her out with, dull, dead eyes. She shivered and lay down upon the mattress, gripping her rifle tight.

She hugged the gun close, as though it were a source of warmth. If anything other than a tool for killing, it was her only friend. It has kept her alive this long, it has kept the abominations at bay, and she cherished it as she would any friend, for without it, she would be lost, alone, and vulnerable.

After what seemed like an eternity, her eyes closed and her body succumbed to sleep.

*   *   *

Samantha wasn't sure how long she slept. She wasn't even sure if it was daylight yet. She had never bothered to seek out a watch during her travel, and up until now, she'd always spent the night in a place where she could see the sun shining the following morning.

But she wasn't tired anymore. The rest had done her some good, and so she figured she might as well be on her way.

She ate her last apple and followed it down with her last soda. She knew she would have to raid a house or two in order to find more food before she left the town.

She hesitated before the door of the bomb shelter. There was no way of knowing what lay on the other side.

Better safe than sorry.

She placed her revolver on the cot within easy reach, and held onto the rifle. She figured she could either shoot or knock aside a single zombie with the rifle, and then fall back to the revolver if more than one attempted to shamble through the door when she opened it.

Steeling herself for the moment, she unlocked the door and chanced opening it a crack. Peering out, she had to squint her eyes against the sun overhead. Then a thin silhouette in tattered clothing rose from the ground, blocking the light.

It reached for the door.

As startled as she was, Sam quickly stepped back and brought up her rifle. She wasn't certain, but it appeared that only one zombie lurked outside the door. She decided she would allow it to enter the shelter and then batter its skull in with the butt of the rifle. Not only would she save a bullet, but she also wouldn't attract any undue attention from the sound of a gunshot.

The door slowly opened, and the zombie strode into view. Samantha swung the butt of the rifle down in an arc at the head of the dead thing.

Exhibiting surprising speed, the zombie brought its arms up in a defensive maneuver. It blocked the attack, though apparently not without suffering some damage to its left forearm. The zombie cried out in pain.

"Ahhh, what the fuck!"

Samantha had been poised to deliver another strike when the zombie's outcry made her pause. Zombies weren't supposed to speak or feel pain.

This zombie also possessed a pair of lively eyes. When they spied the rifle in Samantha's hands, they went wide with shock and fear.

"Ahhh, don't shoot!"

Quickly assessing the situation, Samantha silently cursed herself for mistaking the rather thin and dirty, yet definitely alive teenager for one of the walking dead. Still, with his torn clothing and scraggly hair, and his sudden, silent appearance, it would have been an honest mistake.

Angry with both herself and the kid, she kept the gun trained on him.

"Christ! I almost killed you! What the hell do you think you were doing?"

The teenager was flustered, but tried to compose himself. He lowered his arms, straightened his posture, and smiled meekly. He was still visibly rattled, but did his best to present a calm demeanor.

"Hey, sorry, just doing the same as you, I guess. Looking for a place to camp out for the night. I was scouting out the nearby houses when I saw you go into this yard and then down here. But you shut the door before I could call out to you. I tried knocking, but I guess you couldn't hear me."

Sam glanced at the door. It was very thick, so it was possible the boy was telling the truth.

"So if I wasn't answering the door, why'd you stick around?"

"I was tired. Where else was I gonna go?"

"So you slept down here, in front of the door? Why, when the house is right over there? Wouldn't a bed have been more comfortable?"

"Well, sure it would. But I didn't want to miss you when you came back out."

"Oh? Why is that?"

The kid shrugged. "Well, I was kind of hoping I could go with you. We could be traveling companions!"

"Kid, you don't even know where I'm going. And what makes you think I'd want a scrawny runt like you trailing along behind me anyway?"

The kid flinched. It was obvious Samantha had wounded him with her words. She didn't care. She lowered her rifle and retrieved her revolver from the cot.

"Beat it kid," she said. "I travel alone."

"Why? I thought there was safety in numbers."

"Not in this situation. Alone, I can move quietly. I can hide easier. I don't have to worry about anyone but myself. I don't have to worry that some idiot kid is going to make noise and bring a whole lot of zombies my way. You follow me?"

"Yeah, but..."

"No buts. Just leave me alone. I've got miles to walk to get where I'm going. I don't need to be looking back every five minutes to see if you need your nose wiped."

Sam pushed him out of the way and ascended the short flight of steps.

"Hey!" the kid protested. He chased her up the steps. "I can take care of myself just fine. I may be young, but I'm smart. I'm resourceful."

Sam turned around and scrutinized the teenager. In the full light of the sun, he looked more hopeless than ever. He carried no gear of any kind and the clothes he wore were a bit worse for wear. A pair of dirty, ripped jeans, a tattered flannel shirt, a scuffed leather jacket and sneakers with the laces undone.

Sam shook her head. "C'mon kid, seriously? You can't even keep your shoes tied."

The teenager looked down and saw that his shoes were indeed untied. He dropped to one knee and started tying them.

Every instinct told Sam to just turn around and start walking, try to disappear behind a corner somewhere and leave the kid behind. But then she thought of her son. This kid in front of her was probably about the same age. Wherever her son might be, she hoped that someone would choose to help him if he needed it, rather than turn their back and walk away.

Samantha closed her eyes and sighed. When she opened them again, she beheld the kid standing in place, a hopeful expression on his face.

"What's your name?" she asked.

"Danny," he answered.

"All right Danny. But you do what I say, when I say it. And if I get tired of you and tell you to go away, you do that, too, without argument. Got it?"

Danny's features brightened. He looked extremely relieved. It was obvious then how scared the kid actually was.

"Hey, that's great! Thanks so much. And don't worry, I can handle myself. I've killed a few zombies already."

Sam raised an eyebrow. "Have you? With what?"

"Oh, I had to club one on the head with a rock. And I had a knife, but it got stuck in another one's skull. I couldn't get it out."

"Okay, well, maybe we'll find you something soon, but my plan is to avoid them altogether. I've been sticking to the countryside rather than the roads, avoiding towns except when I need supplies. Which is now. Have you searched any of the houses for food? I'd prefer to find something here, rather than go further into town. Zombies tend to congregate more in town centers for some reason."

Danny shook his head. "I was going to look in this house last night, but then I saw you."

"And you waited. Got it. Well, let's go have a look then."

The kid seemed overjoyed to be included, and eagerly followed closely behind Samantha as she started off for the nearest house.

*　　*　　*

The night was chilly, but Sam didn't want to chance a fire. She and Danny sat together in the midst of a large cornfield, surrounded by the tall cornstalks. She'd decided to camp here for the night and then put Danny on watch for a bit. He might prove useful after all. And even if he fell asleep, any walking corpses moving through the cornfield would likely make enough noise to rouse her from her slumber. She'd become a very light sleeper over the past few weeks.

They shared a can of corn and some warm soda, both acquired during their search of some of the houses in the town they'd left behind that morning. The first two houses they had checked had turned up nothing useful, but the third house had provided a wealth of canned goods, and even some fresh vegetables that were growing unattended in a backyard garden.

Samantha already carried a can opener, so she filled her pack with as much canned goods as she could carry without overloading herself. After scrounging around in the closets, they turned up another duffcl bag, which they filled as well with more cans, fresh vegetables, and some bottles of soda.

They found no guns or ammunition, but Danny helped himself to a hammer from a toolbox. After checking the radio to see if any stations were broadcasting (they weren't), the pair departed and had been walking steadily westward ever since.

Danny spent much of the day babbling randomly about a wide variety of subjects, and Samantha spent much of the day attempting to tune him out.

That evening, as they supped in the cornfield, Danny shared his insight into the zombie phenomena.

"I think it's some voodoo priest somewhere."

"What?"

"You know, those guys from Africa that make zombies out of people and stuff? They have voodoo down south in Louisiana. I'd bet a voodoo priest cast a spell and made all the dead come back to life. If we can find him and kill him, the spell will be broken, and all the dead will be...well, dead again. For real."

Sam looked at him with a mixture of distaste and annoyance. "That's the stupidest idea I've ever heard."

"Oh, really? And how many ideas have you heard? I haven't heard that many."

Sam had to admit to herself she hadn't heard too many plausible theories either.

"I suppose you think that UFOs came down and shot some kind of beam at the Earth that made the dead wake up, like that one news guy said."

Sam shook her head. "It doesn't matter what caused it. We're screwed, plain and simple. Chances are, most anyone you see walking around these days is a zombie. Everyone else is either hiding or got eaten by those rotting bastards. There isn't anyone coming to save us. The government probably went into hiding weeks ago when they realized things were going bad, and the army, well, they probably split too once they realized there wasn't really anyone in charge anymore."

"Okay, so what's your plan then?"

"No plan. I just want to find my son."

"You have a son?"

Sam rolled her eyes. "That's what I just said, isn't it?"

"Well, where is he?"

Sam shook her head and looked at the ground. "I don't know. He was in Freedmont when all this started. With his father. But now, who knows?"

"How come you weren't with them?"

Samantha remained silent for a minute and continued staring at the ground. Then she looked up and stared at Danny. "They left seven years ago. My husband and I, we had...problems."

"Oh." The kid didn't quite know what else to say. Then he had another thought. "What if you get to Freedmont and find your son and he's dead? Or worse, what if he's a zombie?"

Samantha resisted the urge to grab her rifle and clobber the kid across the skull with it. "Then I'll put a bullet in his brain and make sure he stays dead, so that his soul will be at peace." After a second of thought, she added, "And if you mention my son again, I'll kill you, too."

*　*　*

The bright moon stared down upon them, unblinking. Samantha slept, but her dreams were fraught with horrid imagery of jaws full of gnashing yellow teeth pulling apart strips of bloody flesh. Hundreds of mouths chewed and sucked the juices from organs while screaming schoolchildren were torn apart by an unflinching, uncaring crowd of zombies.

In her dream, she was an observer, powerless to help. And then one of the zombies spotted her and broke off from the group. It slowly headed in her direction. She willed her feet to turn and run, but was rooted in place and unable to cry out for help.

The pale, sickly green creature was upon her, its hands groping beneath her clothes, its clammy skin causing her to recoil within herself. Its lips, wet with blood and gore, caressed her cheek and neck, and it exhaled stale air into her face.

Desperately flailing, her eyes fluttered open, and she felt a weight leaning against her side. With the last vestiges of her nightmare still fresh in her mind, she shrieked and pushed away from whatever lay beside her.

She felt a warm hand pull away from her breast, and a mop of hair brushed against her cheek.

Danny scrambled away from Samantha. "I'm sorry! I'm sorry!"

Still slightly disoriented, Samantha felt her neck. The flesh was still intact, but it was wet with saliva.

"Were you...were you kissing me?" A rage boiled up inside her. "What the hell were you just doing, you little shit?"

Danny pushed himself farther away, looking fearful and apologetic. "I'm sorry, it's just...."

"Just what!" Samantha leapt to her feet. Her eyes were dark pits of fury. Her hands were balled into fists.

"You're pretty." Danny lowered his eyes, unable to meet the storm that blazed in hers.

"I'm pretty? So you thought you'd fucking have your way with me while I slept?"

"No! I mean, well, I thought you might...."

"Might what?" she shouted.

"Well, I've never...."

"Never what?"

"I've never been with a girl before, okay?" Danny raised his eyes in shame. "I just thought that maybe if I showed you I liked you, you'd like me back."

Samantha strode over to the whimpering kid and savagely backhanded him across the face. Not completely satisfied, she leaned over and hit him again.

Danny lay on the ground and spit out a thick glob of blood. Samantha thought she might have seen a tooth in the mess.

"Don't you ever touch me again," she said steadily but angrily. "I could kill you right now. No one would ever know. But I'm not a murderer, and there's a shortage of live people around these days. But when we get to the next town, you're gone from my sight. And I recommend you stay gone from my sight forever, because if I ever see you again, I may rethink my stance on murder."

Sam left the kid lying on the ground and walked back to her gear. She sat staring at the cornstalks, fuming. She knew she wouldn't get any more sleep that night, and she also knew that the kid probably wouldn't last more than another day or two on his own.

She didn't care.

*   *   *

They walked throughout most of the morning in silence. Danny tried to initiate a conversation or apologize again on a few occasions, but a withering glare from Samantha quickly silenced his attempts.

When Sam spied a few zombies in the fields some distance away, she and Danny took to the nearby woods instead, using the trees and undergrowth as cover. Shortly before noon, through a small break in the trees, Samantha saw the perimeter of a town nestled in a valley only a few miles away.

Samantha set down her rifle and removed the pack from her shoulders. She opened the pack and retrieved a pair of binoculars. Danny walked over and stood silently beside her while she scanned the town.

"It looks clear," Sam stated. "I'm sure there're a few zombies wandering around, but if you're careful you can avoid them. You'll probably be able to find some more supplies, maybe even a gun."

There was no response from Danny.

Samantha sighed and lowered the binoculars.

She found Danny staring at her with a strange expression on his face. He held her rifle in her hands. It was pointed at her.

Samantha was far from amused. "Kid, put down that gun. We're not playing Cowboys and Indians here. This is real life, and that's a real gun, and I don't feel like having a real bullet blow my brains out just because you felt the need to prove your manhood to me."

Danny opened his mouth to say something, but closed it again. He didn't lower the gun. His eyes watered.

Samantha reached for the revolver at her hip.

Danny pulled the trigger. A bloody eruption on Samantha's chest followed the thunderous roar of the gunshot. She crumpled to the ground.

Utter shock spread across her face, and her left arm moved spasmodically.

Danny stared down at her, appearing just as shocked. His eyes were wide as he observed the torrent of blood pouring from the wound.

"I'm sorry," he whispered.

Samantha's eyes followed the sound of Danny's voice. A trickle of blood escaped her lips. She spoke painfully through grit teeth. "Bastard."

"I'm sorry," Danny said again. "But you were going to leave me." He reached down and plucked the revolver from her hip.

She tried grabbing it away from him as he did so, but her efforts were weak and futile.

"I need these," he said. "I won't make it on my own." His eyes narrowed. "But you knew that, didn't you?"

She rolled over and crawled slowly across the ground, then collapsed. She breathed slowly. Her heavy gasps pushed clouds of dirt into the air.

"So I'm just taking your advice," Danny continued. "I'll travel alone. Look out for myself. But now I have food and guns."

Samantha heard the words as a distant echo. She thought of her son, and wondered for the last time if he was still alive, or if he roamed the countryside, seeking live meat. She closed her eyes.

Standing over her, Danny still spoke. "I can end it now if you want. So that you don't come back. But I don't want to waste any more bullets. I can use the hammer."

Samantha remained silent. She didn't move. Danny frowned. He'd expected a least some reaction.

"What, you think I'm kidding?" he shouted. "You still think I'm a fucking joke now?"

Something touched his shoulder. Danny turned and shrieked as the putrid fingers of a reaching zombie left a trail of slimy dirt along his cheek. The dead thing groaned as it closed its fingers around empty air.

Stepping backwards, Danny tripped over Samantha's prone body and fell. Panicking, he raised the revolver and fired as the zombie leaned over him. At nearly point blank range, the bullet shattered the upper portion of the zombie's skull, painting the ground with bits of brain, bone, and rotting flesh.

His heart pounding violently, Danny nonetheless felt some confidence returning in the wake of the kill. But then another zombie shambled forth from the bushes. It wasn't alone.

A small group of the walking dead steadily marched forward through the undergrowth, emerging into the clearing. Danny fired the revolver blindly, hitting a few of the zombies but felling none of them. Then the gun was empty.

Danny cursed and leapt to his feet. He swung the rifle at the closest zombie, an old, wrinkled woman who looked like she must have once been a kindly grandmother. The butt of the rifle connected with the side of her face. Something crunched, and an eyeball slowly oozed out of the socket. The old woman dropped.

Danny kicked her in the head for good measure, and then did the same to Samantha's body, cursing her before turning to flee.

As he spun around, he found a hulking, shirtless man waiting to greet him with open arms. Danny screamed, and the fat, repulsive zombie growled like a savage beast. It closed its arms around Danny, pinning the teenager's arms to his sides. The zombie gnashed its teeth against his face as it pulled at the flesh of his cheek.

Danny's frightened screams turned to shrieks of agony as half his face was savagely ripped away. The zombie released him in order to consume its meal, but others quickly took its place.

As blood poured down his body, Danny flailed against the tide of zombies that drove him to the ground and tore into him.

His screams slowly faded and he gurgled his last sound just as Samantha opened her lifeless eyes.

ANTHONY GIANGREGORIO

PARADE OF THE DEAD

John Benson, of 328 Forest Drive, peered out his bedroom window at the street below, his dark brown hair falling into his eyes so he had to brush it back.

They were still there.

The zombies.

As difficult as it was to believe, even after more than two weeks of witnessing it first hand, but it was true.

There were dead people walking around outside.

As he watched them, he recognized many of the people moving about. There was Mrs. Cullen, just shy of her sixtieth birthday. She would never reach it now; she would stay fifty-nine forever.

As John watched her shuffle about like she had amnesia, he couldn't help but stare at her withered frame. For she was as naked as the day she was born, with the exception of the shower cap on her head.

She was missing a large part of her lower right thigh and a chunk of her left arm. Coagulated blood seeped from the wounds, coating her in a sticky red syrup that had hundreds of flies feasting on her. John saw she didn't seem to notice.

It was her expression that was the most chilling, though the sagging breasts that looked like two deflated and wrinkled water balloons were a close second. Her blank gaze was chilling to behold. Her mouth sagged open and her jaw was slack, making her look like a dullard. He couldn't see her eyes from his bedroom window but he did see that she never blinked.

And why should she? She was dead after all.

Mrs. Cullen wandered past his house and then turned into a driveway a few houses down. He wasn't worried; he knew she'd be back soon enough.

Next to come by the house like an early morning walker out for a jaunt was Mr. Keelson. He was a slovenly man with a balding pate and a large belly. Only now half that belly was missing, a cottage cheese like substance hanging out, some of it splattering to the road as he walked. It looked like someone had taken a massive drill to his abdomen and had turned it on high. As he walked, John could see into the large hole in his torso and at the glistening organs within.

Mimicking life in death, Mr. Keelson kept reaching into the folds of flesh, rummaging around for a juicy morsel, and then he would shove it into his mouth. He was eating himself piece by bloody piece.

Bits of kidney slipped out of his mouth to land on the pavement, looking like he was leaving a trail of slugs behind him.

He walked past the house and then further down the road. Like Mrs. Cullen, John wasn't worried; he knew Mr. Keelson would be back.

As he shifted the curtain around the window for a better view of the street, John saw the next dead soul come into view.

The ghoul had been a cheerleader once, her yellow and blue uniform hugging her slim form like a second skin.

Only now she wasn't the perky young cheerleader. Now she was a creature from Hell.

She was missing her right arm, the white bone poking through the muscle and tissue, and in her other hand, the only one she had left, she still had her pom-pom. As she walked, the tinsel would swing back and forth, and it looked like she was cheering.

Yay, dead people! Goooo, death!

John watched her hobble by, and though he knew he was being sick, he still admired her shapely ass when she moved off down the street, grinning at the way the material hugged her thighs.

But he wasn't worried, she'd be back in due time also.

Next came Herman, still wearing his postal uniform. John didn't know the guy's last name; to him he had always been just Herman.

Herman was missing his mail bag now, and one shoe was gone, along with a few fingers and toes. Herman looked as if he'd been through a meat grinder and lost, his uniform now hanging in rags. But still he made his rounds, even if he didn't have any more mail to deliver.

John watched the rest of them shuffle by, the other neighbors from down the street, the UPS man, still in brown khakis and shorts, and the newspaper boy who'd delivered his last paper.

They all walked by his window as if on parade.

John stepped away and turned around. He didn't want to because he knew what he'd see lying there in the bed, but he had no choice.

Tied to the bed, all fours limbs secured so she was spread-eagled, was his wife.

Marsha didn't look so hot and there was no amount of makeup that could help her complexion.

She hissed at him as he made his way around the bed, but he ignored her. It had been like this for three days after the dead first began to walk, as it had taken her that much time to succumb to the bite on her right forearm.

She had been at the market when one of the first ghouls had popped up. It made sense, too, as the Mayberry Mortuary was just down the block. The man who had attacked her had worn half a suit, the rear part open to the world, the bare-assed ghoul not at all immodest about his nakedness. When Marsha had stepped out of the store, the zombie had been there and had sunk his teeth into her arm like it was a roast duck. She pulled back instinctively and upon seeing the man's pale and haggard face, had assumed he was a bum.

Luckily a police cruiser was driving by and the two officers had witnessed the entire incident.

As the two cops jumped the dead man, Marsha took her queue and ran away, not wanting to become bogged down with questions and having to go to court later to get the man sentenced to a jail term. She was simply happy to get away from there.

For three days she'd nursed the wound until John knew something was seriously wrong with her. On the third day, she couldn't get out of bed and that night she'd slipped into a coma. Of course by now the news was rampant with reports of attacks by what appeared to be walking dead people.

But John had bigger things to worry about as his wife slipped into death. As he sat on the floor at the foot of the bed he'd cried, not knowing what to do. His parents were dead years ago and he was an only child. The neighbors were dealing with their own grief and loss and had no time for him. So he was all alone with a dying wife and a world going to Hell in a hand basket. Or was that a coffin?

It was as he sat on the floor, his knees curled up to his chest, arms around legs, that he witnessed the dead walk for himself first hand.

He was dozing lightly, trying to rest, when he heard the sheets shifting on the bed. At first he didn't know what he'd heard but soon he was awake, the only illumination the pale light of the streetlamp coming through the main window.

He looked up to see the sheets slowly rising, like a figure from an old horror movie, perhaps Dracula rising from the tomb. It was when the sheets slid off his wife, her face now showing, that he knew there was something terribly off about her.

At first her glazed eyes saw nothing, as if she had woken from a deep sleep, but then when John shifted position, his body brushing the edge of the bed and making noise, her eyes seemed to come into partial focus.

He didn't know what he was looking at as he stared into her dead eyes. He saw something there, though vacant, but he couldn't put his finger on it.

Later, he would come to realize there was a hunger in those white orbs, a hunger he could never hope to fulfill.

She hissed at him and moved to get off the bed and John, sitting on the floor, watching like a child punished for doing something bad, was frozen.

She slowly got up, her arms and legs unsteady, but in a few seconds she had her balance.

Then she came for him, mouth wide, saliva dripping out of the corners to splash onto the carpet, her dead orbs piercing into his very soul.

And John knew she was gone and whatever was in the bedroom with him wasn't his wife anymore.

Though filled with fear and revulsion, he knew if he didn't stop her she would do...what...to him. The news reports said the dead were eating the living, and he could only assume she would attempt to do the same. So he did what he had to do; he defended himself.

When she was standing over him, her mouth so wide it looked like her jaw would unhinge at any moment, he kicked out with his right foot, knocking her to the floor.

She fell towards the bed, bouncing off it to roll onto the carpeting and she was now only a few inches from his left foot.

Her hand reached out like a whip and latched onto the foot as she tried to crawl up his shaking body. She managed to get halfway up, John staring into her dead eyes as she hissed and snarled.

He suddenly realized his groin was directly below her and if she figured this out, he was about to become a eunuch, so with a yell of disgust, he bucked his hips and tossed her off him.

She rolled across the room to come up against the bedroom door and John came to his feet.

His wife was only five-six, not very tall compared to his five-nine, and he pounced on her back, sitting on her so she couldn't get up.

She flailed with her arms and beat her hands onto the carpet, but she couldn't shove off his weight.

The bureau was near his reach, so he pulled each drawer open, yanking out socks, shirts and underwear, looking for something, anything that would work as bonds to secure her.

Then, in the bottom drawer, he found Marsha's scarves. They were frilly things, full of all the colors of the rainbow, and he grabbed them in hand and pulled them to him as some of them fluttered to the floor.

As fast as he could, he tied her hands and feet and then picked her up, dropping her back onto the bed.

All the while her teeth clacked as she tried to bite him.

"Honey, I don't think I'll be sleeping in the same bed with you tonight or ever," he said, his voice cracking slightly as he fought to maintain his sanity.

If she heard him she gave no reaction, but merely tried to bite him again and again.

Not knowing what to do, John left her then, closing the bedroom door behind him, figuring he needed a good stiff drink.

When he returned to the bedroom later that night, he found she was on the floor, wiggling around like a worm on a hook.

He decided then that just having her tied up wasn't good enough, so he transferred her back to the bed and tied her up one limb at a time until she was spread-eagled on the mattress in a perverse position, as if they were about to have kinky sex. But that was the farthest thing from his mind. Since she'd died and returned, her skin had begun to crack, the red muscles and tendons within shining through. Her face had taken on a bluish pallor that gave her the look of a drowning victim. Her lips were now swollen and her skin had grown tighter, making her look all the more cadaverous.

In truth, she was the embodiment of death.

But though she was dead, she was all he had left in a dying world and he found himself returning to the bedroom to be with her.

Wanting to take his mind off her, he'd taken to looking out the window, watching the walking dead as they paraded past his house.

There must have been something in their dead brains that kept them near to where they lived or worked because time and again they would return. They seemed to be walking a route, and when they reached the end of the block, they would turn and shuffle back the other way. All day, every day and night they did this.

He would watch for hours at a time, making up names for the ones he didn't know, the others, once his neighbors, he would actually smile at. They were dead and he was still alive. He was winning in the end.

It was late one night as he stared out at the dead block party, lost in the stories he'd made up for each of them, when his wife got free of one of her scarves.

Whether by design or dumb luck, she was then able to free her other arm, so that her upper body was now able to reach over and grab him.

John, lost in reverie as he stared out the window, turned to check on her to see her sitting up, arms outreached to grab him. Before he could jump away, she pulled him to her and sank yellow teeth into his throat, tearing out a large portion of his neck.

Blood shot out and sprayed the wall crimson and he gagged, punching her in the face as he stumbled away.

His hand reached up to his throat to staunch the blood flow but hot plasma squirted through his fingers, dripping onto the carpet to stain the shag scarlet.

His mouth opening and closing in shock and panic, he stumbled downstairs, hoping to get a bandage and save himself, but even as he stumbled towards the bathroom and the first aid kit, he knew he would never make it.

Already he was growing weak from blood loss, his vision going in and out as he bounced off the walls in the dark house.

He knew then he was going to die, and he had seconds to decide how he wanted to spend eternity.

But it took only a split second for him to decide what he would do, and turning, he ignored the bathroom and half-walked, half-fell towards the front door.

Opening it wide, he felt the cool air blow on his face and he then turned and walked into the living room, each step a chore as his blood seeped out of his torn throat.

Above him, on the second floor, he could hear his wife banging around as she tried to free her still secured legs. He actually grinned then, wishing her well. Maybe she would get free eventually to then join the walking dead outside in the street.

John plopped down in his favorite chair and stared at the open front door, the cool night air washing the stink of the house away. He hadn't realized how bad it had become, the redolence of death filling the walls and floors, seeping into the furniture. Trapped inside with his rotting wife, he had grown accustomed to it without ever realizing it.

He coughed then, spitting blood to stain his shirt a bright red and he couldn't keep his eyes open anymore, they were just too heavy.

Then, closing his eyes, he slipped off into death

*   *   *

Brandon Wilkinson of 456 Forest Drive peered out his living room window, watching the living dead as they shuffled past his house in the middle of the street like an undead parade was going on.

It had been more than a month and a half since the dead began to walk and Brandon had been holed up in his house, waiting for the world to return to normal. But the more he waited, the more he was coming to believe the world would never be the same again.

He was smarter than most and had stocked up well on food and water. He had enough to last him a year if he was careful, not that he believed he would need that long.

The electricity and water was out, the food in the refrigerator and freezer used up weeks ago as he didn't want to waste it and it would be instant milk for the time being until everything got back on track.

To pass the time he did one of two things. One was to read. He loved to read and had a massive library, one that would take two lives to read them all. The other thing that whiled away the hours was to sit at his living room window and watch the walking dead shuffle by his house.

They did this every day and never seemed to leave for long. They would walk a circuitous route by his house to the far end of the street to then turn back around and go the opposite away. All day, every day and night they did this.

As Brandon sat with a warm beer in his hand, he spotted a familiar face.

Mrs. Cullen was still as naked as the day she first appeared, though her withered skin was missing in more than one place as the crows got at her.

Another ghoul came around the bend and he saw it was the cheerleader. She wasn't as attractive as a month ago, but the figure was still there, as long as you didn't mind a little pus with your lovemaking.

Next came Mr. Keelson, more than half his weight gone thanks to a diet of eating himself. Almost his entire set of organs was now missing, chewed up and forced into his ever expanding stomach. Brandon figured it was going to rupture any day now. A family of rats had set up their home in his gut, enjoying the protection and comfort of the meat cave.

Then came the mailman. Brandon had dubbed him Brian, for a friend he'd known years ago. He thought the mailman looked a little like him so the name had stuck.

Oh, yes, all the residents of the neighborhood were out as always, stumbling about lazily. If they saw live prey that would be a different story, of course. There were many bloodstains on the sidewalk and street from where someone had been trying to make a break for it on foot. But once they were cornered by the larger numbers of walking dead, they were quickly brought down and eaten, usually to come back with half a face or a missing limb to join the undead ranks.

So Brandon knew he wasn't going anywhere, at least not until the dead were destroyed. And he didn't have a gun so fighting wasn't an option.

So he would wait and sooner or later the world would go back to normal; it had to.

As he peered through the wooden slats on his window, Brandon spotted a new recruit to the undead army.

The zombie stumbled like a drunkard, its head lolling to the side, the open and jagged wound in its neck filled with maggots and flies.

Brandon watched John Benson for the entire time he shuffled past his window, then he turned his attention to the UPS guy, who was having a problem with a curb on the far sidewalk.

And so the parade of the dead would continue, until either Brandon was rescued or he joined their ranks himself.

MICHAEL SIMON

REVELATIONS

I learned very quickly that hotels were the safest. As a lone survivor, I wouldn't dare pitch a tent in the vulnerable outdoors and leave myself exposed to the undead. Rather, four solid walls and a thick, locked door radiated at least some semblance of security. The smell of mouldy carpets and dusty bedcovers was a small price to pay.

I shifted the TV to the floor and covered the shelf with my sawed-off shotgun and bandolier, Beretta nine millimeter and the knap sack containing the rest of my essentials, flashlight, batteries, matches and what was left of my meager food supply. Not to mention the picture of Jennifer.

I stuck to the second floor exclusively. The rooms were too high for the zombies to reach and yet close enough to the ground in case of an emergency. The doors would stop anything less than a sledgehammer and the peephole allowed for a check of the immediate hallway.

I peeled off my leather jacket and dirty clothes, stained sweatshirt and mud encrusted jeans that had taken me half way across the state. I tentatively fingered the red welt on my shoulder, the result of a collision with a tree trunk outside Rock Springs, and winced slightly. My other blemishes, the various yellow-green bruises on my thighs and arms, the results of other run-ins, were fading slowly. Here, in my fortieth year, I was constantly amazed just how much the human body could withstand, both mentally and physically.

I opened the taps in the sink and whispered a silent thank you when the water flowed. I knew, sooner or later, the pressure in the lines would bleed out and indoor plumbing, like electricity, hot food, and four week vacations would eventually fade into memory.

I put the plug in, grabbed some handy hotel soap and proceeded to scrub six weeks of sweat and dirt from my clothes. Afterwards I hung them over the curtain rod in the shower. Supper was a muted affair as I finished off the last of the raisins and biscuits all the while staring at the faded photo.

Tomorrow I would have to scrounge for more food.

Out of habit, I double checked the door before climbing into bed. Surviving this long meant not taking chances. By now I was well acquainted with the constant ache in my muscles and joints and it was all I could do not to think about hot tubs or saunas. Outside, the western sky was flaming red and the wind howled through the bare trees at times rising in pitch to an inhuman scream. It was the perfect backdrop to another round of nightmares that had infected my dreams since the *change*. I thought about my family for a few minutes, remembering the way it was, before fatigue dragged me into slumber.

*   *   *

I woke to the sound of smashing glass. My eyes snapped open and I found myself reaching for the shotgun even before my mind kicked into gear. It took precious seconds before I remembered who I was or where I was. But by then I had taken the safety off and pumped one shell into the chamber.

There were more sounds coming from outside so I quietly stepped over to the window. Edging the curtain back ever so slightly, I carefully scanned the parking out. A dozen cars littered the pavement, some parked smartly within the lines; some wrapped around telephone poles with doors ajar and decayed bodies hanging out. My Hummer was parked at the far end, exactly where I left it. Facing me across the parking lot sat an identical four story hotel with rows of windows running down the length of the building. I watched a group of shuffling figures congregate around one of the doors on the ground floor. It looked like something had garnered their attention as one of the undead used a rock to smash the large plate-glass window.

I quickly dressed and packed and was about to leave when I heard the first plaintive cry. It sounded almost melodic at first, soft musical notes leaking into the parking lot. Then, in a moment of insight, I recognized it. It was crying. I had almost forgotten what that sounded like.

I hesitated and then realized what I was doing. "Damn," I muttered. Last thing I needed was to get involved.

A scream erupted from the room just as the undead forced their way in.

Now I knew what had attracted their attention. I automatically scanned the hallway through the peep hole before slipping out. My sneakers were silent across the gray, eighties carpet and down the stairwell that was, thankfully, empty. The door leading out into the parking lot creaked as I slowly swung it open, my finger tight on the trigger. However the parking lot was deserted as the undead had migrated to the noise and the possibility of another meal.

Only a few feet away, the Hummer was like a magnet, pulling at me. I spat a curse and dropped my knapsack.

"Because I have to," I replied under my breath. "Because I couldn't live with myself if I didn't try."

I started running. My shotgun was up, safely off, when the two zombies in the doorway spun at the sudden noise. Slowing only enough to draw a bead, I took the top half of the policeman's head off with my first shot, gray brain matter creating modern art on the hotel's stone facade. The second shell atomized the face of a bikini clad blonde and she collapsed on top of the cop in a truly lifeless pile of seeping flesh. I had a brief mental image of the first time I fired the shotgun on that night in the city, pin wheeling backwards as the weapon almost dislocated my shoulder. This time I had the gun jammed firmly in my armpit and the barrel raised to eye level as I rushed into the hotel room, almost impaling a fat man in a tattered business suit who turned and lunged at me. All my eyes registered before the gun fired was a mass of stained yellow teeth and tendrils of membrane-like tissue hanging from his lips like strips of saliva. Only they weren't.

Headless, he flopped backwards on the king sized bed, a geyser of blood shooting across the room. The two female zombies clawing at the bathroom door hissed and started for me. Two shots in rapid succession slammed them against the wall, pulverizing brain matter and bone into a semisolid gel that slowly slid down the stucco interior. The gun clicked on empty so I automatically pulled the Beretta out of my waistband. I was high on an adrenaline rush but I still thought I heard sounds coming from the parking lot.

"Hey!" I banged on the bathroom door. "The room's clear. It's time to run."

When nothing happened I rattled it again. "Look, whoever you are, I 'm not hanging around. This is you're only chance to get out because in about twenty seconds this place is going to be crawling with undead and you don't want to be at that party."

The lock on the door clicked and a dirty, stained face peered out. It looked to be all of twelve.

"Is it...safe?" she asked in a voice so low I had to strain to hear.

"For another fifteen seconds," I said, snapping shells into the shotgun. "You coming?"

Her wide eyes registered the bodies on the floor. Then she nodded.

"Let's go." I slammed a shell into the chamber and started out the door. The closest zombie, a postal worker with the remains of his bag still hanging over his shoulder, took it in the neck. Spraying bits of gristle and blood, he spun to the ground in a slow motion circle. He wasn't down for good but he was no longer a problem. My mind automatically registered the fact a score of undead were converging on the parking lot from all directions, their lumbering, stumbling gaits almost comical.

I bent down and scooped up my pack.

"Wait," the girl suddenly cried. "My dog is still in there!"

I took one quick look at the four story hotel and the mass of zombies and shook my head.

"Sorry, honey, but you got two seconds to get in because I'm leaving." We had as much chance of finding Lassie and getting away as a snowball's chance in Hell, which, by the way, the parking lot was rapidly starting to resemble.

I gave her credit; she barely vacillated before veering around the postal worker who was stubbornly trying to crawl with his head only half attached. She jumped into the passenger seat as I started it up.

"Smart decision," I said, jamming it into gear. Two of the un-dead had closed the distance and took the full brunt of the Hummer as I accelerated. I could actually feel bones crack under its seventeen inch wheels.

The girl grabbed both sides of her seat as I cut hard right, aiming behind the hotel.

"That's not the way out!" she cried.

"Easy," I replied smoothly. "It's an access path that joins up with the main road. I checked it out last night before getting a room." Like I always do. "Besides I'm not even sure this vehicle could force its way through the crowd filling the entrance at the moment."

I saw her shudder. "It's the noise that attracts them," she said.

I nodded. "It's always something."

The Hummer bounced over potholes in a road that had been long neglected even before the *change*. I didn't let up on the gas but managed a sidelong look at the girl, her matted dark hair and pale skin covered by a worn winter jacket and stained jeans. Her hands and clothes were so dirty it looked like she had crawled for miles just to make it to the hotel. Thin and frail looking, for an instant she reminded me of Jennifer, until she turned and caught my eye and I recognized the pain. My daughter never had that look.

"Name's David," I said, extending a hand.

She dropped her gaze to the floor and ignored the gesture.

"I'm Angel," she said softly. "Angel Morrison."

I let my hand fall back to the wheel.

"Were you hiding there long?"

She resumed looking out the window but managed a slight nod between bumps. "A few days. I got in through a broken window and found a master key in the office. I think they spotted my shadow in that room..." She started to tremble.

If she were Jennifer I would have reached over and gave her a hug. However, it was obvious Angel didn't want to be touched so I focused on the road.

"They may be slow," I said. "But there's nothing wrong with their hearing or eyesight. All it takes is a little slip, a noise or moving curtain, and they're all over you."

Angel suddenly dabbed at some moisture in the corner of her eyes.

"Was there anyone else with you, a friend or family member?" I asked.

She shook her head forcefully and rubbed harder at her eyes. I knew what that meant.

I slowed the Hummer down as we approached the main road.

"Which way," she asked.

"East," I said. "I've been trying to get home since it all started."

She turned in her seat and stared at me. "Nobody has a home anymore," she whispered. "It's just us and...Them."

I felt a lump form in the back of my throat. "Maybe," I admitted. Before the last of the stations went off the air, the talking heads said the undead were everywhere.

"I need to know for sure."

Angel seemed to take the measure of me, a preteen sizing up a middle aged man.

"Okay," she said.

I hesitated. "Okay, you want to come or okay, you want to get out?"

"I'll come," she said. "My family's dead."

Her bluntness stung me. I hadn't yet reached that level of acceptance.

"Hang on." I turned right onto the road and accelerated. "Those gunshots can be heard for miles. They'll all be moving this way."

"I know," she said.

We were far enough out of town that only a few abandoned vehicles littered the road. The rest had been left in the breakdown lane or crashed into the gutter, the occasional corpse slowly rotting beside them or already torn apart by animals or worse. On that first night, the freeways out of the city had basically been impassable; the cars stuck bumper to bumper, effectively sealing off all avenues of escape. Those trapped were at the mercy of the undead.

It had taken three days and I barely made it out...

"There! In the middle of the road!" Angel pointed towards a trio of zombies who had converged over something that looked like road kill but was two sizes too large.

I swerved to the right at the same instant they noticed us. Their pale, blood covered faces contorted in a spasm of muscles as they lurched towards the Hummer.

Angel pointed again, this time towards the woods. "There's two more over there."

"I see them," I murmured. To squeeze between the two groups would be... problematic. But if the girl was expecting me to stop and turn around she was about to get a surprise. I shoved the pedal down.

Her eyes widened and she automatically grabbed the dash.

"It's why I chose this vehicle," I said. "It's almost a tank."

In truth I stumbled across it outside Salt Lake City. The driver, a woman by the look of the strips of cloth matted to the pavement, must have actually gotten out of the Hummer. The keys were still in the ignition.

I aimed for the two on the right. They were smaller, almost child-sized and therefore less mass. Their faces were hooded behind a curtain of hair and their clothes little more than ripped shreds flopping in the wind.

The first zombie bounced off the front bumper, cart wheeled over the hood and landed in the ditch, its legs bent in four different directions. The second, somewhat smaller, was sucked under the vehicle.

As we accelerated away, I removed one tense hand from the wheel and wiped my perspiring brow while Angel exhaled and leaned back.

"You all right?"

She took another deep breath and nodded.

"It's just another day in Paradise," I said.

That induced a trace of a smile before she dragged it back under.

I grinned. It was nice to see there was still a little girl in there somewhere.

*　*　*

"Are you sure this will actually work?" Angel eyed the plastic tubing in my hand dubiously before shifting her gaze towards the woods on both sides of the road.

"I've been doing it for a while now," I replied. "It's just a matter of physics. When the gas reaches a high point it will flow downhill, into the Hummer's gas tank."

"But how does it get into the tube?"

"You have to suck it up." I almost laughed at the face she made.

"You're crazy," she said.

I stuck my tongue out at her before feeding one end into the van's tank and the other into my mouth, hoping not to repeat a bad experience. The first time I tried it I swallowed a mouthful and vomited for twenty minutes.

With so many cars littering the roadways there was no shortage of gas. The trick was to find one out in the open where the undead couldn't sneak up on you. We had pulled the Hummer right up to the van and I had the shotgun ready just in case. I gave Angel the revolver even though I wasn't sure she knew which end to point.

Thirty minutes later we had accumulated half a tank. I packed away the tubing and the medical kit we found in the back of the van and continued west, looking for that small roadside deli that was listed on one of my maps.

"The gas station we passed probably had some chocolate bars and chips," Angel said.

I shrugged. "It wouldn't do us much good. We need something more than carbohydrates, some protein and stuff."

"Oh." She obviously had no idea what I meant but after two days she wasn't so quick to dismiss my ideas.

I pulled up just outside the entrance to the deli, the Hummer's tires spraying small stones across the hard packed dirt apron. I kept it in gear as we waited. If any zombies were in the area our arrival was an open invitation and they would come stumbling, lurching, crawling...

As we waited I resumed teaching Angel how the gun worked, how to aim and to absorb the recoil. She actually giggled when I described the first time I fired the shotgun.

"You prefer that over this revolver?" she asked.

"It's got more stopping power," I explained. "Aiming is not important at close range."

"And this one," she patted the Beretta on her lap. "Still has to hit them in the head?"

"Yeah, nothing else will stop them."

It was apparent from the beginning, to kill the zombies you had to stop their brain from working. It all came down to neural activity; as long as some brain cells were firing and impulses were going to the muscles and joints, the undead were still a threat. Shut down all brain activity and they died, just like before the change.

"All right, you stay in the Hummer and hit the horn if you see anything."

"I'd rather go with you."

"And I'd rather just focus on getting food and getting out of here," I said. Last thing I needed was a distraction. "I'll just be a couple of minutes."

Stepping outside the Hummer the first thing I noticed was the heat. It radiated off the ground in waves and mixed with a strange staleness that hung in the windless air. My sneakers crunched loose gravel as I walked between the gas pumps and my eyes flickered warily between the front door and corners of the building.

I swung open the flimsy screen door and was immediately overwhelmed by the smell that waffled out of the diner. The wave of putrid, gut-wrenching decay forced me to turn and retch. I stepped back, took a steadying breath and withdrew the trusty handkerchief from my jacket pocket.

I should have known better.

Wrapping it around my mouth and nose made the smell almost tolerable.

The chairs and tables had been piled against the front windows and the blinds had been fully drawn. Several of the ancient, round stools in front of the counter had been bent over at an angle and looked like drunken sailors on their last legs. I kept my shotgun at the ready as I edged around the counter but all I saw were shards of glass and smashed bottles covering a slew of dark stains on the floor.

After visiting similar buildings, I didn't need to see the splintered front door, cast back on snapped hinges, to know that someone had made a last stand here.

And failed.

The saloon style swinging doors invited me into a kitchen that seemed in relatively good order if one ignored the pan of rotten meat over the cold burner and the blood stains on the floor. Still, the pots hung in orderly rows above the stove and neat piles of dry goods were stacked by the stainless steel freezer door. As I stepped closer, I noticed strange scratch marks on the steel and a blood trail that ran out the back.

The handle on the freezer door was bent slightly and wouldn't budge.

"Damn thing," I cursed, gripping it tightly with both hands before giving it a solid heave. At six-four I was never accused of being weak, only stupid.

The seal broke with a sudden *whoosh* and I staggered backwards, just out of the reach of the three zombies who practically jumped out of the freezer. Frost covered and wrapped in frozen clothes, they shocked me into a fatal moment of uncertainty. I had a fleeting vision of yellow teeth and frostbit fingers, of a girl with her face caved in and one eye budging precipitously over a crushed orbital bone and a fat, middle aged black man sporting a white tux and cracked sunglasses.

In that moment of panic, my finger tightened on the trigger and the shell amputated the black man's leg below the knee. He collapsed sideways, tripping up the third zombie, a teenager with a blood encrusted face and a large gaping hole where his jaw should have been.

The girl fell into me with teeth and claws searching for the soft flesh of my face. I twisted around but was off balance and we stumbled to the floor. I felt teeth sink into my leather jacket, biting and ripping like an animal. I slammed an elbow into her face and, following that, the butt of my gun. Broken bits of teeth flew across the floor.

I twisted and kicked with both feet. My finger tightened on the trigger and the shotgun blast blew a hole in the ceiling. I felt more teeth sink into the leather jacket and reflexively pummeled her with the gun again, crushing more bones in her face. Undeterred, she lunged for my face just as the teenager gained his feet and jumped from the other side. I swung the gun across in time to tear his face down to the bone, exposing a thick flap of muscle and hair. The blow sent him careening into the wall.

My handkerchief was suddenly ripped from my face by a scarred, claw-like appendage, my leather jacket torn by hungry teeth that sunk deep, seeking flesh. I realized in a moment of clarity I had only seconds to live so I swung my hammer like fist. The girl flew backwards but the teenager was back, clawing at my legs and the black man was hissing as he hauled his mangled frame across the floor. He managed to get a hand on the barrel of my gun. I kicked him once, twice in the face, spraying the floor in a fan-shaped arc of congealed blood but his grip was iron clad. The girl slowly climbed to her feet and hissed at me.

My God, I thought. This is it.

The teenager suddenly ripped a hole in my jeans just as the girl lunged for my face. I smelled her putrid breath, like meat long spoiled in the midday sun, as her teeth clacked together inches from my face. I shoved her back at the same instant the gun was hauled from my grasp, effectively dashing my last hope.

And in that moment everything abruptly slowed down, the teenager trying to avoid my kicks as she sought the vulnerable meat on my thigh, the black man clawing at my arm and the girl arching her back for one final lunge at my face. My mind blanked for a split second and then clicked back into gear as her head exploded in a cloud of red mist.

I thought I was dreaming.

The headless girl teetered momentarily before collapsing on the floor. I immediately shoved the black man away and focused on keeping the teenager off me. He straightened, hissed through rotten teeth just as the left side of his head disintegrated in a mess of pulp, grey matter and protruding bone.

This time I registered the sound of a gunshot as it echoed around the room and the corpse fell backwards. I saw Angel standing in the doorway, both hands wrapped around the Beretta.

The black man saw her too and began crawling across the blood-stained tiles. She shot him in the shoulder but it barely fazed him. She tried twice more, the first a harmless gut shot, the second went wide into the wall, her aim thrown off by the gun's kick.

She screamed and dropped the two pound revolver as the black man grabbed her foot. I kicked out and something in the zombie's side cracked and caved inwards. I grabbed the gun and slammed the stock repeatedly into his face, until he finally stopped moving and a layer of cartilage and mucus covered my arm.

I leaned over and vomited.

Angel collapsed in a heap and began to sob like a real twelve-year-old girl. I struggled out of the ripped jacket and passed a hand over my arms and legs. No cuts. I breathed a sigh of relief and then reached over and hauled Angel into my lap.

"It's okay now," I whispered into her matted hair. "We're safe. You did good, real good."

I sat on the stained and bloodied floor, between the mutilated bodies of the undead, and listened to Angel's muffled sobs. I rocked her gently in my arms for a long time.

*　　*　　*

"What happened to your parents?" I asked as the Hummer consumed the country miles.

Angel frowned as she slowly finished the last cracker and followed it with a mouthful of lukewarm orange juice. She unconsciously passed a hand through recently cleaned brown locks.

"My brother turned first, a week before you found me," she said in a low voice. Her eyes didn't meet mine but rather stayed fixed on the road. There were few abandoned cars to be seen and, so far this morning, no zombies.

"He got to mom first, before anyone had figured out what was happening. Dad stopped him with a baseball bat but not before he was cut real bad."

"Oh." I swallowed, knowing what was coming next.

She took another sip of the juice, wetting her tongue. We had gathered a month's worth of supplies from the Deli and that included a healthy portion of orange juice. I found out early that the twelve-year-old loved orange juice.

"Dad lasted five days before he turned in the middle of the night and came for me..." She shuddered and I patted her arm reassuringly.

"Did he try and treat it?" I asked. Not that it would make a difference, the more damage the zombies inflicted, the faster the victim changed.

She nodded. "I saw him pour all kinds of medicines into the cut."

"But it didn't help?"

Angel turned and stared at me and I recognized a steely resolve that went far beyond her years.

"It was horrible? Once it gets into your system it starts corrupting from the inside."

"It wasn't his fault," I said.

"I know." She glanced back at the road and I realized in that moment she'd achieved a level of acceptance I hadn't yet reached.

"You did good the other day," I reminded her.

She smiled. "I dropped the gun."

I laughed. "We'll do some more practicing later today," I promised.

I watched her smile slowly disappear and in the morning light I couldn't help but marvel at how much she resembled my daughter.

"I'd like that," she said softly and we both quietly watched the miles pass.

*   *   *

It looked like Santa's sled had blown a tire outside Rawlins and spilled its contents across the road. Dolls, plastic toys and a score of board games covered the road like pieces of a dissembled puzzle, spilling out of the open doors of the transport truck that had flipped on its side. As we approached I saw Angel's eyes widen and couldn't resist a smile.

"Would you like to stop?" I asked wryly.

Her head bobbed. "Sure."

I let her play with the toys for a little while before I told her it wasn't safe to linger.

"Can I keep this one?" she asked, holding up a brown haired Barbie. I hesitated. She had dressed it up in a dark coat and jeans, exactly what she was wearing. The similarity was striking.

"Absolutely," I smiled.

We were interrupted by a low moan down the road and my shotgun was instantly in both hands. A big, hulking zombie was crawling out of a ditch. Clad in worn coveralls that were stained with overlapping blotches, he looked like he'd just stepped off the farm. He moved towards us in halting, jerky steps.

"David."

"Take out your gun, Angel," I said calmly. He would intercept us before we got back to the Hummer. "Remember what I taught you. He's no different than the others except maybe a little bigger." I patted my gun and glanced down at the girl. "Your turn," I said.

She grimaced but slowly put down the Barbie before pulling the revolver out of her waistband. She aimed with both hands.

"The safety," I reminded her.

She grinned sheepishly and clicked off the safety. The first shot hit the zombie in the chest and staggered the big farm boy. He seemed confused and his hand probed the new hole in his breast-bone. The second and third took him in the stomach and shoulder and his step faltered but only for a moment.

"David." She was more insistent.

"Focus," I said calmly. He was big, a good four inches bigger than me and heavier. He hissed evilly as he lumbered.

"Aim for the head."

Another bullet tore a chunk out of his neck, spinning him around. Up close, I could see the blotches on his overalls were semisolid parcels of flesh that oozed green slime with every step. His hands as well were covered in some kind of noxious substance. The eyes were red rimmed, his mouth a blood-encrusted hole that sent bile surging in my throat.

"David!"

My finger tightened on the trigger just as a squeal escaped her lips and a bullet entered his skull above the right eye and traveled transversely across the skull until it exited behind the left ear, blowing a three inch crater and spewing chunks of grey matter and bone all over the road.

There was an ear splitting moment of silence.

"Good shot," I said quietly.

Angel wiped the tears from her cheek and picked up the Barbie. Without a word, she walked back to the Hummer.

I felt like I had just corrupted the last good soul on the planet.

*　　*　　*

The Hummer carried us east, past the burned out towns of Elk Mountain and Arlington, past the abandoned vehicles and mutilated husks of corpses that now formed the fabric of the country and perhaps the world. Angel played with her doll while I kept an eye out for zombies.

We came upon the accident just before noon. It looked like the van had lost control and sideswiped the tractor trailer that was blocking the right lane before flipping over and coming to rest on its side in the left breakdown lane. It left a trail of broken glass and shattered plastic and the crushed torso of something that might have once been human.

Judging by the three zombies clawing at the van windows, I figured at least someone was still alive inside.

"Are you going to stop?" Angel asked.

My eyes swept across the road, calculating, and into the rearview mirror where I could see several more zombies stumbling out of the woods.

I shrugged. I had already made one stupid rescue attempt.

"Why not." I angled the car towards the wreck and skidded to a stop twenty yards away. Immediately two of the creatures, a baseball player with one arm missing and a woman in a ripped blue blouse, turned and started for the Hummer. Bits of tissue and bodily fluids matted their hair and smeared their albino faces.

It made me sick just to look at them.

"I'm ready," Angel said.

"Take the girl," I said. She was slower, struggling on an ankle that had bones sticking out.

A single shotgun blast turned the baseball player's head to mush. It took Angel three shots to kill the woman but by then I had sprinted to the van. The third zombie was using a rock to crack open the windshield. He was naked with long deep lacerations down his back that exposed the depth of muscle and thighs that dripped blood onto the pavement. He turned in time to eat a shell from three feet away.

I looked inside and saw two very anxious faces staring out at me.

"You got about twenty seconds before a crowd of them arrive," I yelled. "Time to get out now!"

"We can't," The man hollered. "The door's jammed!"

"Cover your eyes." I smashed the window with the butt of my shotgun. "Come on."

"David!" Angel fired two shots.

"Coming!" I hauled the woman out and then ran for the Hummer. Angel fired again and a saw a boy in blue pajamas pitch backwards. Two more shots staggered a man in a three piece suit but he kept coming until my shotgun blew a fist-sized hole in his neck.

"Everyone, get in!" I picked up Angel and threw her in the front seat with me before dropping the Hummer into gear. The couple jumped into the back seat, closing the door just ahead of two flesh seeking claws that rattled the window.

I hit the gas and buried a zombie under my wheels.

"Not bad, young lady," I whispered and gave her a quick hug as we sped away.

*　*　*

John and Sarah had been running since their wedding reception in Saratoga turned into a bloodbath. As far as they knew, they were the only survivors. At a small, out of the way campground, John relayed the horrors of the past several weeks over a meal of crackers, spam and bottled water.

"It's a wasteland out there," He waved his arm in an all encompassing gesture. "There is no safe haven. If you didn't come along we'd be part of it too. I want to thank you for that."

"Forget it."

"I mean it." He resumed biting his nails. I could tell from the start the swarthy Italian was the nervous type. Still, he seemed sincere enough.

"Then you're welcome," I said, glancing towards the Hummer where Angel was showing off her Barbie to Sarah. Small boned, with long blonde curls and a big nose, Sarah seemed nice and more importantly, unruffled by the new reality.

"I... we don't want to impose but we're not sure where to go... Where are the police or the army?"

I smirked. "Haven't you noticed? The undead are composed of everyone, including our vaunted police and army." I laughed at his incredulous expression.

"Then what do we do?" he asked meekly.

"Beats me. I'm going home...if it's still there. You're welcome to join Angel and me. At least until the food runs out or we start eating each other." I gave him a smile to show I was only half kidding. "So grab a few hours sleep. I'll take first watch and wake you in three hours. Sarah can spell you after that."

He nodded glumly and went over to talk to his wife who was still playing happily with Angel. I had a quick memory of my wife playing with Jennifer in front of the fireplace...

Sarah caught my eye and waved. I forced a smile, grabbed my shotgun and silently wished for a zombie I could shoot.

*　*　*

Two days later we found some dry goods in an abandoned drug store in Laramie and even managed to sneak away before the undead noticed us rummaging through their backyard.

Angel fell asleep in the back seat after lunch and Sarah leaned over from the front seat and covered her with a blanket. John was next to Angel, staring out his window.

"You're pretty good with her," I said with a slight nod. "Makes me think you've been around kids."

"I had younger siblings," she said in a quant southern drawl. "But she's a cute kid to begin with. Is she yours?"

I smiled. "Nah, I found her hiding in a hotel."

"So that's why she thinks you're the best thing since sliced bread."

I laughed. "And to think for the first few days I could barely get a word out of her." I glanced briefly at Angel's sleeping form.

"Well, she sure can talk up a storm now," the blonde said. "Too bad she's not feeling so hot."

"How's that?"

Sarah shrugged. "I figured you noticed how pale she's looking and she's slept most of the last two days."

I shook my head. She always seemed to nap during the long stretches of driving. "Maybe she's caught a flu bug or something. Can't say we've been eating healthy these past few weeks."

"Yeah," she nodded, causing her blonde curls to bob. "She probably needs some time to get over it."

"Don't we all," I said.

* * *

"Sorry to interrupt you guys but it's time for a quick bite before we leave."

Angel made a show of rolling her eyes and Sarah laughed.

"He's such a party pooper," she whispered conspiratorially. "There's never any time to play."

Sarah stood and soothed out the wrinkles in her pants. She picked up the Barbie and helped Angel up. "There'll be time later," she said. "After we fix Barbie."

Angel stuck her tongue out at me and walked slowly back to the Hummer.

"What's wrong with her doll?" I asked Sarah.

She waved a hand dismissively. "Just a rip in its clothes," she said. "Nothing that can't be fixed."

"Oh." I picked up the gun and followed them over to the vehicle. For some reason I suddenly didn't feel like eating.

* * *

"She's definitely not feeling well," John stated matter-of-factly as we unpacked the sleeping bags.

"Definitely," his wife chimed in. "She's got a fever now and her color is worse."

"Hmmm." I tapped my chin thoughtfully. "Maybe we can search for some medicine tomorrow. We're coming up to another small town on the map called Buford."

"Good idea," John said. "I know a little about pharmaceuticals so I'll give you a hand."

I nodded as they turned in. I had first watch again so checked my gun and strolled over to where Angel dozed fitfully by the Hummer. I almost smiled as I noticed the Barbie tugged under the blankets next to her pillow and the revolver next to that. On impulse I reached down and pulled out the plastic doll. Sarah was right; there was a small tear in the tiny jeans. But rather than an incidental tear, the rip was straight, scissor straight and underneath there was a curious black stain on the molded plastic.

I hesitated. This wasn't feeling right.

Angel's leg was partially exposed and I couldn't stop myself. I pulled back the cover slowly and... almost choked. The skin was black from the ankle to the thigh and stretched tight like a balloon caught in a vice. An effusion of purulent ichor leaked out of the tissue and dried in a golden smudge and I could detect the faint odor of decay. To stop the groan from escaping my lips I bit my lip until I tasted blood.

When I finally looked up Angel was staring straight at me.

"My daddy scratched me before I got away," she said quietly. "I tried to keep it clean but it kept getting bigger."

"Why...why didn't you tell me," I stammered.

"You were busy keeping me safe," she said and then tilted her head quizzically to one side. "Daddy turned bad after a while. Do you think I'll turn bad, too?"

I choked back tears. "No, Angel. You'll never turn bad. Tomorrow, we'll go into town and get some medicine for you. And then I'll take you to my home and you'll meet my daughter, Jennifer. She's got dolls too so you guys can play together."

She smiled and yawned. "I'd like that, David. Maybe Sarah can play with us, too."

I gently took her in my arms as she faded back to sleep. She was hot, burning up with fever and a poison that would steal more than her innocence. My tears fell unabated and I couldn't stop the tremor that shook my entire being. Her steady breathing reminded me of a better time, of a better world. I felt as if I was about to lose my family all over again.

I held her for a long time, until the sun crept over the eastern horizon, until the well of my emotions had run dry.

It was an unconscious act to pick up her revolver.

WHEN THE DAY IS DONE

YOUR CHARACTER IS ALL YOU HAVE LEFT WHEN
YOU'VE LOST EVERYTHING YOU CAN LOSE
E.C. McKenzie

Boston was in turmoil.

He had just come in from Paris, landing at Logan International in the midst of a city in chaos. Television stations in Europe covered the problems that were plaguing the country, especially in Chicago where the first incident took place.

It was a camera crew led by a man by the name of Castlin that captured the first real look at what was besieging the nation. At first Jack thought that it was the trailer to a new horror film about zombies. CNN played the Castlin film over and over, showing the dead walking the streets of Chicago, killing innocent people at random. That was when Jack Sagen knew he had to get home.

His wife and daughter lived in Worcester, Massachusetts, alone and unprotected. He should have been there all along and not hopping planes from one country to the next.

Jack left for France a week earlier on a business trip, visiting an atomic energy facility that his company invested twelve billion dollars into. That night at the hotel, he saw the Castlin footage for the first time on the French 2 station.

He was shocked at what he was looking at.

It was a grainy piece that looked even worse on the news. The beginning of the film showed several of the Chicago Police trying to detain a pale man who was biting a woman he'd just attacked on the street. The woman was screaming as the man tore at her throat. Blood was everywhere as the police tried desperately to pull him off her. Finally, one officer shot the man, point blank in the chest, knocking him backwards away from the woman. Not knowing if he was dead, they approached cautiously. Suddenly the man sat up to the surprise of the officers, especially the one trying to pull the woman's lifeless body back toward one of the cruisers out of harms way. They fired again, at point blank range, knocking the man back down to the pavement in a spray of blood and gore.

The camera from inside the cruiser captured the lifeless woman slowly getting up, her face locked into a rigorous death mask, blood streaming from her torn-out throat. The officer who pulled her to safety suddenly backed away, his initial warning cries ignored. But by then it was far too late. The woman attacked him, bearing down on him like a rabid animal. He couldn't draw his weapon to fire as she completely covered him with her bloodied body, ripping and biting.

The film ended there and the news anchor, face pale, began relating how the *plague*, that's what they're calling it on the French news station, was spreading throughout America.

The dead were rising and Jack was stuck in Paris.

So he caught the last flight out before the ban on all inbound and outbound flights took effect. At Logan he didn't even bother to get his luggage, but ran to catch the first cab available. The cab driver, a balding, squat looking man, was reluctant to leave the city to travel the hour it would take to get to Worcester. But Jack quickly offered him five hundred dollars. The man was hesitant at first but the money was too good to pass up. On the turnpike the traffic was heavy, people trying to get home, or to get away from the plague that was now in Boston.

According to the news coming over the cab's radio, the dead were walking and killing. The reporter, in a voice filled with tension, related several incidents in the downtown area. Sirens could be heard in the background, mixed with gunfire. To Jack, it sounded like a report coming out of Beirut or some other war-torn country. The cab driver reached out to shut the radio off when a person suddenly stumbled from the shoulder of the road into their lane on the highway.

The cab driver swerved to avoid hitting the man standing in the center of the highway as he hit his horn for good measure. The man looked drunk as he swayed back and forth, his head cocked to one side. Jack glanced back as the cab sped past and saw that the man had only half a face, his jaw hung downward, gore dripping onto his shirt, brains showing through a cracked skull. The sight was confirmation of the news reports that seemed so unbelievable, and he immediately vomited onto the back seat, making the driver curse.

The stench was overpowering, making Jack vomit again. The driver yelled back to him to stop or else he would drop him off right in the middle of the turnpike. The driver's voice was trembling as he drove on at a crawl in the ever thickening traffic. Jack swallowed, trying not to get sick again.

It was true, though they were dead, they were walking.

God help us, he thought.

He reached into his pocket and threw another hundred dollar bill toward the front seat.

"Get me home!" he yelled at the cab driver.

The man looked at the hundred dollar bill crumpled on the front seat and shook his head in resignation, but he picked it up and continued on.

Jack sat back and thought about his wife Sophia and his daughter Dianna. No doubt Sophia had seen the news as well. How could she not? It was on all the stations. He couldn't imagine the fear she must be feeling right now. He'd tried calling her from the hotel in Paris but the lines were busy and had still been busy when he got into Logan and had tried again. He tried a thousand times to get through, but the busy signal sounded persistently.

His family lived in a beautiful home just outside the city limits. The house was his gift to her, four thousand square feet of total luxury. It was built according to her designs which had been given to an architect to reconstruct per her approval. It looked like an Italian villa and the cost was phenomenal. It almost broke him to build it. The trip to Europe was necessitated by the fact that he needed the extra money to finish paying for it. He actually grew to hate the house since it took him away from his little girl. But now he wanted to see it, to be in it, to hug and hold his family inside its walls.

Something was holding up the traffic. Tail lights blared red as they neared a toll booth. Loud noise in the distance made the cab driver lower his window.

It was the sound of people screaming.

Jack could see the driver's face turn pasty white in the rear view mirror. Taking off his coat, Jack laid it over the vomit-stained seat and scooted forward, leaning over the front divider.

"What's happening?" he asked.

The balding driver, a man in his late sixties, turned to him, eyes wide, fear showing on his face. He shook his head. The locks in the car automatically clicked into place. Jack tried to look ahead, beyond the other cars. The toll booths up ahead seemed overly active. People were moving outside them, in traffic, past cars.

"Hold on!" the driver yelled as he shifted gears and squeezed by a small foreign car, scraping his massive bumper across the passenger door, trailing bits of paint and a side mirror. The people inside the car were screaming at him to stop.

"What the hell are you doing?" Jack screamed from the back seat, feeling metal crunch metal in the sudden collision.

The driver turned for all of a second, his eyes panic-filled orbs.

"I'm getting us out of here! Look, look!" he said as he pointed toward the toll booths.

Finally, Jack saw what made him react the way he did. The walking dead had found easy prey at the toll booths. The long lines of stopped cars, the toll takers locked in their tiny boxes were like McDonald's Happy Meals. The screaming was coming from them, the dead people swarming like locusts, killing everything they were able to catch.

Oh God, thought Jack as he watched in horror. The zombies were tearing them to shreds. People were leaving their cars only to be trapped by more of the dead, shambling things. More animated corpses were climbing over the guardrails, heading right for the stopped, jammed vehicles. The screaming intensified as people were being dragged from their cars and butchered. They didn't have a chance in Hell.

The cab driver rammed another car in the far right lane, pushing it like a toy and driving past it toward the main state highway building to the right of the toll booths. Other drivers tried to follow the cab, seeing that it was making its way through, only to be rammed by other cars trying to do the same thing. Jack closed his eyes to pray, to beg God to get him out of this mess, to help him get home.

When he opened his eyes, a man with only one arm, his bloody ribcage protruding through his side, started to pound on his window. Blood and what looked like a clotted mass of congealed tissue slid across the glass as the cab driver jammed his foot down hard on the gas pedal. The dead man spun crazily down the side of the cab and fell to the ground as the cars behind following the cab drove over the body. They made it past the main toll building and through the first booth.

And suddenly they were free, the road in front of them open. Jack looked behind to see hundreds of zombies moving in tandem past the booths to the waiting cars filled with people who had no clue as to what was coming their way.

"Now I can't go home. Because of you I can't go back. I should kill you for tempting me with your filthy money, you bastard!" yelled the cab driver, spittle coming from his clenched teeth.

Jack stared at the old man's eyes as he looked at Jack in the rearview mirror. Tears were streaming down the man's face.

Jack didn't care what the man thought. He'd paid him and the driver took the job. Now he wanted to get home.

"Look, were safe, you got us through, just get me to my destination, please," Jack said as calmly as he could, though it probably sounded a bit high and shaky.

The driver said nothing in return, just kept driving, wiping his eyes as he did so. The road was still clear for the next several miles then more red lights lit up the roadway ahead.

"Shit..." the old man spat out.

Jack quickly began to look down the road and noticed a maintenance exit that was gated at the top and led to a small town road. He pointed it out to the cab driver who turned toward it. The cab pulled up to the gate and stopped. Both could see the large padlock and chain.

"Only one way through," Jack replied from the back seat and the cab driver nodded.

It was no longer a regular fare to cater to anymore. It was a matter of survival on both their parts. The old man backed the cab up a good fifty feet and stopped. He sat there as the car engine rumbled softly.

"I can't believe it's come to this. It's like a waking nightmare," said the old man while shaking his head, not really speaking to Jack, but mostly to himself.

Jack realized the sacrifice the old man made bringing him out of the city. But how was he to know that it would be like this?

And now he was asking the man to drive his company vehicle through a locked fence.

"Do you know where we'll be once I go through that fence?" asked the driver.

Jack thought about the question and reached for his phone. It came with an optional GPS system. He turned it on and looked at the signal, which was strong. Hitting a few buttons, he got the GPS mapping device and watched as his address came up and then a colorful cartoon roadway which showed where they were.

"Yeah, I know where we are. I can still get us to my house," he stated as a matter of fact.

The old man nodded and turned in his seat to face Jack. His face had a stern, troubled look to it and Jack was expecting the worse from him. Instead, the man held out his hand and Jack took it.

"My name's Jonas Patel. I'm sorry I yelled at you back there. It was one of those *in the moment* things."

"Jack Sagen," he replied back as they shook hands. "I'm sorry also, Mr. Patel. I just want to see my family again. I had no idea that we'd be fighting for our lives to get out of the city. How could anyone ever guess that something like this could happen? Also, I'm sorry about messing up your cab. It's just, seeing that man..." Jack couldn't finish and Jonas patted his hand in understanding.

"Yes, well, let's just get us out of here alive. I don't have family in Boston, thank God. But I do in Springfield. So, despite my outburst, I'm glad we'll be heading in the same direction."

Jack smiled and thought about their circumstances. They were at least forty miles from Worcester and preparing to leave the most direct way there. If things were bad on the main roads, what would they be like on the secondary roads? Patel seemed to read his mind and looked at the phone in Jack's hand.

"Once I get you back home, God willing, will you let me have the phone to find my way to my sister's house in Springfield?"

Jack thought about handing his precious phone to this stranger. It had all his personal information on it. But the man was already risking his life for him. It seemed a very small price to pay in return.

Jack nodded. "Yes, no problem. It's yours as soon as I get home."

That seemed to make Jonas happy and he turned in his seat, once again facing the maintenance road leading to the gate. He gunned the engine and threw it into drive. The car sped forward rapidly and Jack prepared himself for the collision. It came fast and hard and the gate exploded outward as the taxi tore through it headlong. He heard glass tinkling on the ground as the cab's headlights shattered. He felt more than heard the crunch of metal on metal as the gate swung back, swiping the side of the cab.

"Right or left!" Jonas yelled as he jammed on the brakes.

"Left," Jack said, his heart rate beating wildly.

Jonas turned left and accelerated down the road. It was suburbia with plenty of huge, wealthy residences. Jack noticed one of the houses was on fire. Smoke was rising into the sky in thick, black plumes while several people were running down the street. Not far behind them was more of the walking dead. Jonas groaned in horror at the sight of several of the children being pulled along by their frantic parents, the kids falling over each other. The parents tried to get them up quickly but the zombies were upon them in an instant. Jack couldn't look back, didn't want to know. He thought of Dianna at that moment. He couldn't imagine her going through an experience like the one he just witnessed.

"Intersection just ahead. What direction Jack?" Jonas yelled again, his voice panicked. The voice jerked Jack back to the real world, horrible as it had become. He looked at his phone and told Jonas to take a right.

Two figures came out of the woods by the passenger side of the cab and slammed into it, pounding against the glass as they tried to get in the vehicle. Jack could tell they were dead. One was a man, or what was left of one, and the other was a woman. Both were cadaverous looking with bloody, seeping wounds that no one could survive. The man's face was burnt black with no eyes or skin and the woman had only one arm with her intestines hanging from a gaping hole in her stomach.

"Oh, God!" Jack yelled as he slid as far from the two zombies as possible even though they couldn't get inside the locked cab. Jonas cursed loudly and gunned the gas, making the tires squeal. With dirt spewing behind the tires, the two zombies were left in the dust.

They continued down the road for several miles and suddenly came to another intersection.

"Tell me where to go please. Hurry, we shouldn't remain in one place for too long," complained Jonas as he looked in every direction.

Jack told him to continue straight for the next ten miles.

"Why is this happening? How are the dead coming back to life? It's impossible! What in hell is going on, Jonas!" Jack yelled.

Jonas drove on without saying another word. When he finally spoke, it was with a slow steady voice.

"I don't know, Jack. But I do know that God would never do this thing. What's happening is against all natural laws. I believe that man did this thing, that he brought this destruction upon himself. At least that's what I wish to believe."

Jack placed his face in his hands and prayed to make it home to his family, to find them safe and whole. That's all he wanted.

The cab drove on.

* * *

With the sun quickly descending, dusk fell across the land.

As they drove on, Jonas spotted a light in the distance. As the cab drew closer, he could see a large factory building on the side of the road, flames licking out its windows. In the parking lot, cars were burning and bodies littered the pavement. Moving dead people were feeding on the corpses. It was a scene straight out of Hell.

As the cab passed by, several of the animated dead raised their heads to look at them, their faces covered with the remnants of their feast.

"At the next light take a right, Jonas, that'll bring us directly into Worcester," Jack replied, his voice cracking. Even Jonas was quiet while passing the gruesome, bloody carnage.

The cab came to the intersection and didn't stop as Jonas turned right. He would no longer stop for anyone or anything until he got Jack home. The streets were wreathed in shadows now that the day was coming to a close and the sunset was blood-red. The city lights glowed in the ominous atmosphere, casting an eerie radiance that made everything look surreal. Jack could hear sirens in the distance and watched as people ran down a side street. A gunshot near their position made Jonas speed up, not wanting to get caught in the crossfire. Something very bad was happening here, both sensing it immediately.

The deeper they got into the city, the clearer the evidence became. Bodies lay everywhere, the dead not far behind. Police cars blocked streets and fired upon the walking dead in an ongoing battle.

"We must get out of here, we can't continue on this route," Jonas said as he started to turn onto a side street that looked dark and empty. The GPS on the phone re-calculated the new route and Jack told Jonas to drive straight for a half mile and take Foster Street. They were now on streets Jack had never seen before, a part of the city he never wanted to visit. This part was noted for high incidents of crime and violence.

"Jack, when I get you home, you need to show me how to work that GPS device. Otherwise I'll be lost," Jonas said, his voice drifting to the back seat where Jack watched the streets with wide eyes.

"No problem, just get us the hell out of this section of town. Turn left and then right onto Park Street, we're almost there."

Jonas did as requested, and as the cab swung around the turn, both men saw the huge pile-up of vehicles blocking the intersection to Park Street. Several nearby buildings were on fire after the fuel from the cars and trucks ignited, sending flaming debris through store windows and onto cloth awnings. Bodies littered the street with dozens of the walking dead zeroing in on them.

"This won't do!" Jonas yelled while slamming on the brakes.

Jack knew where he was now and told Jonas to go down a one-way street to their right. Jonas was about to turn when one of the wrecked cars exploded, followed by another, larger explosion, the blasts lifting the cab a few inches off the ground and pushing it backwards. The driver's window imploded inwards, making Jonas cry out in pain as the small bits of glass cut his face in several places. Minutes passed and Jack found himself on the floor of the cab, his arm pinned beneath him. He got up slowly, his arm painful to move, and looked out to see a nearby gas station in flames as a nuclear-looking mushroom cloud rose high into the sky. The tanks must have blown and the car had been only a few hundred feet from the explosion.

He was bleeding and touched his head to find glass embedded above his left eye. He pulled the tiny shards from his head and looked over the seat to find Jonas lying very still. Jack looked out the front windshield which was broken and hanging inside the car. Beyond the windshield, flames were moving toward them like living wraiths. The dead were on fire, undaunted on their quest for human flesh.

"Jonas, get up, damn it, get up now!" Jack screamed, grabbing Jonas and shaking him. But the old man wouldn't move and the human torches were getting closer by the second. Jack got out of the cab and opened the driver's side door and fell to the pavement, his legs weak. Getting to his feet, he moved to the driver's door.

Jonas' body lay across the front seat, his face bleeding in several places. Jack tried to lift him, pull him out, but he wasn't strong enough. He could see the reflection of the approaching zombies in the passenger side glass only fifty feet away and knew if Jonas didn't wake up, he was going to die.

Jack turned Jonas over and realized why he wouldn't wake up. A large sliver of the windshield was driven into his right eye. The man had been killed instantly. Jack closed his eyes, knowing the poor man would never see his sister in Springfield. Jonas died trying to get Jack back home and no amount of money he had could bring him back.

Or so he thought.

Suddenly, Jonas' remaining eye began to twitch, and with a hiss, he sat up. Seeing Jack, he moaned loudly and tried to bite Jack's hand.

Realizing Jonas was now one of *them*, he backed away, shaking his head with disbelief.

The other walking dead were almost upon him so he turned and ran.

Darkness was coming. He was so close, only a few streets away. He saw the Miller's house along with Steinbrenner's massive home. Both were dark and empty looking. He passed more homes that he was familiar with, all dark and foreboding. Something wasn't right. There should be some kind of activity in at least one of the homes.

House after house looked abandoned and that only made him run faster. Jack knew he must look quite a sight, covered in his and Jonas' blood.

His street was the very next one and he pushed himself to run even though he was exhausted beyond reason from the day's events. The darkness was all pervading now with only the street lights casting their caustic glare. Several houses had lights on and he picked his out immediately. The front light was on, the living room light shown through the closed drapes. Someone must be home.

God, Jack thought as he made it to the front steps, *you listened to my prayers. You got me home.*

He fumbled in his pocket for his keys and finally got the right one in the door lock. He opened the door and called out to his family. The keys jangled against the door, making it the only sound he heard in the eerily quiet house.

"Sophia, Dianna, I made it home!" he yelled again, getting no response.

He stood in the living room and began to look around for the first time. *Really* look at what was about him. One of the lamps was on the floor. Glasses during a meal, shattered. It was then that he noticed the blood stains on the door jamb, the fingerprints along the hallway. He took a tentative step into the kitchen, looking down the hallway that led to other rooms in the house. On the floor in the distance was something bulky, something wet around it. He caught the cry in his throat as he approached, fearing the very worst. It was the family dog. It was a small breed, its body now ripped into unidentifiable pieces. The only thing he could actually make out was the snout and collar.

Tears ran down his face as he moved more carefully through the house. He wanted this nightmare to go away, to wake up and all of it to be gone.

A thump from upstairs drew him to an immediate halt, his heart was racing and his fear suddenly doubled. He was about to call out and he stopped himself.

The stairway was in the living room and he moved as silently as he could to the bottom of the stairs, looking up into darkness. Sudden movement made him draw back. A shadowy figure swayed back and forth, its balance off. The movements were jerky, like something unhinged. The shape began to move down the stairs, one at a time. Jack knew he should run, but something held him in place. A wet, sticky sound came from the shape as it descended.

Light from the living room finally gave Jack the first real glimpse of the form coming down to him. The legs were bloody with bone glimmering through. Soon, the sight of a torn dress appeared, which led to a midsection that looked so very wrong.

Jack began to cry, his voice sounding strangled. When the stomach of the form came into view he saw it was gaping open for all to see. The rest, to his horror, was what he had expected.

It was Sophia, her face a ragged display of ligaments, hanging flesh and teeth. In her arms lay Dianna, his daughter, her body mangled and distorted from numerous feedings.

He cried out, his anger and fear mingled as his voice rose into madness as he fell to his knees.

Behind him, in the darkness of the doorway, his neighbors waited, ready to feast.

ALICE

She studied herself in the spotless mirror, stared at the crow's feet around her eyes, at the gray intruding at the roots of her otherwise short, auburn hair, at the jagged scar that stretched from her right earlobe to the corner of her mouth.

She bumped her finger over its jagged length and remembered that day—the day her face was forever changed. She had been in the center of their long-abandoned town, nestled in the heart of Maine, trying to find some bandages for Sister (her younger sibling) and Phil, who were both hurt and waiting in the car. As she rummaged through a stockroom at Charlie's General Store, one of those things snuck up behind her and grabbed the back of her neck. Shocked, Alice had turned quickly, and seeing the creature, lost her balance and crashed through a glass display of Valentine's Day gifts beside her; a shard of glass severing her cheek in half.

She didn't remember much else about what happened in that store—didn't remember how she made it out of there alive, didn't remember making it to the car to see that Sister had died from her wounds, didn't remember crying as Phil unlatched her door and pushed Sister out before she had the chance to turn. They drove home then in blood-splattered silence, a sorry sight the two of them were: Phil with his sprained ankle and Alice with her new split face. It was just ten minutes later when Alice had haphazardly repaired the gash herself, with all the care and skill of a butcher on a bad day. Sister was dead and Phil had passed out from the pain from his ankle, not to mention the events of the day.

Her hands were shaking, and those things were pounding on the door just behind her, moaning, intent on getting in and finishing what they had started. With nothing by her side but Phil's fishing kit, a Zippo she'd found in the car they'd been using to get around after theirs had been flipped, and a bottle of Wild Turkey, she had stared into the same mirror she was looking into now and stitched her wound closed.

She wasn't prepared to mend such an awful injury, but who would? Who knew that the world was going to fall apart? Who knew that she would be barricaded in her own house with a horde of flesh eaters just outside, hammering at the blockaded door and the reinforced windows with their dead hands? As Alice slid a lighter-sterilized fishhook threaded with fifteen-pound test fishing line in and out of her skin, she bit back screams and tears. She thought oddly of their family doctor, a young, wet-behind-the-ears little runt named Dr. David, wondering what he would think if he could see her now, sewing her face closed with Phil's fishing gear and slapping herself silly with Wild Turkey to ward off infection. Her half-assed surgery was a hack job, and it would forever leave a set of train tracks barreling across her face, but Alice wasn't planning on signing up for any beauty contests any time soon.

In fact, she'd read in one of those trashy magazines that the former Miss New Jersey had been spotted chasing a group of Girl Scouts down the streets of Camden; Girl Scouts who had been out selling their overpriced Thin Mints when the shit really hit the fan. She'd read how the dead beauty had pursued the girls down the length of Martin Luther King Boulevard and then into a 7-11 as she swiped at them with her fingerless right hand and chewed on some poor, anonymous soul's bottom lip.

But this was before anyone really knew what was going on.

This was before *Armageddon*, as Father Luccio called it. This was before the universe had opened up and dumped all of the horror and the depravity and the ghosties and ghoulies and long-legged beasties that our parents had always told us never existed right into our world.

Alice ran her fingers along the length of her scar one more time, an early morning ritual. She did it to keep herself grounded, to remind herself that the nightmares she faced when darkness fell didn't end when she woke in the morning. And it was morning now. She stood looking into the mirror she cleaned obsessively, tracing her scar, this rough terrain of mutilated skin that felt so foreign on her otherwise smooth, pink face.

Yessiree, Bob. A real hack job, this is, she thought. And all the while my needles and thread sat just in the bathroom under the sink, ready to go. But I reckon no one would fault me for not thinking clearly. Those monsters had just bitten off Sister's left thumb and clawed a strip of flesh from her body the size of a laundry sheet, after all. Who would think clearly after all that? Not even Jesus Jumped-Up Christ himself.

"Maybe today's the day," she muttered, sighing, despair prevalent in her words as she lightly fingered her scar. "Maybe today could finally be the day." She grasped the sides of her head and massaged her temples.

Another headache. They were getting worse and worse.

Alice always got headaches this time of year, when leaves were beginning to line the trees up and down Warwick Avenue, and when the garden old Ben kept in front of his kitchen window just across the street would start to pucker with purple Verbenas and black-eyed Susans.

She sighed and walked over to her calendar.

Classic Tractors of Northern Maine; Phil had picked it out. She remembered asking him if he purposely picked the most boring calendar at Charlie's General. He didn't answer her. He never did when she picked on him, when she alluded to his poor taste and his uselessness. As her eyes danced over the rustic old barns in the background of the tractor photo, she sighed again. She could have been nicer to Phil, sure. Could have actually listened when he told her about his day, could have been less hurtful when it came to his weight. But he could have tried to be a bit more of a husband, too. To be interesting, and loving, and intimate, and not so... nothing.

Coulda, shoulda, woulda. Shit in one hand and regret in the other and see which fills up first, she thought.

She picked up the calendar pages and let them fall one by one, the Xs she had scrawled over each date blending together in the motion to create a blurry black mass. She had never been one of those people who X-ed out each day. At least back during the normal days, anyway. She always considered it tantamount to counting down to the end of your life. And why do that? Why wait to die? That's something Phil would do.

The first X was placed over February 3rd. It wasn't the first day when things started going screwy, but to Alice, it seemed it was the first day things would never magically revert back to normal; the first day when TV stopped broadcasting emergency press conferences with the President and members of the scientific community who stressed safety precautions, but who also proclaimed their optimism that this virus—or whatever it was, no one knew for sure what made the dead walk—could be subjugated and defeated. Actually, it was also the first day TV had stopped broadcasting anything at all, except for that blue message with the high-pitched tone that begged people to have patience and to await the return of normal broadcasts after they had sorted out their array of technical difficulties, complete with a cute little cartoon man in a beard and overalls holding a wrench in one hand and scratching his helmeted head with the other.

The calendar was a thick mess of blank ink, and terribly out-dated, yet she kept it hanging next to the series of new calendars she had scrawled on the white wall next to the window. It had been months now. Months of fear, of scavenging for food, death, the most horrendous of smells, and even boredom. Almost six months of compulsively cleaning the same spots in her home over and over, something she had done back before the world was turned inside-out. But then it was for reasons of hygiene and respectability, and not to keep her mind off the things wandering around outside that used to be her friends and neighbors.

And it had been long lonely months without Phil, and even longer without Sister, but she didn't need the calendar to remember that.

She grabbed one of the many thick, black markers from the jar on the windowsill—the kind of marker that temporarily clouded your face with that pungent, chemical smell, one that always reminded Alice of her art class at St. Dominic's High School—and X-ed out yesterday's date. She stole another look at the obsolete calendar, but she wouldn't throw it out. Couldn't throw it out. She kept it hanging because of those tractors; those stupid, red tractors that looked the same on every damn page.

Looking at them always sent pangs of guilt battering through her heart, but it was her chance to remember Phil, too.

"All right, Alice, enough of that," she said to herself, blotting out the tears that formed in the corners of her eyes. "This is nothin' new, you old bitch. Don't start lookin' for sympathy because there's no one left to give it. So you knock that shit off." She wiped away the last tear and shook her head.

She picked up her black, military-issue walkie-talkie from the charger. One of many Phil and her had swiped from a store when doing a weekly supply run last year. They had given the rest to the few remaining neighbors. She held the transmission button and spoke into it.

"Mornin', mister. How is it out there? Over."

Radio static was her only response for a moment, and she began feeling that familiar sense of dread creeping into her stomach.

"Come in. You're still kickin' over there, ain't ya?"

A few more seconds of silence greeted her, and then Ben picked up.

"Morning, Alice. It's not bad today. There were a bunch of them out there earlier, but they must have found something to snack on down the street. Maybe George Hunter. I haven't seen him for a while."

"If old George Hunter finally bit it, then they'll be snackin' on him all week," she said.

He laughed in response. "You're a real gas, Alice."

"Don't I know it. Buzz me if you need somethin' later," she said.

"Will do. Good luck today. Out."

She smirked and put the walkie-talkie back into the charger. Ben wished her luck every day. It was his way of signing off, of beginning a new day.

I'll take whatever I can get, she thought.

She turned and strode across her cluttered house and opened the pantry door. Her eyes panned across her collection of canned food and freeze-dried coffee, carefully arranged with their labels facing out. She dreaded this every morning, this feeling of inevitability. She had been quite the housewife, and while most would find that an empty and pathetic attribute, she prided herself on it. She enjoyed cooking, and enjoyed keeping a clean home. She knew a lot about food, and not just about preparing it, but she also had a keen sense on when something was spoiled, or when that Use-By date could be ignored.

It was all just a way for them to steal more money from you, anyway. Sure, make the expiration date a week earlier than what's necessary. The quicker the expiration date, the quicker people will restock. Bastards. Taking advantage of decent, hardworking...

Scanning across her small pantry of old food, some of it past the expiration date she had always been able to best, her keen skill to predict the edibility of expired food was now a gone-but-not-forgotten luxury. She grabbed a bag of freeze-dried coffee and lifted it close to her eyes. Phil had found most of the coffee in a storeroom in the back of an old store two towns over. It was old when he found it but he grabbed it anyway, not taking the time to read expiration dates.

Her glasses had broken not too long ago, and though she could get by without them, she definitely missed them at times like this. She raised and lowered and raised again the bag close to her face, but her fifty-eight-year-old eyes were unable to make out the expiration date. She grabbed another bag, and then another, but she couldn't decipher the tiny print on those, either.

Well, guess there's only one way to find out, now ain't there? she thought.

She carried a bag over to the coffee grinder that Phil had built entirely by himself (it had been the talk of their small town; at least until all the rotting people-eaters, that is) and ripped the top seal off the bag. She breathed in the aroma, but with the beans still whole, it was hard to tell. It was always hard to tell.

She poured in just enough for two cups and hit the button. The grinder's gears turned harshly, decimating the beans into a fine blended mix. She always hated this part, this process she had to follow, the fear she had to endure: five seconds of grinding, and thirty seconds of silence as she waited and listened for signs that the creatures out in the streets had heard the ruckus and would follow the sounds directly to her front door.

Nothing so far.

Five more seconds of grinding. Thirty seconds of waiting.

Recently, she noted the increasing number of creatures lurking around the neighborhood for the better part of three weeks, so it had been a while since she had been able to enjoy a cup of coffee. Today there didn't seem to be that many of them, so she decided she'd earned the right to risk it.

The last five seconds of grinding passed and she listened for thirty more.

Nothing.

She exhaled heavily and carried the fresh blend over to her coffee maker.

What a shit this is. Living in fear in my own home. Can't even make a cup of coffee without shitting my old lady pants, she thought.

She dumped in the contents and pressed the button, the little orange light in the bottom left of the control panel greeting her warmly. She shared another quick moment of relief.

She knew the day would come when her electricity would stop, and she dreaded it, but that day would not be today. In the first few weeks after she and Phil had installed several locks on each door and covered their windows, knowing things were obviously not going to get better, Alice had anticipated the electricity disappearing soon after. But it hadn't. She didn't know why, but the why didn't matter. She still had it, and that was all that did matter. The water was off, sure—had been for a while—but she could live without that. She had plenty of bottled water, and once that went bad, she could boil it, anyway.

Sitting down at her kitchen table, Alice lifted the mug to her nose, and inhaled. Smelled okay. Not exactly fresh, but not something that would send her to the morgue, either. She sipped. She swished. She waited.

And she spat.

It tasted like one would expect coffee to taste if it had been left to burn for several days in a coffee maker no one bothered to clean. It was a rancid taste, almost akin to what those *things* smelled like after mummying around in the sun for three days straight.

Almost, anyway. Let's not get carried away.

She stared at the mug, disbelieving. The day had come. Her coffee had finally gone bad. She'd never have another cup of fresh coffee for the rest of her life.

"Well, shit. There's one less reason to be upright and breathin'," she said, bitterly. She sat a moment longer, but then hurled the mug across the room, shattering her collection of ceramic thimbles that were meticulously displayed in a glass cabinet affixed to the wall. She and Sister had collected them together for years, from yard sales, from craft fairs, even from Dolly's Antiques down on Fifth Street. She always thought it weird that Sister had insisted that Alice keep them in her home, but as she explained it to her years ago: "You love that shit. You keep them."

She missed Sister. During the days not clouded with death and chaos, people always laughed when she would introduce her sister, Sister, to them. They loved the name, and loved that it served as a clever double-meaning. Their father had always told them that their mother had very much wanted their second child to be a boy, and when a girl was delivered instead, they had decided Sister to be the perfect name. This was one of the few memories they had of their mother. She had died of cancer when they were little girls and they lost their father to the same cancer, like a sick joke, just ten years later.

Staring now at the shattered remnants of her and Sister's collection of thimbles, Alice felt large waves of sobs begin to force their way out of her stomach. They always started down there, deep, and when she felt them coming, she would shut her eyes and swallow. Over and over. She would keep them down there with yesterday's lunch and yesterday's after-lunch shot of Wild Turkey and whatever else that was swilling around down there that she was over and done with. That's how she always looked at it.

Mourning and regret are just as useless as yesterday's meal. They're gone and can't affect anything, so just wipe your mouths and your asses and let's move on already.

She walked back to the walkie, picked it up.

"Coffee went bad, Ben. No more coffee for Alice, ever again," she said in a cracked voice.

Ben picked up, almost immediately this time. "Aw shit, I'm sorry, Alice. I don't drink the stuff, but I know I miss my morning cup of tea. You know if I had it to give, I would."

"I know. I just needed to complain. Out." She dropped the walkie back into the charger.

Her head throbbed suddenly and she shut her eyes again, tight at first, until that sent a small shockwave of pain around her skull, so she relaxed them, massaging her temples, moving her finger tips around in circular patterns. Phil had always told her to lightly squeeze the bridge of her nose instead, but what did he know? He never got headaches. Not like these, anyway.

She looked across the room and saw a framed picture of Phil holding up his prize catch from his yearly fishing trip with Thor Harmon and Sam Kensey. A twenty-inch tuna hung suspended from his fishing line. Phil had on his typical wide grin and wore that brown sloppy hat covered with bobbers and pins hailing Boston College's football team, the Eagles. Thor and Sam stood on his left, holding their cans of Pabst Blue Ribbon and without any caught fish to be seen. They loved to fish, but Phil was the only one who ever managed to catch anything. When he did, he acted like he was King Shit, whereas Thor and Sam were more interested in seeing how many six-packs of PBR they could hold in their fat guts before shooting it back out of their mouths over the side of Water love, the boat Phil kept down at Wharton's Dock.

"Where are you now, Phil, huh?" she demanded, holding the frame in her old, wrinkled, exhausted hands. "No more advice on how to get rid of these headaches I get? You should've listened to me, you dumb bastard! You'd still be here! You'd be driving me nuts, but you'd still be here!"

She dropped the frame back on the small table situated near the back door and wandered over to the front window. She peered through one of the few eyeholes in the old wooden closet door nailed over the window and stared hard into the corner of the front yard where she buried Phil almost a year ago.

There was no tombstone, no flowers—no nothing. Just a mound of dry dirt overtop the body of her husband, and overtop her first life; the life she fancied she would live until her peaceful death in bed; and not for years to come.

*   *   *

Despite the chaos around them, Alice and Phil were able to make a new life for themselves while the world was falling apart, waiting for the sky to finally crack open and bring forth the apocalypse of which those left alive had long anticipated.

Despite the weight of earth's demonic rebirth, and despite the loss of Sister, they managed to live life safely and peacefully. That is, up to that point, anyway.

It was as Phil and Alice were sitting at the kitchen table one morning, enjoying a cup of coffee, a bout of silence between them, that the sound of a dying truck engine and a shrill scream trespassed into their small, cramped, one-story rancher.

"What on God's green...?" Phil asked, rising quickly to his feet.

He limped over to their barricaded window and peered through the eyehole.

"It's a girl!" he yelled, leaning his hands on the worn door. "And there's a dozen of them things after her!"

Alice lifted herself from her chair and joined her husband at the window, peering through another eyehole. It had been several months since they had seen an outsider, as the neighbors called them. These were unknown people who would occasionally wander into town seeking help or supplies, or at times, to loot and vandalize. A few neighbors on their block had remained, and while they all kept an eye on each other's property and warned of any oncoming attacks with their walkie-talkies, they all basically stayed out of each other's lives.

No need to live in cramped quarters. This wasn't the Depression, after all.

Alice saw the old brown truck immediately. It was much too large and quite uncharacteristic for the petite blonde girl driving it. Its engine finally petered out its last grind and the rickety vehicle stopped dead, rolling down the naturally declining Warwick Avenue before crashing right into Ben's tan Oldsmobile parked in his driveway across the street. The girl leapt from the truck almost immediately and ran screaming from the small horde of zombies stumbling after her. Peals of their moans filled the street, and as this poor girl pleaded for help from the front yards of people no longer living, Alice could see in her husband's face his overwhelming desire to want to intervene.

"No, you don't, Phil Hardy. You're gonna stay right here with me. You're not goin' out there."

Phil continued to watch intently through the eyehole, his body jumping and convulsing as he reacted inwardly to the girl's anguish.

"She needs help, Alice! That girl's alone, and she'll never make it if we don't get to her!"

"She's already dead, Phil," she replied firmly, as if scolding him. "She's as dead as Sister, and your brother, Roy, and old Mr. Barnes, and most of the world. And if you go out there, you'll be dead, too. And then I'll be alone."

"We can't just sit here, Alice."

"Yes, Phil. We can."

For the first time since the girl appeared, Phil turned to look at his wife. Within her eyes, he saw sparkles of tears, but he also saw fierceness and her unyielding stubbornness, which he knew all too well. He returned his gaze to the outside world and began to look frantic. "I...I can't see her anymore!"

"Because she's gone, Phil. It's too late for her."

He moved away from the window. Insistent. Frustrated.

"I'm gettin' the shotty, Alice, and I'm goin' out there. And you're gonna stay here."

"You're gonna go out there and play hero, Phil? With that bum leg of yours? What good could you do? And for what? She's dead! She's just one more dead person among the hundreds of thousands or millions of people who are already dead! One more life won't save the world! One more death won't be a tragedy!"

She grabbed her husband's wrist and held it tight, fueled by her feeling of dominance bastardized by love and concern. "You're not goin' out there! And I won't say it again!"

"Alice...watch the damn door."

Phil stormed across the room to the closet where he kept his guns. He flung the door open and pulled the shotgun from the rack nailed to the wall. He checked its shells, cocked the gun, and walked over to the front door, handing her a pair of binoculars.

"Watch my ass, would ya?" he said.

"Phil, if you leave me a widow, I'll never forgive you."

"I'll see you soon, Alice. I promise you," he said as he cupped her scarred cheek, then giving her his crooked smile, and taking one last look at his shotgun to look for any signs of wear or defection, he got moving.

Alice unshackled the front door, opened it, and watched Phil lumber out, grasping his gun. He waddled across the street and began firing at the ghouls pursuing the young girl in the yard across the street—the Watkins' yard— the next-door neighbors of Ben.

Alice watched from the door with her binoculars, utterly terrified, more for Phil than herself, or for that stupid girl who was threatening to destroy their lives. Everything she feared, and everything that she had warned Phil about...well...it would take less than ten seconds for it to all to become a reality.

Phil blew shot after shot into those human- shaped creatures, sending clouds of blood and flesh into the air. He made his way over to the poor girl who was now lying motionless on the ground in the Watkins' front yard, fending off attacks from the advancing ghouls.

"Phil!" Alice screamed, spotting one slowly creeping up behind him.

As if he heard her warning, Phil spun around and beat the creature in the face with the butt of his gun. The ghoul stumbled back, and Phil flipped the gun and fired point blank into its face. The entire head evaporated into pink mist and puzzle piece-shaped bits of skull bone, while its scalp—still intact and covered with thick, black hair, went flying, landing on the hood of a car. The scalp sat there like some kind of cartoonish joke, and from where Alice stood, she remembered thinking it looked like an old cat, sunning itself in the hot summer day.

As Alice watched, the walkie-talkie in the charger behind her came to life.

"Alice! What the hell is Phil doing out there?" It was Abel Watkins, the man whose yard Phil was currently battling in. "Alice? Get him out of there!"

She ignored Abel's commands, training her eyes only on her husband.

Phil fired a shot at another ghoul, shearing away most of its neck. The head fell to the side, coming to rest on its shoulder, still attached to its body by just a sliver of skin, before crumbling at the knees into a jumbled pile of dead, clothed meat.

Alice gripped her binoculars tightly and watched Phil reach the girl on the ground. She looked to be about sixteen or seventeen years of age, Alice guessed as Phil knelt down and checked for signs of life.

He tried to rouse her, but there was no response. Alice could see that the girl's shirt was stained with blood, but she couldn't spot any wounds. Phil shook her again and her arm, which had been draped across her midsection, fell limply to her side.

That was when Alice spotted the chunk of flesh missing from the palm of her hand and saw Phil grimace when he saw it too.

Alice had been right. It was too late for the girl.

Another ghoul, it was Jerry James, the local mechanic, approached from behind Phil, and Alice screamed again. Phil looked behind him, saw the dead man and took aim. But before he could fire, the girl suddenly sat up behind him, snarling, drooling an inordinate amount of spit.

"No!" Alice cried from her place at the door.

The girl grabbed Phil's meaty arm and she took a sick, wet bite from his shoulder!

Phil screamed in response and mashed the girl in the face with the butt of his shotgun, knocking her to her back to the grass. He hammered down on her face several times until it was a cavern of red gore, now rapidly filling with blood. He stared in shock at the mess he'd made, seemingly transfixed. Everything was a mangled mess of bone and meat, and the only thing that was recognizable was the girl's tongue, which, despite the mutilation it sat in, looked surprisingly clean; a pink boat amidst a sea of blood beset in her caved-in face.

And then they fell on him, a tidal wave of ghouls swelling around him, clamoring clumsily against each other, desperate to get at this warm meal before them. Phil did what he could to fight them off, but it was no use. Alice screamed bloody murder from her door, took two tentative steps towards him, but then backpedaled into the house and slammed the door.

She shackled it back up, and then leaned against it, sobbing. She slid slowly down the door, her butt plopping on the floor. She remained there for several hours, long after Phil's blood-curdling screams had subsided. She cried softly and occasionally hammered her elbows into the door in response to the pounding coming from the other side, from the ghouls that had killed and eaten her husband, and were now hoping to kill her, too.

* * *

"Jesus, Alice! Oh my God. I'm so sorry. What the hell did he think he was doing? Why did you let him go out there?" Abel demanded through the walkie-talkie. Alice threw the binoculars at the radio, knocking it off the table and silencing Abel's accusatory tone. She laid her head in her crossed arms and cried with such intensity her eyes momentarily blacked out, giving way to stars that danced before her only to dissipate into nothingness that had now become her life.

She stayed like this all day and eventually fell asleep in the mid-afternoon hours. When she awoke, sounds of moaning were still outside the front door, but it was just one voice now.

It was Phil's.

She recognized him immediately—and not because she knew if one of those things bit or killed you that you just came back like one of them—but because she'd spent so many years listening to that very same moan. Phil would utter it when he got out of bed or his favorite chair, or on those nights he'd come home having drunk to excess with Thor and Sam. Then he would throw himself into the bathroom and fall to the toilet so he could heave out thirty dollars worth of beer from Donny's Bar.

It was a noise she'd grown to hate, and that hadn't changed, but now it was because it suddenly meant something new. It no longer meant Phil was old, or tired, or hung-over.

It meant Phil was outside.

Sure, he was dead, but he was outside, and he knew she was in the house. He could probably smell her, too.

Alice got up, pressed her ear against the front door, and listened while Phil continued to beat his fists against it and emit those awful noises. She hobbled over to the eyehole in the window, her knees weak from the position she'd remained in for close to six hours, and peered out.

Despite Phil's hooting and hollering, it was surprisingly clear of any other ghouls.

She made her way over to the closet and slowly opened the door. Phil's shotgun was lying on the ground outside in a pond of his blood, but there were a few other guns still in the closet for her to use. She spotted the six-shooter at the bottom of the gun rack and knelt down. She opened the chamber, saw it was fully loaded, and snapped it back into place.

Alice had never fired a gun in her life, but she'd helped Phil clean them a few times. There wasn't much to a six-shooter, anyway. She was certain she would be okay. Reasonably certain. Maybe.

She closed the closet door and walked back to the front door, the gun now in her hand. As Phil continued to beat against the door and make those awful noises, she grasped the gun in both hands and began crying again. She held the gun up and rested her head against it, trying to calm down. She screamed in fury after a moment, and then unlocked most of the door. With one lock left still securing the door, she stopped again. She turned around and walked swiftly into the living room, which Phil had insisted on decorating years ago with a Southwestern theme. It was filled with cacti plants and paintings, dream catchers and pottery, turquoise and tan; a room where she was now forced to spend her life alone. She stopped in front of the cream-colored couch and arranged some throw pillows woven with Native American tapestry designs so that they were stacked in front of each other. She moved back several steps, took aim at the pillows, and fired.

Nothing but an empty click greeted her.

She stared at the gun and began fumbling with it in her hands, looking for what could be halting the bullet from firing. She checked the chamber again just to make sure and saw all six rounds were in place, ready and waiting. It was then that she spotted a switch—the safety—just above the chamber wheel. She clicked the switch, and aimed the gun again. She pulled the trigger, sending a bullet through three of her best throw pillows, her couch, and into the wall behind it. The bullet's propulsion sent the gun exploding up into her face and cracked her in the chin. Blood almost immediately soaked into the jagged cut left by the gun, and she made a gasping sound. Momentarily losing her footing from the blast, she nearly fell down on the glass coffee table behind her. After steadying herself, she went into the kitchen and grabbed a dish towel. Attempting to turn on the faucet, she remembered the water had stopped flowing months ago, and she slammed it once with her hand and ran over to her tea kettle. She poured some water left within out into the dish towel and held it to her bleeding chin.

The sound of the gunshot had agitated Phil, and he began beating even harder against the front door, now only secured by one lock. Recalling this, Alice gripped the six-shooter securely in her right hand as she held the towel on her bloody chin with her left.

She took three quick breaths, walked hurriedly over to the door, unlocked the last lock with her gun in hand, and stepped back.

Phil continued to batter the door and make those wet, guttural sounds. Seeing this was just going to continue, she walked up and spun the knob very quickly, freeing the door from the jamb. She stepped back, aimed the gun, and waited.

Phil beat against the door a final time and sent it crashing in.

Alice, ready to fire the moment she had a clear shot, was caught off guard by the nightmarish figure of her husband before her. The man she remembered was gone, replaced by something from her nightmares.

A deep gouge in his stomach had let loose a torrent of intestines, and an end strand, which was hanging several feet out of his body, had somehow been tucked into his belt like a morbid pocket watch. As he moved closer to her, his shambling feet crushed the other intestines that were dragging on the floor in front of him, and with each step, he pulled a bit more out of his gut with a sick, greasy slide. One eye—his left—was completely gone, as was a large and almost-perfect circle patch of flesh around the eye socket. The staggered patterns at the edge of this skinless patch, caused by the unevenness of a set of teeth, made it look like a red, sloppy cloud. His nose was also gone, a gaping, dark hole, serving as what seemed to be the unending source of blood pouring down into his mouth and down his chin.

As Phil lurched slowly after her, she was suddenly assaulted with the memory of Bugsy, their old Bloodhound. At fifteen years of age, the dog's time had come where he could no longer get up off the floor. Their pet, not eating or drinking, was wasting away. Despite Alice's sobbing and her selfish begs for Phil just to let him be, Phil had taken Bugsy into the woods and shot him near the fallen tree where they would walk him everyday.

Phil had argued that Bugsy was suffering and in pain, and while Alice knew this, it made her hate her husband just a little bit.

Phil moaned again and she inhaled one sharp breath, centered the gun on Phil's face, and put three bullets into his forehead.

Alice buried Phil that day without much fanfare or ceremony. She dug a hole two feet down, laid him face up, and covered his face with the dish towel that was soaked with her blood. A little macabre but appropriate. Part of her should be down there with him.

After throwing the dirt from the yard back on top, small clumps cascading off the bigger ones as they bounced off the sandwich wrap she'd used to keep his intestines inside his body, she packed the mound with the shovel and said simply, "Goodbye, Phil, I'll miss you," and went inside.

*   *   *

Her head was pounding now, and it was getting unbearable. She turned and walked into the bathroom, her hand reaching for the medicine cabinet. Squinting her eyes from the pain, she lifted up each bottle and held it close, trying to read their labels. Finding the one she wanted—a bottle of generic sinus and allergy medicine—she was greeted not with the sound of a few loose pills clattering around inside, but with the sound of nothing at all.

Empty.

"Damn it," she muttered, throwing the bottle behind her into the shower she hadn't set foot in for months. Bottled water heated over her electric stove had been her only means of keeping clean for some time now. Not that it mattered. Who was around to smell her?

No one.

No one at all.

She strode back into her empty living room and looked around. She looked at the dark, musty, disgusting house where she'd spent the six months of her life entirely alone, with no company at all except for the random warnings from Ben, her only remaining neighbor across the street. All the other neighbors—the Watkins, the Davies, and the Georges—had either been killed or had packed up and driven off, attempting to escape the insanity of this horror story their lives had become.

Alice sauntered over to the table, picked up the framed picture of Phil and his fish, and stroked his face, smiling, remembering the time years ago when he'd come home drunk and insisted on building a dog house for Bugsy. He'd made it as far as outlining the entrance on the front piece of soft pine before going to bed, citing simply, "screw Bugsy".

She carefully set the picture down and turned, her eyes washing over the hideous Southwestern décor and at the smashed ceramic thimble collection which had taken close to twenty years to amass, yet only three seconds to destroy.

She gazed at the splash of expired coffee soaking into the carpet, at the walkie-talkie wrapped in duct tape and stuck in the charger, and the red light blinking from across the room. She looked at what her life had devolved into. She could scarcely dissociate the events of yesterday from the events of last week, the days and weeks blending together in her mind.

And with that, epiphany cascaded over her like warm bathwater.

Enough's enough.

She walk to the small candy dish she kept on the counter near the front door, grabbed the set of keys for Marlene Watkins' car that she had been using since Marlene was eaten by the mailman, and turned to Phil's picture again.

"I'm goin' to the store, Phil. I need some goddamned head pills. Want anything?" She even waited for a response before she turned, opened the door, and strode out of her house.

She walked to her car, which was parked crookedly across their front yard, its driver's side door just a few feet from the front door of their house. For a fast getaway, she had decided. It's not like there were any neighbors left to call Constable Barton and complain. And it's not like Constable Barton was taking any calls today, anyway. The last time she had seen him, he was stumbling down the banks of Kennebec River with a hole in his belly the size of a cantaloupe.

She opened the door, slid in, and closed it behind her. She turned the key in the ignition and the car started without a problem, the gas gauge needle shooting up to read a full tank, courtesy of Jerry James' filling station.

She sat back, waiting for the engine to warm up, not bothering to take a quick look and see if there were any of those things out there that could pose a threat. She didn't even do a quick scan from the safety of the car.

One of those things, which had been staring at a mangy cat sitting perched on the roof of a nearby house, suddenly turned, hearing the car's engine. It moaned once, rubbed the back of its hand across its mouth, and sauntered on down the yard and into the street.

As Alice busied herself in her tape collection, which she kept in a box on the seat beside her, the creature lumbered over to the passenger side window and started clumsily slapping on the glass.

"Oh, look, company," she said, not the least bit concerned, her head still down over the box of old cassettes. "What's your poison, sailor? I've got the Platters in here, some Glenn Miller. Oh, wait, I've got just the thing." She grabbed a cassette, held it close to her eyes to verify it was the one she wanted, and popped it into the tape deck, which whirred and threatened to quit on her for a moment before it began to play one of her favorite songs: *Time of the Season.*

She rolled the passenger side window down and she tossed the tape case into the ghoul's face. He pawed at where it struck him, confused and agitated.

"You should give these kids a listen, you undead good-for-nothin'. It took me a little while to get past their hippie crap, but they've really grown on me."

She shifted the car into drive and roared forward, plowing through the white picket fence surrounding her front yard. The dead man, which had been holding onto the window jamb, flew off, rolling limply down the lawn. Alice bounced the car over some bushes, tore up the long-dead Millers' front yard, and splintered the Georges' mailbox before she ended up in the street.

"I'm off to the store, Ben!" she called out the window. "I'll bring you back a sirloin!" She laughed at her joke and continued her trip into town.

The ghoul she knocked off her car got up slowly, stared at her as she drove off, and then began walking after her. Other human shapes that had been wandering around backyards, or lying pathetically on their backs waiting for something to happen, followed suit. Soon, a small horde of walking dead had formed and were soon plodding after the car disappearing down the street.

As Alice drove, she sang along with the song, softly, peacefully. Her headache was starting to go away, but she knew it would be just a matter of time, whether it be the next day or the next week, before another one would rear up and assault her poor noggin.

"Better safe than sorry," she said, adjusting the rearview mirror and seeing a crowd of the undead following slowly and dumbly behind her.

"A thing needs doin', and I intend on doin' it. I won't sit here and suffer like an animal. And if it's my time to go, then it's my time to go." She shifted the mirror down so she could see her scar. She took one hand off the wheel and ran her finger down the long, jagged reminder of her horrid, empty pseudo-life.

"Today's the day, I think," she said loudly, sighing, despair no longer prevalent in her words. "I think today can finally be the day."

She shut her eyes softly, smiled, and thought of Phil; of his salt and pepper hair, of the picture of him and the tuna, of his wide grin.

"I'll see you soon, Phil," she said. "I promise you."

VALLEY OF DEATH

As a town, Los Pueblos doesn't offer much. And what it does have comes in limited quantities. There's one bank, one grocery store, one service station, and one feed store. When any of the 187 residents get hungry, they can choose from three barbecue places, Rosie's Coffee Shop, or the taco stand that can be found most days out on Route 3.

And when folks die, they usually make a stopover at Hudson & Family Funeral Home, which is not just the only funeral home in Los Pueblos, but the entire valley. Los Pueblos loses people at a clip of about one or two a month, so the place stays pretty quiet.

This suits Anderson Jacob just fine. At only 15, Anderson is well on his way to realizing a future that does not include this town. He's scheduled to graduate from Pueblo Valley High School two years early, but not soon enough as far as he's concerned. More than a part-time job, the funeral home for Anderson is a library without the books. But it was better than a library because most days he's left completely alone to study. Not like his house, where his four younger sisters kept the place in a perpetual state of chaos.

Gabby Hudson had hired Anderson to work part time, keeping the place tidy and doing some heavy lifting. Despite the name on the sign, Gabby was the only Hudson left after Carl died, and managing the place, even in a ghost town like this, was too much for a 72-year-old woman to handle alone. But even an old bird like Gabby was quick to recognize that Anderson was as smart as he was courteous. Pretty soon he was not only doing the muscle jobs, which included digging the graves and keeping the kudzu under control out at Valley Rest Cemetery, but he was also handling most of the day-to-day business.

On one of his first days on the job, while cleaning out a store-room, Anderson came across a discarded computer. Until then he'd assumed the most advanced piece of machinery on the premises was Gabby's 20-year-old Texas Instruments calculator. When he asked Gabby about it, she told him that Carl had bought it one day years ago after seeing a 60 Minutes story about how computers were going to make everyone's lives easier.

"I swear, that jackass would have hired a freighter of chimps if somebody told him they'd do his work for him," she'd told Anderson at the time.

So Anderson dusted it off and spent an entire weekend writing a piece of software that was so simple even Gabby would be able to use it to automate purchasing for the funeral home. He even made the numbers extra large so she wouldn't have to use her reading glasses, which she was always leaving downstairs in the parlor anyway. She wanted no part of it at first, but after he showed her how all she had to do was click on the item she needed more of and it would show up a few days later, she couldn't have been more excited than if he told her Elvis Presley himself would be delivering this year's order of cavity fluid.

But with Anderson proving bright beyond his years, she left those responsibilities to him. And she would spend her days either shopping over in Santa Domingo or playing golf at Royal Ridge. That is, unless they had a client. That was one part of the operation Anderson had absolutely no interest in. In fact, he went to great lengths to avoid the parlor at all costs, a disposition that Gabby found very amusing. Anderson was so polite, and helpful beyond reason for a boy of 15, that there was never a time he didn't offer to do for Gabby whatever it was she was in the middle of. That is until one day when she forgot her glasses down in the parlor. She'd been down there working on Maria Diaz and came upstairs complaining about her back, stooping over the table for long periods of time always aggravated it. And poor Maria had been in a head-on collision with a logging truck and needed quite a bit of work. But Anderson never offered to run down and fetch them, and Gabby knew it wasn't likely that the thought didn't cross his mind. He was apt to tie your shoes if he noticed one was undone.

Gabby picked up on this and used it endlessly to tease him.

"Anderson, sweetie," she'd say. "Be a dear and run down to the parlor and round up my glasses, will you? You'll find them next to Mr. Fogarty."

Usually, Anderson would find himself too preoccupied with whatever he was doing, whether it was emptying trashcans or restocking the Kleenex, to even acknowledge the request. Or he'd push his nose even further into whatever book he was reading and pretend not to hear. He even got to where when Gabby came upstairs without her glasses, he'd get started on some outside project that took him out of earshot, short-circuiting the situation before Gabby could even ask.

But this week had been a busy one and today Gabby was here, working on Mrs. Hollandsworth, another casualty of Route 3. That stretch of highway that connected Los Pueblos and the rest of Pueblo Valley was responsible for about 10 percent of Hudson & Family's business. Which is to say about once or twice a year someone would hydroplane off the Pin Oak Bridge or fall asleep and cross the yellow stripe at just the wrong time.

Jessup Nelson was currently occupying the viewing room, decked out in his United States Air Force uniform and, over that, the very finest Hemingway coffin his wife Madison could afford. In just a couple of hours the Nelson's would file in to say their good-byes. This was the first time since Anderson had been working at Hudson & Family that they had an intake and a viewing in the same day, so Gabby was working harder than she'd had to since hiring Anderson.

While Gabby was downstairs with Mrs. Hollandsworth, Anderson was at the front desk studying for a chemistry final. It would be his last test as a high school student, which meant he was just one more summer away from leaving Los Pueblos for good. He suspected this would be a fine place to visit, lots of people do after all, but to grow up here is to know the true meaning of despair.

It was late in the afternoon when Anderson was startled by the sound of something metal crashing to the floor downstairs. Anderson listened, but the clang was followed for a few seconds only by silence. Then in the softest voice he'd ever heard her use, Gabby called to him.

"Anderson?" she said, in a tone that sounded like she was trying to wake him from a nap without startling him. "Anderson...can you come down here, *please*?"

Her tone frightened him and he was sure she'd fallen down. Certain he'd be calling 911 very shortly, he grabbed the phone off the cradle and took it with him. About halfway down the stairs he realized this would be the first time he'd set foot in the parlor. The fumes were already assaulting his senses. As he cleared the final step, he saw that Gabby hadn't fallen. She was standing next to one of two embalming tables, the long metal cannula resting at her feet. This must have been what Anderson heard. Gabby very briefly looked at Anderson, then looked toward the adjacent wall. He followed her gaze to where Mrs. Hollandsworth's body was standing upright, facing the corner, like a kid sent to time-out.

For a fraction of a second, Anderson thought Gabby had really gone all-out with this one; propping up poor Mrs. H. in the corner like that and luring him down here to mess with him. But then he noticed she wasn't just standing in the corner, she was moving. He watched for several seconds while Mrs. Hollandsworth took a slow, lurching step into the wall. She bumped into it with her head and chest, bouncing back a little. Then she'd try it again, like a wind-up toy unable to turn around.

Anderson looked back at Gabby, who was still standing there looking at Mrs. Hollandsworth. He'd read about how people used to be so afraid of being buried alive that their headstones would be equipped with bells. A string was tied to the bells and attached to the person's hand. If the person woke up, they could ring the bell from their casket and be rescued. He never thought in a million years this was still possible.

He started towards Gabby, and then out of the corner of his eye saw Mrs. Hollandsworth turn. He looked at her and one glance told him Mrs. Hollandsworth was as dead now as when they pried her from her Toyota Prius. Her eyes were open, but vacant. And there was a huge hole in her neck where Gabby had been using the cannula to inject embalming fluid into her carotid artery. He dropped the phone and the sound of it shattering on the tile floor sounded like it came from miles away.

Without thinking, he jumped over the stainless steel table and ran to Gabby. Her eyes ballooned and he looked back to see Mrs. Hollandsworth's corpse fix her gaze on them and approach. He picked the cannula off the floor and reared back like he was about to take batting practice. This didn't seem to threaten Mrs. H. because she kept coming, reaching out her arms like a blind man expecting to bump into a wall. The corpse's teeth shown and Anderson thought he saw flecks of blood there, probably left over from the accident.

Anderson gave Gabby a gentle shove toward the door, hoping she'd take the hint and run. To his relief, she did. She was already to the steps before Mrs. Hollandsworth knew she was making a move. She turned toward Gabby, but she was too slow and too far away now to pose a threat. She started like she was going to follow her up the steps and Anderson slammed the cannula on the table with a crash.

"Over here!" he yelled. "Hey, you, over here!" He moved a little closer, watching how she moved in slow jerky motions. Whatever was happening to her, it hadn't reversed the effects of rigor mortis. For a second, Anderson thought Gabby was probably on the phone with the police by now. Then he saw the phone in pieces on the floor. His cell phone was sitting next to his chemistry book upstairs, but even if Gabby thought to look for it he didn't give her much of a chance of figuring out how to use it.

Mrs. Hollandsworth turned back toward Anderson, first her head, then her body followed with considerable effort. Once she was aligned, she began moving in his direction, her dilated pupils locked on him. At the rate she was going, it would take her several minutes to reach him. Anderson considered cracking her in the head with the metal cannula, but decided that would probably finish Mrs. H. for good and he wasn't about to make such a permanent decision with the limited information he had. He waited a few seconds before making a break for the door, for Mrs. Hollandsworth to get a couple of steps closer, that way he'd have a better angle on her should she decide to go after him.

Anderson bolted, closing the door behind him and making sure it clicked. Upstairs, he found Gabby sitting in a chair, crying into her hands. He put a hand on her shoulder and knelt down beside her.

"Mrs. Hudson," he said. "Mrs. Hudson, what happened? What's wrong with Mrs. H?"

She looked up at him and for a second seemed confused and disoriented, and Anderson thought she might have hit her head downstairs. Then he saw the flicker of recognition in her eyes.

"She was just lying there," she said. "I had that metal rod shoved into her neck pumping her full of chemicals. Andy, I was ready to plug her up when she sat right up. I mean she sat up on the table!" She sobbed again into her hands. "My God, I've never seen anything like it," her voice was quiet again, the way it was when she called to him from downstairs.

Anderson reached for his cell phone and saw that he had three missed calls, all within the last two minutes and all from his house. They could hear Mrs. Hollandsworth bumping around downstairs and Anderson wondered how long it would take her to open the door. Based on the vacuous look in her eyes, he suspected that turning the knob might never occur to her.

Gabby jumped at a thundering crash coming from the viewing room. Anderson ran to the doorway and saw that Mr. Nelson's casket had fallen from the platform and was lying upside down on the ground, a crack splintered down the center of the open lid. Under the overturned casket, Jessup was writhing around face down, his uniformed arms and legs splayed out from underneath the casket like some kind of macabre turtle. And he didn't seem to me making any progress.

The fact that a man who just an hour ago was not only dead, but was now two days removed from having every orifice sewn shut, his blood drained, and his empty carcass filled with chemicals, suddenly didn't seem all that odd to Anderson.

Gabby came up behind him and gasped.

"I'm calling the police," he said as he closed the door. "Someone will know what's happening."

"Andy," Gabby said. "What *is* happening? You know about science, right? Carl and I've run this place for more than 50 years and I've never seen anything like this."

"No, Mrs. Hudson," Anderson said in the most measured tone he could muster. "I think this is new."

He walked her back over to the chair and sat her down, dialing 9-1-1 on his cell as he did so. *All circuits are busy,* he said after several seconds. "Look, I need to go back downstairs."

"Andy, no!" she said, her face lighting up in fear. "You can't, why would you want to go down there?"

"I left the phone down there and we might need it to call the police. Now, I'm going to be okay, but I need you to stay put."

"I wish you wouldn't," she said. "We have your phone, what do we need that old cordless for?"

"Well, for one thing the Nelson's will be calling soon to confirm Mr. Nelson is ready for the family to see him. They'll be arriving shortly, and, well, I think we might want to postpone." She smiled at his attempt at levity and he was glad for it. "Stay right here and I'll be back in 90 seconds, okay?"

She nodded and he bounded down the stairs. He put his ear to the door to see if he could still her Mrs. Hollandsworth rattling around. He couldn't, so he opened the door carefully, just enough to peek through and give the room a quick scan. She was standing in the middle of the room, her back to him, looking at the whirling ceiling fan as if she were solving a puzzle. Anderson looked down and saw the phone. The battery compartment and the rest was close by and he entered the room, scooped them up and started back up the steps after closing the door once more.

He hesitated, then turned around and headed back down again. He opened the door and watched her stare at the fan like it was talking to her.

Curiosity overwhelmed him and he decided to get a closer look. After all, he wasn't sure she wanted to hurt him. And if she did, an elderly woman had been quick enough to get away. He moved around Mrs. H so he could see her face. Her dead eyes watched the fan and he thought she would ignore him completely until she lowered her head in his direction. It startled him, but he stood fast, looking at her. He wasn't sure if she was seeing him with her exploded retinas, but he was positive she knew he was there.

"Anderson," Gabby called from upstairs. She sounded afraid and Anderson felt suddenly guilty for leaving her alone.

"I'm okay!" he yelled back. If the dead woman couldn't see, she certainly could hear because she cocked her head, first toward Gabby's voice then back to Anderson. Mrs. Hollandsworth lurched toward him and stretched out her arms in that blind man's way of hers.

"Well, get up here then!" Gabby yelled back. "I think Jessup's gone!"

Anderson bolted toward the door, closing it behind him. He had the phone reassembled before he made it to the top of the stairs, but stopped cold when he got there. Gabby was not in the chair where he'd left her.

"Mrs. Hudson?"

"In here, Andy," she said from the viewing room. Anderson walked in and saw the smashed coffin but no Mr. Nelson. "Where did he go?"

Just then a uniformed hand reached out from underneath the casket and grabbed Gabby's ankle.

She screamed and fell to the floor, a sickening thud pounding through the room as her hip shattered. Anderson grabbed her under her shoulders and tried pulling her away from Mr. Nelson's grip. Then from under the casket, Mr. Nelson reached toward Gabby's ankle and opened wide, the stitches Gabby used to keep his gaping mouth closed ripping the flesh around his lips. He sunk his teeth into her ankle and the parlor erupted in her screams.

Anderson loosened his grip on Gabby and kicked Jessup in the jaw. This broke his hold on her and Anderson brought his foot down hard on the zombie's head, causing it to split in two. He drew back his foot and it was smeared with the little remaining soft tissue that was left in Mr. Nelson's skull.

That must have turned out the lights for good, because he stopped moving. Anderson grabbed Gabby again and dragged her toward the door. She was screaming and crying, and her leg was bleeding horribly. Judging by the trail of blood they were leaving behind them, Anderson suspected she'd be dead in a matter of minutes unless he could stop it somehow. Once in the lobby, he dropped her and shut the door to the viewing room just to be safe. Then he whipped off his belt and tied it around her leg.

"Mrs. Hudson," he said. But she didn't respond.

Between the broken hip and the blood loss, Anderson knew she was probably in shock. More to himself than to her, he said, "This is going to hurt like hell, I'm sorry." Then he slung her over his shoulder and carried her to the intake room where there was a nice big couch. As gently as possible, he set her down, but she was completely out by now. He checked the makeshift tourniquet and tightened it. Then he covered her with a blanket and went back to the lobby.

Somewhere in the distance he heard a siren and walked outside. It was coming down Route 3, headed his way, so he ran to the street. In a few seconds he saw a sheriff's car speeding in his direction. He waved his arms as it went by but it thundered by without even hesitating. In the distance, in the direction the sheriff's car was heading, a column of smoke was billowing into the air. Near it, Anderson could hear the sirens of several emergency vehicles congregating.

He dialed 9-1-1 on the cordless phone and again got the all circuits are busy message. Then he tried his cell. Same result. He dialed his house and his mother picked up.

"Anderson, thank God!" she said breathlessly. His sisters were crying in the background, which was nothing new around his house, but there was something more to it now. His sisters had a distinct cry for when they were scared and until that moment he'd never heard them all go off at the same time.

"Mom," he said, again trying to muster a calming tone. "Something's happening down here at the funeral home. Mrs. Hudson needs an ambulance."

"Oh, God, Andy," she said in a tone that suggested her worst fears had been realized. "I don't know what's going on, but it's happening everywhere. People are coming back. Dead people!" she said. "I haven't heard from your father and they're saying not to get on the roads."

"What do you mean, go on the roads?" he asked.

"They're telling us not to drive. If you're not home by 5, you have to stay put."

Anderson looked at his watch. "Mom, it's almost 6."

"I know, and it's just me and the girls here on the ranch and I don't know what's going on!"

"Okay, Mom, settle down," he said. "It's going to be okay. Dad was going out to Exeter Bluff today, he's probably on his way back now. I mean, they'll let him come home if he's out right? Have you tried his cell?"

"He left it here," she said. "He left it here and now I have no way to know where he's at or if he's safe. Andy, have you seen any of *them*?"

He thought about how to answer, then remembered lying was out of the question because he'd already told her Mrs. Hudson needed help. "Yeah, I think so. I mean, the two bodies here were raising hell."

"The head, Andy," she said. "The news is saying that if you hit them in the head, or shoot them in the head, that seems to kill them. Permanent, I mean."

"Okay," he said. No way was he going to tell his mother that only a few minutes ago he'd figured that one out by himself. "What else are they saying?"

"That they don't understand anything," she said. "I mean, it's happening everywhere. People try talking to them, but it doesn't do any good. People in hospitals are getting hurt."

"What hospitals?" he asked. St. Joe's was the closest and that was way over in Cecil County.

"All over, Andy," she said. "I mean, this thing is happening all over. They keep showing security footage from a hospital in China."

When his mother said that whatever was happening was happening on a global scale, it was the first time Anderson got good and scared.

"Mom, lock the doors and windows. The ranch is so far off the beaten path I doubt you'll have anything to worry about, but just in case. This is exactly the type of thing that makes people feel like they can just take what's not theirs. Keep a gun close, just in case. And keep the phone charged."

"Andy, you gotta come home, okay," she said with a desperation that made Anderson's blood run icy.

"I'm going to try to, Mom. I have to make sure Mrs. Hudson is okay and I'll need to bring her with me."

"Okay. Please be careful."

Anderson ran back to the intake room. He could hear Mrs. Hollandsworth bumping around again downstairs. Maybe she'd solved the mystery of the ceiling fan. He threw the door open and Mrs. Hudson was sitting up, her head looking down at her lap.

"Mrs. Hudson," Anderson said as he approached and sat next to her. He put his hand on hers and it was cold to the touch, a side-effect of the shock. "Mrs. Hudson, the ambulance isn't coming so we need to go to my house. We need to take the van, okay?"

She turned and lunged for him, giving him just an instant to get a hand on her forehead. Her jaw snapped shut within a breath of his neck. He pushed her away and stood up. She stood up, too, but her stance was wildly off-kilter due to her fractured hip. She reached toward him and popped in his direction in a grossly deformed gate. With each step, he could hear the bone in her hip crunching. Her eyes weren't dilated the way Mrs. Hollandsworth's were. Mrs. Hudson's eyes looked alive, like there was something firing away behind them.

He looked around the room and grabbed a heavy silver candlestick from a table. "I'm sorry, Gabby," he said and then swung the base end of the candlestick into her temple. The contact caused a massive crack to explode on the side of her head and she collapsed in a heap. As soon as he saw the wound, he understood why Gabby had that look of comprehension that Mr. Hollandsworth seemed to lack. About 75 percent of Mrs. H's brain matter had been removed, at least as much as Gabby could get out with the cannula.

He stared at the blood pooling around her head for a few seconds before snapping back to reality. Back in the lobby, candlestick still in hand, he grabbed a keychain hanging from a hook on the wall, pausing for just second to look back at the staircase leading to the parlor. Mrs. Hollandsworth was getting louder. He considered going down to finish her, but decided two homicides was enough for one day.

With the keys in hand, he started toward the front door, but stopped stiff when he saw three people congregating in the parking lot. He recognized Veronica and Dom Nelson, classmates of his at

Pueblo Valley High. The third person he didn't know, but assumed it was also a member of the Nelson family.

He started outside again, but again stopped when he recognized the slow, jerky movements they were making. Then he noticed that there were no cars in the parking lot, so he figured they must have walked here.

Anderson recognized the vacant stares immediately, but there was something intentional in the way they lumbered toward the building. Not like Mrs. Hollandsworth downstairs, who seemed to move in no particular direction.

Near the street, he noticed two more men and three women. All five were dressed like they were going to church, or a wake, and all moved in that undead way Anderson had come to recognize.

Veronica was the closest and Anderson could now see the flesh had been ripped from her cheekbone. Dom's mouth was covered in blood, but Anderson didn't see a wound. There was a large gash on his upper arm though. In fact, all of these new arrivals had similar mortal wounds on their arms, necks or faces.

Anderson ran to the door and locked it, wondering how many of those *things* pulling in the same direction it would take to bust it open. But he doubted they'd be able to figure that out. Whatever they were, they seemed to be operating on instinct rather than logic.

Her heard a popping sound and saw Dom fall to the ground, motionless. The others didn't even notice and kept moving toward the door. Veronica was the first to reach the door, but she didn't even try the handle. She just bumped into the glass like she expected to walk through it. Then she put her hands on the glass and felt around, like a mime. Another pop rang out, and Anderson saw one of the ladies' heads explode in a fine red mist before she fell. Another pop and a puff of smoke floated up from across the highway.

He recognized his dad's hat first, the same Pueblo Lumber hat he'd worn for years. Aaron Jacob was kneeling behind a rock, his rifle leveled toward the funeral home. Anderson fought the urge to run to him and instead stepped away from the door. His old man was a crack shot, but better to be safe than sorry.

Anderson dialed home again.

"Andy," his mother said, just as rattled as before.

"Mom, Dad's here. He's with me."

"Oh, thank God," she breathed into the phone. It sounded like she'd been holding her breath for days. "The roads are closed, nobody's coming in or out of the valley."

"Keep the doors locked and don't let anybody onto the ranch. No matter what. We'll get there when we can but it's going to be a while if the roads are closed."

"Okay, but you be careful," she said.

He said he would and hung up the phone, then turned back toward the door to see that the shooting had stopped. And the reason why stopped his heart.

There must have been 50 or more people lumbering towards the funeral home's door. All of them were dressed in their finest threads, and all of them were stone-cold dead.

A booming knock filled the lobby, coming from the back door. Anderson ran to the door and without giving it any thought, opened it. Aaron barged in and closed the door behind him. He was breathing hard and Anderson noticed the stock of his rifle was matted with blood, hair, and bits of skin.

"Wow!" Aaron said. "Can you believe this?"

"Jeez, me and Mom were worried sick. How'd you get back from Exeter Bluff with the roads closed?"

"I was back in the valley when the shit hit the fan. Listening to the radio, I thought I'd better get back to the house. Then I remembered you were working today and I thought your mom and sisters were probably safer on the ranch than you were in a funeral home."

"What'd the radio say was happening?" Anderson asked.

"Can't tell crossbows from elbows," his dad answered. "But it's bad, Andy. People are getting hurt something awful. If they bite you bad enough they can kill you, rip you apart like wild animals. And when you die, you don't stay dead for long."

"I know," he nodded toward the door to the viewing room. Aaron followed his look and gave him a curious stare. He walked to the door and opened it.

"Yeah," Aaron said as he looked at the formerly reanimated corpse of Jessup Nelson. "I guess you do." He shut the door and looked to the front door.

"Why do you think they're coming here?" Anderson asked.

"I guess they were on their way here already. And whatever happened didn't change their minds."

"There's so many," he said. There were probably a hundred or more piling up against the building now. He could here the low moaning sound seeping in from outside.

"Gabby keep any weapons around?"

"Just this," Anderson said, holding up the candlestick he'd used to bash in Mrs. Hudson's brains.

"Those things out there," Aaron started as he engaged the bolt action on his rifle. "If they get in, we're as good as gone. They're here to say goodbye to what's left of their friend. Let's send them to Hell so they can say it in person."

THE HOUSEWARMING

It was nearly midnight, and Josh Harrison had a lot on his mind.

Leaning against the railing of the front porch, taking a long drag off a Marlboro Light, he couldn't help but think how the housewarming party he had so meticulously planned was a resounding dud. Josh doubted if the assorted guests could even pack a minivan. What was intended to be a bash to rival his fraternity days ended up devolving into little more than a small gathering of old friends.

And that would have been totally fine if Amanda had shown up, Josh mused. *Shit, I probably wouldn't have bothered with the whole thing if I knew she was going to blow me off without so much as a phone call.*

"...for this place, Josh?"

"What was that?" Josh asked, torn from his thoughts by a question coming from across the porch.

"How much did you pay for this house?" Laura repeated as her petite form approached through the darkness. Lost in his own melancholy musings, Josh hadn't heard her come outside. She joined him at the porch's edge.

"I got a good deal on it," he answered, tossing the cigarette over the railing and onto the front lawn. "Government foreclosure."

"It's nice. A little big for just one person, but nice."

Josh sighed. "I'm hoping it will fill up, someday."

"No Amanda tonight?"

Even through the gloom, Laura could see the sharp look Josh shot her way.

"What?" she asked. "Don't play dumb. Not with me. I saw the way you two were ogling each other in the bar last weekend."

"She said she would be here."

They fell silent, Josh's answer conveying volumes. Laura's eyes wandered over the car-filled driveway, then out across the country road at the small oval and square shapes covering the ground.

A violent shudder snaked its way through her body. She rubbed her bare arms, trying to rid herself of the goose bumps which had suddenly broken out up and down her skin.

"What's wrong? You need a sweatshirt?" Josh asked.

"How can you live across from *that*?"

Josh followed her gaze. "What, the graveyard? It's kind of a peaceful neighbor, actually. I've been here for about three weeks, and today was the first time I've seen a funeral procession drive by."

"I couldn't live here," Laura said, her lip turning up in disgust. "Constantly being so close to all of those headstones, all of those dead bodies...it would just give me the creeps."

"Well, I guess it's a good thing you don't have to worry about that. We've already been down that road, and I, for one, don't plan on going back."

"Like I would take your chain-smoking ass back anyways," Laura replied, playfully punching Josh in the arm. "How many packs a day are you up to?"

"It's a coping mechanism. In high school I didn't know the meaning of the word stress."

"Excuses, excuses," Laura said. She had a smile on her face, but it quickly faltered when her eyes returned to the cemetery. It might not bother Josh (his lack of imagination was one of the things she could never get over), but something about the way the light of the full moon softly reflected off the cold gray of the headstones made her queasy. She turned back towards Josh. "How about we go inside and enjoy your party? It feels like a class reunion in there."

"Is Davey christening my toilet with vomit yet?"

"He's on the way, she grinned. "I think Paul and McDonald are having a heated debate about who had more rebounds in the senior game."

"I guess I better get back in there. I had more rebounds than both of those clowns."

Laura laughed, and the two friends (and former lovers) went back inside the house. The world would be a far different place the next time they passed through the door.

The scene hadn't changed much during the time Josh spent outside in the vigil for Amanda's arrival. The coffee table was littered with empty cans of Budweiser, shot glasses, and quarters, evidence of the drinking game of the same name. Most everyone was gathered in the living room. Kirk was standing in the corner with the long legged blonde he'd brought along. Josh didn't know her, but apparently Kirk had designs on becoming very well acquainted with the girl. Josh hadn't seen him once leave her side, not even to take a leak. His dedication was either impressive or pathetic; Josh couldn't decide which.

Paul, Granderson, and McDonald were seated on the couch, jostling about as they recounted past glories on the athletic fields of the alma mater. Davey's lanky form was stretched out in the recliner, a bottle of Jack Daniels between his legs and a smile on his face. He gave Josh a thumbs up as he walked into the room with Laura. Josh chose to ignore whatever his thoroughly intoxicated friend meant to imply with the gesture. Megan and Brittany's trip to the kitchen for another drink was ongoing, as the two kept their own company in front of the fridge.

Some bash, Josh thought as he and Laura took a seat on the vacant sofa. He was quickly dragged into the discussion raging at the adjacent couch.

"Hey, Josh, what's your take on this little bet we got goin'?" McDonald asked. "Granderson is trying to convince us he hit more than twenty homers our last year of JV ball. Me and Paul, we're taking the under. What you got?"

Josh considered for a moment. Granderson's thick frame was a stone wall, his face about as revealing as that of the Sphinx. "I wouldn't put anything past Beefcake," Josh said. "He actually looks smaller to me now than he did in the ninth grade, if that's possible. I'll take over."

Granderson cracked a smile, while Paul and McDonald erupted with jeers.

"Shit, we'll never know the true answer to this now that Mr. Dutch passed away. The bet's off!" Paul exclaimed.

"Wait, what happened to The Dutch?" Josh asked, bewildered.

"You didn't hear about that? He had a stroke last Tuesday, running around the track in the morning just like he did when we were in school. Shit man, they buried him today in Oak Hill Cemetery. And that's right across the road from your house. I was gonna go to the funeral but Leo wouldn't let me off work. I thought you knew."

"No, I didn't. I guess I don't read the newspaper enough," Josh said, his voice trailing off.

Davey suddenly sprang to his feet, his head dangerously close to the swirling blades of the ceiling fan. He tottered back and forth, as if the floor was swaying on stormy seas. He righted himself and raised the bottle of Jack Daniels into the air in a toasting gesture.

"To The Dutch!" Davey hollered. The men who had suffered through the arduous baseball practices of Coach Dutch raised their drinks in salute. "May his piss poor treatment of his players be revisited upon him sevenfold in the afterlife," he concluded with a flourish. He took a healthy swig of Jack and collapsed back into the recliner. Megan and Brittany glanced over with a *silly boys* look and resumed their conversation.

"Man, Davey, The Dutch used to ride you harder than anybody," McDonald said.

"Yeah, a couple times there, if he'd put just a little bit more rum and a little less coke in his thermos before practice, I'm pretty sure he would've ripped my head clean off when I goofed around," Davey replied. "He made me realize that guys like me are better suited for the basketball court."

"By *guys like me*, do you mean tall, uncoordinated, Big Bird look-alikes?" McDonald interjected, and the discussion moved back towards basketball.

The subtle sound of scrapes on the window, resembling a tree branch blowing in the wind, didn't begin until around one a.m.

Truth be told, Josh's senses were still tuned to any sign of Amanda's arrival, and his ears immediately keyed on the slight rasp. He initially thought it was coming from the side window, where the overgrown branches of a willow tree occasionally brushed against the house.

As the noise continued unabated, Josh began to think it wasn't emanating from the side of his new home at all, but from the front. Two windows looked from the living room out onto the porch. Curtains were drawn over both, shrouding any view of what was causing the soft scratches.

Josh was about to write it off as nothing more than his mind teasing him when he noticed Kirk's companion staring intently at the window closest to the door. As if sensing his gaze, she looked at Josh and raised her eyebrows in a quizzical expression that said, *It's your house.*

"Quiet!" Josh said loudly, ending a comical recounting of Davey's lack of skills on the hardwood in mid-sentence. "Does anybody else hear that?"

The noisemaker, whatever it was, didn't disappoint on the big stage. With all ten pairs of ears now straining to pick up any sound that was out of place, it actually seemed to increase in volume, the rasps becoming more desperate.

The sound reminded Laura of a movie she had once seen. Some poor sap had been buried alive, and the slow scraping on the window brought to mind an image of the man in his last moments, feebly scratching his tomb as the oxygen ran out. Not for the first time that night (and surely not for the last), Laura's body was rocked by a shudder of fear.

"Is somebody trying to get inside?" Brittany asked from her stance in front of the fridge.

"Sarah said she might stop by if she could get Rick to watch the baby," Megan remarked.

"Why wouldn't she just knock on the front door?" Paul wondered aloud.

"Sara Parker? Where is that hot mama?" Davey said, jumping to his feet and moving to the window. He ripped back the curtain, his large frame blocking everyone else's view and gasped loudly with surprise.

"Holy shit, it's The Dutch! I guess the reports of his demise were greatly exaggerated!" Davey said with wide eyes.

Davey was over to the front door before anyone could process his preposterous statement. The porch didn't have an outside light, and neither Josh nor any of his guests could see anything through the window, least of all a man who was supposed to be deceased.

Davey swung the door open. "Come on in, Coach Dutch!" he said with a cheer only the heavily inebriated can muster.

Josh was dimly aware of Megan muttering, "Stop it, Davey, that's sick," from behind him. From their vantage points, nobody could see more than a foot outside the house.

Davey stuck his hand through that invisible threshold, as if to pat a friend on the back. His body suddenly jerked forward, the look of drunken mirth on his face instantly transformed into stark terror. He screamed in pain and stumbled back a step, now bereft of his index and middle finger. He looked at the digits in disbelief for a brief moment, before an arm reached through the door and grabbed hold of his **Shit Happens** t-shirt, pulling him onto the porch and out of view.

Everyone froze, shocked, not knowing what to think. Davey screamed once again, and it was the high pitched wail of the ninth grader whom The Dutch had terrorized so often. It ended abruptly. There was a gurgling noise, and then silence.

Josh and Granderson were on their feet simultaneously, bounding to the doorway in a few quick steps. The rest of the party crowded behind them.

"Holy Mother of God," McDonald whispered.

The sight before them, an impossible sight, sent Brittany running towards the kitchen sink, vomiting. The Dutch, decked out in his finest suit (although large, dark splotches suggested he had been crawling through mud, or worse), was bent over Davey's prostrate form, taking swiping chunks out of his former pupil's neck. Davey's head had almost been cleaved from his body, the bites were so greedy. It hung on by a thin thread of flesh. A growing pool of blood was sinking into the floorboards of the porch. The Dutch paid no mind to the stunned faces looking his way. All of his focus was on the meal at hand.

Granderson brushed past Josh. He seized The Dutch by the collar and threw him off the porch in one quick motion, as if he was nothing more than a bag of trash. The Dutch did several summersaults through the grass, his neck making a sickening, crunching sound during the second revolution. He came to a stop for the briefest of moments, and then squirmed back to his feet. His head was now twisted to the right at an insane angle, Davey's blood staining his face like sauce from a toddler's first foray into the world of spaghetti eating, and still he came towards them. His steps were halting, uncertain, but his eyes never left the cluster of people on the porch.

Josh, for his part, displayed a similar fixation on what had once been his baseball coach. This was the guy who kicked Davey off the team for lying down and pretending to take a nap in the outfield, the guy whose hand he slapped in a celebratory high five dozens of times, the guy who had a stroke and fucking died four days ago.

"He's gone," Granderson was saying as he leaned over Davey's mutilated body. "Davey, Davey, Davey." Coming from Granderson's mammoth frame, the desperate whispers took on an especially frightening cast.

"Watch out!" Megan shrieked. "He's coming back!"

The Dutch had shuffled his way to the first step of the porch. He bumped against it twice before he realized the need to raise his leg.

Granderson's face hardened into a countenance of suppressed rage. He turned towards The Dutch, who had gotten both feet onto the first step. Moving with a surprising quickness that matched his grizzly bear body, he sprang to his feet and launched himself towards the outstretched arms of The Dutch. He grabbed hold of the support beams at the last possible moment, using them to swing off the porch, landing a powerful kick to The Dutch's chest in the process.

The man went flying, thrown backwards several feet. Granderson hit the ground running, heading towards his truck parked in the driveway.

"What the hell are you doing?" McDonald called from the porch, a question that was posed in some variation by the majority of the onlookers.

Granderson ignored them. He hastily dropped the tailgate of the truck and leapt into the bed, the metal frame sagging slightly beneath his weight. He grabbed the axe from the other tools of his logging trade. Not thinking about what he was intending to do, not daring to think, he ran to where The Dutch was slowly getting back up.

He swung the axe down with practiced precision. It cleaved through The Dutch's neck like it was nothing more than a piece of tissue paper. The Dutch's crew-cut head, long the bane of generations of students, went flying into the air. It bounced against a nearby maple tree, rolling over the grass before coming to a stop facing the crowd on the porch, frozen in one last sneer of disapproval and...what was that? Hunger?

Brittany, who had just returned to the deck, started retching all over again. She ran back into the house, a thin trail of vomit making its way down her chin. Granderson took a seat on the steps of the porch and promptly buried his head in his hands.

"Can somebody tell me what the hell just happened?" Kirk asked, his confused gaze darting from one person to another.

Josh almost laughed. At least now he knew what it took to get Kirk's eyes to leave the blonde. "Davey was killed by The D... by a dead man," he said simply, trying to get his mind around the outrageous implications of that statement.

"Would somebody please tell me I drank too much tonight and that I'm just dreaming all of this?" McDonald said. "Tell me I'm gonna wake up on Josh's couch, and the worst thing in the world I can imagine is a brutal hangover."

"I don't drink, and you're not dreaming," Kirk's mystery companion said.

"I'm getting outta here," Kirk said. "Something Twilight Zone weird is going on and I don't dig the vibe."

"You can't leave," Josh said, disbelieving. "We have to call the police. Davey's dead, in case you haven't noticed."

"Tell them I left before the shit hit the fan. Or don't. You can do whatever you want, but I'm hightailing it back to civilization. Are you coming?" he asked the blonde.

"I'd rather not add *leaving the scene of a crime* to my rap sheet," she said, drawing stares from everyone but Granderson.

"Whatever," Kirk answered. He ran to his car and took off without a second glance.

"I always thought he was an asshole," Paul said. "Sorry," he added to the blonde. She waved her hand dismissively, implying she'd reached the same conclusion hours ago.

"Paul, would you take the blankets off the couch and cover him up?" Josh requested. "And Laura, it's probably best if you call the police, whether your dad is on duty or not."

They went about their tasks, and the rest of the party retreated into the house. Josh slowly approached Granderson's still form. "How you doing, big guy?" he asked.

Granderson grunted.

"You know you did the right thing, right? I have no idea what type of nightmare we just slipped into, but that Dutch wasn't The Dutch we all knew."

Granderson raised his head, placing it on his interlocked fingers. "I know," he said. "That wasn't anybody, but killing him still brought back memories I've done my best to forget."

"Iraq?"

"Afghanistan. Iraq was a picnic by comparison."

"Come on," Josh said, patting Granderson on the back. "Let's move the body out of sight."

They were finishing up the nauseating job when Megan and Brittany burst through the front door of the house, with Laura following closely on their heels, saying something about *doing the smart thing*.

"What's going on?" Josh asked as the women approached.

"We're leaving," Megan said curtly.

"Nine-one-one is busy," Brittany exclaimed. "Busy! How does that happen?"

Josh turned to Laura for greater illumination.

"I had to call my dad's cell phone," she said. "He told me they've been getting a steady stream of calls for the past hour. The P.D. is stretched beyond its limits trying to get a handle on whatever's going on. I could tell he didn't want to say too much, didn't want to scare me, but he insisted that the best thing we could do for ourselves is lock the doors and stay inside."

"Screw that!" Brittany shouted, on the verge of tears. "I've got a family to get to."

Granderson's deep voice interrupted the argument. "Josh, were you expecting anybody else tonight?"

Josh glanced towards the driveway. A cloud had drifted over the moon, cutting visibility in half, but he was reasonably certain of who was on the other side of the row of vehicles, slowly walking towards them.

"I think that's Amanda," he said, but his mind didn't stop there. *Yeah, it's Amanda, all right*, he thought. Not too many girls around these parts stand five-nine with curves in all the right places, and have lustrous black hair flowing halfway down their backside. *Wait, she brought somebody with her? She brought a guy to my housewarming party*?

"Yeah, that's Amanda, but I don't know the sap walking behind her," Josh said with a twinge of jealously that seemed petty under the current circumstances. The look Laura gave him said exactly that.

Josh chose to ignore it. Man, he needed a cigarette.

"Good," Brittany said. "We can tell them to turn right around on our way out." She went striding towards the driveway without another word.

"I'm sorry, guys," Megan said as she walked backwards, slowly following Brittany's flight. "We'll call you when we figure out what's going on."

The last word hadn't been out of Megan's mouth for more than a second when a scream erupted from the driveway. It was Brittany. She had walked right up to the late arrivals, no doubt intent on spreading her brand of panic. Amanda was now bent over Brittany, looking for all the world like she was giving her a hello kiss. Brittany violently jerked away, blood peppering the suddenly vacated air between them. Brittany's blood. Half of her nose had been ripped off, and the chomping motion of Amanda's mouth suggested exactly where the other half had gone.

Josh was frozen in place. His brain was a jumbled mess, vainly trying to make sense of the insane images his eyes were feeding it.

This isn't happening, this isn't happening, he thought in a continuous loop as the scene in the driveway unfolded.

Not satisfied with a mere bite of nose flesh, Amanda lunged at Brittany's screaming face. Brittany dodged to the side. Amanda's mouth came down slightly below her collarbone. Blood oozed through her shirt as Amanda's jaws clenched shut with the power of a snapping turtle.

Megan got to her first. She yanked on Amanda's skimpy, spaghetti-strap tank top in a desperate attempt to dislodge her grip, nearly ripping the shirt off but accomplishing little else. Josh was pulled out of his stupor by the suddenly visible sight of a gaping flesh wound just above Amanda's formerly oh-so-fine left breast.

Megan refused to let go of the shirt. Amanda's companion, a guy that Josh didn't recognize, took advantage of her single-minded focus. He sauntered around Amanda, sized up Megan's outstretched arms, and sunk his teeth into the meat of her left forearm like it was a piece of chicken breast.

Megan screamed in pain, finally relenting her grasp on the shirt. She tore her arm away from the man but a chunk of flesh refused to move with her; it remained lodged in the man's gnawing incisors. As if wanting an easier meal, he shifted his focus to Brittany, his outstretched arms knocking her to the ground.

Granderson and Laura arrived a few moments later and Granderson's trained eyes quickly assessed the situation. Brittany, a girl he'd had a summertime fling with once upon a time, was a goner. The life was already draining from her face as the ravenous attackers had their way with her.

Movement from the road caught his eye. Three more shapes were shuffling across the gravel. Granderson cursed to himself and turned to Megan, who was clutching her bleeding arm.

"Let's go," he said, softly grasping her wrist.

"But Britt..."

"She's gone. And we will be too if we don't get back inside the house."

Megan resisted for another moment before, she too, saw the encroaching figures in the road. She allowed Granderson to guide her through the yard, where Josh had the dazed, frightened look of someone waking up in a strange place. He turned and followed them without a word.

McDonald, Paul, and the blonde were standing on the porch. They'd moved Davey's cloaked form away from the doorway.

"What's going on? We heard screams," Paul said. "Wait, where's Brittany?"

Granderson ignored him. "Josh, do you have any medical supplies?" he asked, intent on taking Megan directly inside with no unnecessary pit stops.

"There's a first aid kit in the bathroom cabinet," Josh answered.

"Would somebody tell us what the fuck is going on?" Paul demanded.

"Laura," Josh said, and their eyes met in perfect understanding. Josh, slowly getting his wits back about him after the brain-freeze, followed Granderson and Megan inside while Laura recounted how things had turned from bad to worse. Josh ran to the second floor, taking the steps two at a time. He bounded to his bedroom closet, tearing open the door and tossing aside the piles of clothes he'd neglected to properly unpack as he searched for something important.

For one terrible moment, he thought maybe he'd forgotten them in the move, but then his hands felt the .357 buried under a Metallica t-shirt he hadn't worn in years, and the long barrel of the .12 gauge a moment later. He pulled them out of the closet with relief. It took another minute of rummaging to find the ammunition boxes. He seized them with an exclamation of victory, piled up the firepower, and rushed back downstairs.

Granderson was on one knee, tending to Megan's wound. The rest of the party (Party? This stopped being a party the second that damned scraping on the window started.) stood around the living room, in the middle of an intense debate.

"People don't eat other people," Paul was saying. "Not in America. That can't be what you saw."

"Go outside and look for yourself. If anything's left," Laura shot back. "They did the same thing to Brittany that The Dutch did to Davey, and they're still out there."

"They? You're talking about our baseball coach and a girl Josh was trying to take home a few days ago, not a bunch of crazy ex-cons."

Laura paused for moment, measuring her response. "I know they looked like people we know, but that wasn't them. I don't know how to describe it."

"They're dead," Granderson said without looking up from his bandaging job.

"Yeah, because that makes a lot of sense," Paul replied.

"The Dutch was, is dead. We know that much for sure," McDonald added.

"I didn't get a good look at the other guy, but Amanda had an open wound the size of a softball on her chest. Maybe something happened to her on the way here," Laura suggested.

Josh, busy loading the .357, fumbled several of the bullets to the floor.

"So just what are you saying?" Paul asked. "That the dead are coming back to life? Just come right out and say it so we can get the laughing out of the way and move to the part where things start making sense."

"Listen, I know it's a lot for your small town mind to comprehend, but everything we've seen tonight suggests something really strange is going on. You might have to think outside the box for once in your life."

"Ah, screw off, Laura, you grew up in the same..."

"I hate to interrupt," the blonde said from the recliner, "but I just remembered that the back door was open the last time I went to the bathroom; before the dead started walking. Or didn't," she added, looking at Paul.

Everyone fell silent, all eyes shifting to the kitchen, which led to the dining room and then the downstairs bathroom.

Josh snapped the chamber of the .357 shut. "I'll check it," he said.

"You sure?" Granderson asked.

"Yeah, I'm the dumbass that left it open trying to keep the house cool. I haven't invested in air conditioning yet."

"I'll go with you," the blonde said. "I could have shut it."

They departed the living room, leaving Paul and Laura to continue their argument. Josh swept through the kitchen, gun raised. Nothing was out of place. Empty beer cans and the occasional bottle still littered the countertops. He moved into the little-used dining room, the blonde following closely behind him. It was similarly deserted. No member of the dead sat at the table with a napkin tucked into its shirt, eagerly waiting to be served a three course meal of foot, finger, and face.

They came to the hallway that led to the backdoor. It was wide open, practically inviting anybody stalking through the night to come in and join the party. Just bring your own beer.

It's my party, but the drinks aren't on me, Josh thought and snickered to himself.

"Something funny?" the blonde asked.

"No, not really. We're gonna have to clear all of these rooms before we can shut the door. I don't want anything surprising us from behind."

"I got ya, cowboy. This isn't my first rodeo," she said, brandishing a long butcher knife she must have grabbed on the way through the kitchen.

Josh cracked a smile. "I don't think I ever got your name."

"Tara."

"Tara, I don't know what's happened to the world to turn it upside down like this, but if we get through the night you're going to tell me your entire life story. Something tells me it's worthy of an Angelina Jolie movie."

"Deal," she said.

Three rooms lined the hall between the dining room and the backdoor: a closet, the laundry room, and the bathroom. Josh quickly opened the door to the first. Nothing but cobwebs lingered in the closet. He shut the door and moved down the hall to the laundry room. He eased into the room, doing his best impression of every action hero he had ever watched on the big screen.

"It's clear," Josh said, and all of his focus moved to the bathroom, where he reckoned any ambush was most likely to occur. It was closest to the open backdoor, and even the slow-moving bastards outside couldn't be slow-thinking enough not to realize that somebody would have to use the facilities at some point in the near future, especially if they had any inkling of how much alcohol had been consumed that night.

The door was three-quarters of the way shut, the light off. Josh took a deep breath and gently nudged the door with the short barrel of the .357. It creaked open, light softly spilling across the floor.

So far so good.

Josh reached his hand around the corner, feeling for the light switch. He shrieked at a sudden noise from within the bathroom, nearly firing off a wild round before realizing what had disturbed the silence.

"You should get that fixed," Tara said from behind him.

Embarrassed, Josh flipped on the light and boldly walked into the bathroom. The toilet was still running. He resisted the urge to pump a few bullets into its shiny, almost mocking surface.

"It's an old house," he said.

They went out the backdoor. The moon had returned, illuminating the expanse of the back yard. It was still peaceful, bearing no knowledge of the macabre events that had taken place on the front side of the house. Standing out here, Josh could almost convince himself everything was still normal, that two of his friends hadn't been brutally murdered, that the woman he'd had his eyes on for the past month wasn't less than a stone's throw away, possibly still feasting on the body of one of those friends. Josh couldn't resist any longer; he lit up a cigarette and offered one to Tara. She declined.

"You probably don't think much of us," he said. "Nobody cried over Davey or Brittany. Everyone just started looking to cover their own asses."

"That's a little harsh. I only saw what happened on the porch, but that scene was enough to send anyone into shock. Then, when you throw in the alcohol and the sheer insanity of what's been happening, I don't think that leaves much time for contemplation."

As if seeking to prove the prescience of her comment, shouts started to come from the living room. Josh and Tara's gaze met for the briefest of moments before they simultaneously set off for the front of the house at a dead sprint. Shotgun fire reverberated off the walls as they ran past the dining room table. They burst into the living room, only to find it abandoned. Josh was halfway to the open door when he noticed that the room wasn't quite as deserted as it had appeared. Megan lay on the couch, curled up under several blankets. Her face was drained of color, her breath coming in short gasps.

"Outside," she croaked, raising one shaking hand towards the door.

For the second time in less than an hour, Josh was taken aback by the sight waiting for him on the other side of the doorway. It was as if the door of his home was really a window to a parallel reality, one where the fundamental laws that governed the world had been perversely changed.

Maybe this nightmare wasn't happening at all. Maybe —

The terrified screams told him that the view outside the door was as real as the .357 in his hand.

They were coming from Paul as he struggled to free himself from the grip of a handful of...Josh didn't really know what to call them. They looked human enough, at first glance, but a closer examination revealed the muddled motor skills, the lack of speech, the sickly pallor, and the lifeless eyes; eyes that had the same dull, perpetually hungry sheen of a shark. The fact that they were walking around, killing, eating, suggested they were living people (that they had to be living people), but at the same time they appeared dead (clearly so, in the case of The Dutch).

The living dead, Josh was vaguely aware of thinking.

The shotgun roared to his right, hitting an attacker wearing a Dallas Cowboys shirt in the gut. The man stumbled backwards a few steps, struggling to re-find his balance, before he started right back towards Paul, oblivious to the hole the spray of buckshot had punched in his stomach. Granderson cursed.

Josh stepped through the door to get the full picture. Granderson stood at the far right end of the porch, drawing the .12 gauge down for another shot. Laura and McDonald were behind him, their faces riveted on Paul's fight to avoid being overwhelmed by the crowd of living dead. Several motionless bodies littered the porch. Josh was reasonably certain one of them was Mrs. Bryant, the widow that was his closest neighbor. Her head had been blown into mush, but the rest of her features were dead-on.

Dead. Josh was quickly tiring of the word.

Granderson fired at the Cowboy's fan once again, this time scoring a head shot that dropped him in his tracks. Josh hadn't used the .357 in years, but he tried to remember everything his father had taught him as he squeezed off a round at the skull of

Paul's closest assailant, a shirtless and obese man. It missed wildly, but the tightly packed circle of attackers made for an easy target. The bullet went through the ear of a nearby woman and he tried not to ponder the implications of the resounding *thud* of the woman's body as it fell to the ground,

Josh moved the crosshairs onto the fat man. His meaty arms had finally seized Paul's squirming body.

Josh pulled the trigger. He had aimed low in an attempt to counter the powerful kick of the pistol, but the bullet again failed to connect with the fat man's head. It struck him in his bare shoulder. The man shuddered like he was hit by an electrical shock, but otherwise easily absorbed the bullet, not even grunting in pain. He began to pull Paul's neck towards his mouth as the other hungry figures slowly encroached.

Cursing, wondering why the hell Granderson had quit his own barrage, Josh readjusted his aim and fired as quickly as he could manage. The shot was true. It hit the fat man in the back of the head, forever ending his quest for more food, for another meal.

An exclamation of victory died on Josh's lips as the fat man's body lurched forward, crashing to the ground and burying Paul beneath its considerable weight. For a few terrifying moments, Josh was convinced the bullet had traveled through the fat man's skull and into Paul's face, but Paul's struggles to get free of the dead weight quickly dispelled the notion.

Perhaps it would've been best if the bullet had continued its fatal journey.

As Paul lay trapped under the fat man, hopelessly pinned to the ground, the growing crowd swarmed over him. Josh fired wildly into the throng, his scream of desperate anger merging with Paul's agonized howls. An arm was torn from his body, then a leg. Josh kept pulling the trigger, but the .357 produced nothing but a hollow clack as he helplessly watched the horde begin to feast upon his friend, scavenging over Paul's limbs like a pack of coyotes.

Arms closed around Josh's waist and pulled him inside the house. They sat him down on the edge of the same couch Megan was on.

"We have to leave," Laura said, pacing around the room.

"Leave?" McDonald asked. "Your dad told us to lock the doors and stay inside. How about we finally follow his advice, before those fuckers get any more of us."

"No," Laura replied. "We can't afford to just sit here anymore. Megan needs medical attention."

Megan mumbled indecipherably from under the blankets, underscoring Laura's point.

"Whatever we're going to do, we better do it fast," Tara added from her vantage point as she looked out the door. "There's about fifty people coming this way and it looks like they're eager to join our little party."

"How is that possible?" McDonald asked.

"The graveyard and the mortuary on the north side of it," Laura said softly, looking Josh's way. He avoided her gaze, choosing to focus on reloading the .357.

"Then shut the door and draw the drapes," Granderson said as he pumped a shell into the chamber of the shotgun. "Let's not give them any more incentive than they already have."

"I have an idea!" Laura shouted. "Leave them open. Leave it all open. Let's get as many as of them as possible into the house."

McDonald snorted. "Did you miss the Survival 101 class at that Ivy League school you went to for six years?" he asked. "When people are trying to kill you, it's generally a good idea to stay as far away from them as possible."

Laura went on as if McDonald hadn't spoken. "We lure as many of them into the house as we can. Sure they're brutally violent, but they're also slow, and they act pretty stupid. If we can get them clustered inside the house, then lock the back door on our way out, I think we should have a relatively easy path to our cars."

"What do you think, Beefcake?" Josh asked of Granderson.

"I've heard worse plans," he answered.

"Okay, let's do it!" McDonald said, slapping his hands together. He went over to the stereo sitting on one of the end tables. At the girls' request, they had shut the music off hours earlier. "This ought to get their attention," he said, hitting play and cranking the volume.

The powerfully twisted guitar riff of *White Zombies': More Human Than Human* was soon blaring through the house. Josh thought the riff, the lyrics, the entire song seemed strangely appropriate.

The tune was nearly over when they were forced to shut the door. The porch was now crammed with the walking dead. They weakly smacked the windows, jostling about like concertgoers trying to get the best view of the musical act. Instead of rock stars on the stage, the six frightened survivors of Josh's housewarming party stared back through the thin glass, wondering what had the power to turn these people into mindless killers and cannibals.

"Okay, let's move," Granderson said, breaking the spell. "Josh and I will give them plenty to lick their lips over while the rest of you get to the backdoor."

Josh put his hands on the door handle, waiting for Granderson to give the signal. Granderson waited until they were through the kitchen before nodding his head. Josh quickly pulled the door open and gasped as Amanda stumbled into his living room, nearly falling into his lap.

Josh jumped back reflexively. Amanda's beautiful brown eyes were deadened, but they still burned with desire, although not of the variety Josh had previously longed for.

He had another moment to take in the sight of her blood-stained body before his trigger finger seemed to move of its own volition, firing off one clean round into Amanda's brow. Chunks of brain, blood, and flesh splattered the wall, forming a grisly montage that Josh couldn't seem to take his eyes off of.

Granderson gave him a slight nudge, getting him moving towards the kitchen. They inched backwards as the walking dead streamed into the house, bumping into furniture as they slowly pursued the meat that was tantalizingly close to them. The living room was as jam-packed as a fraternity house on a Friday night by the time the two men reached the kitchen. Amazingly, more bodies were still entering.

"I think it's time to make our move," Granderson suggested when they got to the dining room.

"You don't have to tell me twice," Josh answered.

They ran the rest of the way to the backdoor. Tara and McDonald stood there, propping Megan up between them. She was still wrapped in a thick blanket.

"She can't walk," Laura said. "All of her strength is gone."

"I'll carry her," Josh said, handing the .357 to McDonald. He would be happy if he never had to touch the thing again.

McDonald led the way outside, followed by Laura. Josh cradled Megan in his arms, his adrenaline-laden body barely feeling her weight. Tara followed behind him while Granderson guarded the rear.

The backyard was as deserted as before when he'd enjoyed a few puffs of a Marlboro Light, before the night took another turn for the worse. McDonald stopped at the edge of the house, took a quick peek around the corner, and then turned around and gave them a thumbs up.

Megan began to stir under her cotton shroud, mumbling something Josh couldn't understand.

"Hold up," he whispered to McDonald. "What did you say, Megan?"

He gave her a soft shake when his question went unanswered, but her body had gone limp in his arms. He bent over and laid her on the ground, unraveling the blanket. Her face was deathly pale in the moonlight, her eyes shut.

"Shit," Josh said.

He grabbed her wrist, searching in vain for a pulse. He dropped his head to her chest, hoping to find the slightest trace of a heartbeat. Nothing. Josh was raising his head back into the air when Megan's eyes suddenly snapped open; the same look in her eyes that had stared at him from Amanda's face.

Dead, but so alive.

And hungry.

She reached up and seized Josh's neck, pulling him down even as she began to rise. Josh stared into those dichotomous eyes, transfixed, a dim voice in his head asking if this was going to be the last thing he ever saw. Megan's mouth was now mere inches from his throat. Josh winced, tightly closing his eyes in anticipation of the inevitable bite.

It never came. There was a soft thud, and then silence. Josh forced his eyelids open. Megan was on the ground, a butcher knife buried deep into the side of her head halfway to the hilt. He looked up at Tara, who stood perhaps five feet behind him. She'd tossed the knife like a throwing dagger.

"A little trick I picked up in the course of my travels," she said simply, favoring him with a slight smile.

Laura was quickly at his side, worriedly looking him up and down to see if he was hurt, and when satisfied he was fine, she helped him to his feet.

Then they all heard the now all-too familiar weak slapping sound of hands on glass break the silence of the night seconds later.

"They're at the back door," Granderson said. "We need to get to the vehicles before they start wandering back outside."

"Wait," Josh said, overcome by a sudden flash of inspiration. He walked to the lawnmower parked behind the house. The gas can still sat next to the front wheels, right where he'd left it that afternoon.

Was that really today? Not a lifetime ago? he thought.

He doused the side of the house with gas as they walked towards the driveway. Several of the living dead were picking over what was left of Paul's corpse, a few more were loitering on the lawn. The first pioneers were beginning to tire of the empty house and shuffled back to the front porch.

They decided to stick together in one vehicle and take Laura's Cherokee. Josh made a trail of gasoline thirty feet from the house. He threw what was left of the can onto the porch, where it hit the growing crowd and fell between their feet. Josh lit up a cigarette, sizing up the mind-boggling scene at the first home he'd ever owned.

He was suddenly aware of Laura by his side.

"What did I tell you about those things?" she asked, referring to his smoke.

"That they're no good," Josh said, and with a sigh, flicked the cigarette into the gasoline trail, igniting it instantly.

The flames quickly raced towards the crowded home, and the red and orange tendrils seemed to leap onto the house, growing exponentially across the side of the wood paneling.

"Let's go," Laura said, taking his hand.

They clambered into the back of the Cherokee and Granderson punched the jeep into gear. He accelerated down the road as everyone else watched the flames reach the gas can on the porch. A tremendous fireball erupted, setting the entire house aflame, taking the majority of the dead with it.

"Well, Josh, you sure put the warm in housewarming," McDonald said from the front seat.

Josh actually laughed.

He was alive in a world where the dead suddenly walked the Earth.

What else could he do?

G.R.MOSCA

RED SKY IN MOURNING

Izzy could smell them even before she could see them. It was the smell of a thousand garbage heaps, of dead dog and rotting flesh. Her nose wrinkled and her stomach visibly heaved.

She had to keep the nausea at bay, for her sake and the sake of her baby. They were coming and she needed to think clearly, not let fear freeze her into inaction or the wrong decision. This was life or death, and the walking dead were unforgiving when it came to killing.

She looked around her but didn't see many options. Her group had chosen this building because it offered protection; solid walls, no windows and one entrance. It had been a storage warehouse, not a large one, but in their flight from suburb to country to small town, this was the best they had come across. As she looked around, their best defense was turning into their worst nightmare.

She heard a scream from the other side of the wall. Agony and fear was in that scream, and then silence followed by gurgling and chewing. It froze her blood. They would be through that door very soon. Her eyes widened as she started to pace around the tiny room looking for anything; a way out, something to block the door, a weapon. Her panic mounted when no ideas came to her. All she could concentrate on was the sound of flesh being gnawed and bones cracking. She was losing it now. A string of obscenities softly came from her mouth, punctuated by pleas to an almighty that had stopped listening since the dead began to walk.

A soft thud hit the door, followed by another and another until the entire room she occupied reverberated with it.

Then silence.

Izzy listened carefully, her eyes widening, her hope rising just a bit with the possibility of survival. The seconds of silence stretched into a minute then another. Her heart slowed, her breath eased and she let out a soft sigh. Everything was going to be fine. She would live another day, and if all went well, she would bring new life into the dead world; and soon.

A loud crash made her spin around to see the door exploding inward as a crowd of ghouls poured in. Their hands were so soft, yet strong as they pawed at her, grabbing at first then ripping. Izzy watched as whole chunks of her biceps came off in a ghoul's grip. She screamed then was quieted as another ghoul reached for her tongue. Pain melted into the unfathomable realization that she was being torn apart. Yet she felt powerless to fight back until they reached for her swollen stomach. Only then could she scream and kick and lash out. Blood jetted out of her wounded mouth, her body bled but still she fought; gouging eyes, kicking and screaming.

The last thing she saw was her baby being ripped from her stomach. The fetus, so small and precious was now in the grip of a pale, dead hand. The owner had once been human but now was something else. She thought she heard the baby begin to cry but Izzy's world turned black.

She woke up biting back a scream and looked around. The room was quiet and dark. Four other people lay sleeping around her; she could hear their soft, rhythmic breathing, the occasional grunt in the night. Her breathing, ragged at first, returned to normal as she started to cry into her pillow.

Just one more nightmare to add to the countless others.

* * *

When the group awoke the next morning, they found Izzy packing her belongings into a well-used duffel bag. She advised the rest of them to do the same thing and quickly. She didn't intend for herself or the others to spend another night in the building.

The group had learned over the course of the previous months to listen to Izzy's recommendations as she almost always had good cause for her actions, and if not good cause, she was always right somehow.

Her brother Sam stared at his older sister with heavy eyes.

"You okay, sis?"

Izzy tried not to look back at him by hiding her face in the duffel bag.

"As well as can be expected in this crazy world. I just don't like this place anymore. It feels like a deathtrap. The sooner we get out of here, the safer I'll feel."

The others began to wake up and climb out of their sleeping bags. Jim, an elderly gentleman and his wife Stella had been neighbors of Izzy and Sam's before the dead began to walk. It was only with their help that Jim and Stella were alive today.

Mallory turned over in her bedroll and uttered a big yawn. She was only ten but had managed to survive on her own in Baltimore for who knew how long before Izzy and the rest of the group had found her. Mallory had been hiding in a dumpster in an alley they were running through to escape the city when Sam had heard a sound. They found her hiding under trash bags and discarded clothes, shivering and afraid, but alive. She still wouldn't or couldn't talk but she seemed to feel safer now.

"Come on, sweetie, you have to get up. We're leaving this place," Izzy said to Mallory with a smile. Mallory looked over at Izzy and smiled back, her wide eyes taking in the room and all her companions. Izzy noted how Mallory made a check to see that everyone was accounted for before she started to breathe normally again. Izzy thought to herself, *That is one smart little girl.*

Stella said in a huff, "Izzy, why are we leaving this place? It's safe here and a good place to settle down for a while. Where're we goin' in such a doggone hurry, girl?"

"We need to leave here today. Trust me, it isn't as safe here as you think!"

"Why you say that girl? I'm just startin' to get used to it here and now we have to pick up and leave for God knows where."

"Come on, honey," Jim interjected, "hush up and get packin."

"Don't you hush me, mister Jim Stratton. I ain't no child and I certainly will not be told what to do by this little girl." Stella pointed an index finger at Izzy as her face began turning an angry shade of red.

Look, *Miss Stratton*, if we don't leave here now; then tonight when we're sleeping, this little warehouse you feel so safe in is going to be surrounded by more zombies than you can count. When they finally get into this warehouse (and trust me, they will), they'll start with your husband and finish with you. Do you know what they do to you? *They crack your bones and suck the marrow out of them like you were some kind of a steak dinner*! Is that a good enough reason to leave?" Izzy was red-faced herself at this point but Stella was cowed and even a bit teary.

"You're just trying to scare me," Stella responded in a quiet voice.

"I wish."

"Come on, honey," Jim repeated as he gently put his arm around his wife and led her away.

*   *   *

The sky was always overcast and soot-ridden now, partially from the damage to cities and towns but mainly from the burnings. Where people survived there was always the necessity to burn the dead and the smell of burnt flesh seemed always to be present. It was the only means of ensuring the dead would not be coming back.

Izzy's group had been traveling for a number of days since leaving the warehouse. They stayed mostly on small roads that turned from two lanes to one as they moved further away from towns and into rural villages and farmlands.

The road they had been traveling now split into two. One road would take them up a hill into a high wooded area; the other would take the group down into a flat field thick with tall, dry corn as far as they could see. Izzy stopped and the group stopped, too.

"Izzy. Which way do we go?" Sam asked.

"I don't rightly know yet." She glanced toward a stand of trees and pointed. "Let's take a break over there. We could use a rest and I don't see any danger around here."

"Are you sure?" This from Jim.

"I'm certain."

The group moved towards the trees.

They settled down under the shade of the big elms, each putting their packs down and stretching out in the cool grass. Around them, birds and locust chirped in the warm sun. It was close to high noon, the warmest part of the day still ahead of them. From this vantage point the big cornfield seemed like a waving, brown ocean crowding their field of vision for as far as they could see. The path they had taken now lay behind them up the hill, but in this valley they felt as if they were on the ocean floor.

Izzy felt hot; and dog-tired as she looked at the others Mallory was searching her pack for a granola bar, but Jim, Stella and Sam were both looking at her expectantly.

Izzy returned their gaze. "What?"

"What're we gonna do now?" Stella asked as Jim patted her hand to keep her calm.

"Can we stay here, sis?" Sam asked.

"Yeah, I think we can stay here at least for a few hours. It might be better to get some rest and head out when it's cooler."

"Thank the Lord," Stella half-mumbled, Jim's hand patting becoming a little bit more vigorous at her outburst.

Izzy smiled at the same time Stella did. The two women looked at each other and laughed.

"You crack me up, Stel'."

"Yeah, you, too, sweetie."

Izzy leaned over and hugged the woman. Stella returned the embrace while Jim and Sam smiled.

"Friends again?" piped in Mallory.

Izzy, Sam, Jim and Stella stopped and looked over at Mallory. She was busy eating a granola bar. They looked at each other amazed.

"Well, I'll be," Izzy said.

* * *

The sun was beginning to lower in the afternoon sky. The heat of the day causing an odd shimmering against the horizon making the cornfield seem as if it were moving of its own volition. Izzy and her friends took this quiet time as an opportunity to rest, or just reflect.

Izzy slept, but not well.

In her dream, she was under the stand of trees, but as she looked for her companions she realized she was alone. Glancing upwards, she saw the sun was quickly disappearing below the horizon. She only knew that because the cornfield was backlit by a crimson light. Izzy felt unsettled and uneasy.

Something was going to happen. Something she couldn't stop. Her breathing became hurried and shallow. She looked around knowing there was something she needed to see. A breeze gathered strength and the leaves of the trees rustled quietly at first and then more loudly.

The sound caught her attention and she looked up into the branches. It was difficult to see at first, but there it was...a zombie. The dead man was as big as life sitting on a high branch, staring down at her and mocking her with a smirk on what was left of his rotting face. Izzy's blood froze, her breathing became more labored and she felt a dull ache deep in her belly.

The dead man's head turned to the horizon and he pointed to the cornfield. With his head askew, he stared at Izzy with dead eyes and the mouth opened as if to speak, the jaw hanging by a stray sinew.

Izzy could sense the dead man was laughing at her but she wasn't sure what he wanted. Then he lowered his arm and raised it again in the direction of the road. When she followed his gesture, she looked and saw a multitude of zombies shuffling down the road her companions had just taken. A thousand thoughts ran through her mind at the same time.

Was this real or just a dream, was it a future yet to happen and, if it was to happen, then when? She looked in the direction of the road going past the cornfield and saw more zombies advancing from that direction. The sky seemed to deepen to a red color and the dull ache began to change to a sharp pinching in her belly. She looked up and the zombie was again looking at her with tilted head and mocking gaze. He pointed across the tree to a space behind her. Izzy turned, and sitting on a branch opposite the zombie was Stella; only it wasn't Stella. It was Stella with half of her neck gone, wearing a blood-soaked dress and vacant eyes. As Izzy looked, Stella turned towards Izzy and snapped her jaws and screamed.

Izzy heard herself scream in response as a knife-like jab of pain twisted through her stomach.

Izzy wanted to waken, wanted to run as fast as she could to leave these terrible images, this terrible life that she found herself in, but there was more.

She turned back towards the tree branch that held the grinning zombie and faced him again. His head was askew and she could feel him grinning at her, enjoying her discomfort, her pain. Again he lifted his arm and pointed towards the cornfield. She turned and looked at the field; its tall, brown stalks gently waving in the evening breeze, the risen moon casting a gray pallor over the field. Then the strangest thing happened; the sky turned a crimson red coloring the entire cornfield. Her fear heightened as the wall of crimson seemed to advance towards her with no stopping, closer and closer. She looked up to see the zombie, his gaze focused away from her now, facing the crimson tide. His jaw slacked open and his thin arms rose as if to protect himself.

Then the light turned into a blinding flash and she was awake again.

She saw her friends and brother standing around her with concerned and alarmed looks on their faces.

Her brother Sam stepped forward. "Iz, are you okay?"

Izzy was still a bit disoriented, as is often the case with a vivid dream. She looked around again, at the branches above her, but this time she couldn't make out anything in the trees. It was dark and there was a soft breeze blowing but the air had chilled considerably.

"What time is it? How long have I been sleeping?"

"Not long, Iz, the sun went down about a half hour ago but you've been napping for a while."

"You really had us goin' chil'," Stella piped in. "You must have had some dream. "Um, um, um!"

"You sounded really scared," Sam added. "Your breathing was really heavy and you kept repeating over and over: *They're coming, they're coming.* Lucky thing too, you woke us up."

"I was so damn tired, I would've slept till morning," Jim added.

Mallory surprised everyone with a low and serious whisper. "We have to go, don't we, Izzy?" She sounded concerned, frightened and anxious all in one short breath.

"Yes, we do."

"Soon, right?"

"Yes, sweetie."

"Who's coming?" Mallory asked, looking worried.

"I don't know, sweetie, it was just a dream."

Stella stepped forward and put her face close to Izzy's, "Honey, I don' wan' to alarm you, but you're bleedin'."

* * *

While Izzy lay under the trees with a blanket over her and a sweater under her head, Mallory couldn't help feeling anxious. She couldn't sleep and stood at the edge of the stand of trees, keeping a watch over the road and cornfield.

She listened for any sound that might signify an unwelcome intrusion upon the evening. It was not until nearly daybreak that Mallory truly became frightened. It happened with the smallest of occurrences. At first she wasn't sure what she was seeing, but moving down the road at a fast speed was a small rabbit. Mallory's curiosity caused her to wonder what might be chasing the rabbit, until a fox appeared speeding down the middle of the dirt road. But then another rabbit was soon followed by two small raccoons; followed by a number of opossums, then larger numbers of animals joined them until the road was crowded with all manner of creature regardless of whether they were predator or prey. Deer, field mice, rabbit, rodent, dog, wolf none of whom seemed interested in the other, but all seemingly determined to move forward as fast as they could. Birds soon followed the larger beasts then swarms of insects both crawling and flying. Mallory's heart pounded faster at this sight until she smelled the stench of decomposition and death trailing on the breeze.

She ran over to where Sam, Stella and Jim lay sleeping, and in a frantic voice pleaded with them to get up, her sense of urgency heightened by what she'd just witnessed. The three sleeping people were slow to awaken however, and it was Sam who saw how visibly upset Mallory seemed. He jumped out from under his blanket and ran to the edge of trees. When he looked onto the road, he could barely make out the last of the animals passing by, but the stench was unmistakable.

"We have to go, right now! No time, no time. Get up and get what you can! Mallory, wake Izzy up. Hurry!"

The small camp was pitched into a frenzy of activity, however, Izzy proved difficult to awaken. She had lost some blood, and although the bleeding had abated, she was weakened and had slept like the dead that evening. When Izzy did wake, she was disoriented until she smelled the stench of decay in the air. Her eyes widened and she became alert once more.

"Mallory, Jim, Stella, get the backpacks! We have to cross over into the cornfield! Now!" Izzy yelled.

The others quickly began to break camp. Sam came over and put his arm under Izzy's shoulder.

"You ready, sis?"

"You bet your ass. Let's get the hell out of here right now."

The five of them quickly made their way from the stand of trees to the road. On either side of them the road wound around the tall cornstalks, obscuring their line of sight. In front of them stood the tall brown stalks of the cornfield.

"Which way, sweetie?"

Izzy thought for a second, trying to keep the panic that was just below the surface of her mind at bay. "Into the corn, right now!"

The field soon swallowed up the five of them. They were only a few feet inside the corn but they may as well have been in another world. The air was thick and suffocating, the light was dim and filtered. Although the sun was beginning to rise, within the corn it was still dark and the stalks were close and as sharp as razors. It probably occurred to everyone at some point that perhaps this hadn't been the best idea. They hunkered down low to the ground while watching the road; waiting.

They didn't have to wait very long. The sight of the first zombie chilled them as it shambled down the center of the road in the breaking dawn light. The thing had been a young woman at one time but was now something else. Her hair was long and matted with filth and dried blood, flies flitting about her scalp by the dozens. The dress she had been wearing was torn in places and caked with blood and gore. A bone jutted out of her shoulder where the right arm had been. As she shambled forward, she limped slightly in a weaving motion. Behind her were at least two dozen more; each in a similar state. The dead woman was almost parallel to where Izzy and her group were lying when she suddenly stopped. At the same moment the other zombies stopped as well.

As some swayed in place, others seemed to become frozen in space and time.

Izzy's heart stopped and she felt Mallory's tiny hand slip into hers as Mallory let out an almost inaudible whimper. Izzy glanced over and saw small tears streaking Mallory's cheeks. She looked to her brother Sam who returned her gaze with a determined expression on his face.

Sam's expression said, *We'll get through this.*

The *thing* in the road began to sniff the air, moving her head one way, then the other. She shambled a few steps towards the opposite side of the road and repeated the sniffing. Then she changed direction as if finding nothing and took a few steps again towards Izzy's side of the road and began again to sniff the air yet again. Behind her, other zombies shuffled slowly forward, the undead crowd seeming to become agitated. Some murmured and groaned then a small zombie, once a young girl, began to moan, then stopped.

Izzy looked over to Stella and Jim and saw the chilling effect this was having on them. Stella had a look of absolute terror on her face, which had drained of all color, and she was physically beginning to crawl backwards to get away from the road. As she did this, she was pulling Jim along with her without him realizing what she was doing. Izzy waved her arm to catch Stella's attention but all she heard was Stella softly begin to pray under her breath. Jim seemed in a state of shock at the sight of the zombies and he was allowing himself to be dragged further into the cornfield.

Izzy closed her eyes for a second as she saw the cornstalks behind Stella and Jim begin to bend and sway. The rustling seemed to echo and boom and Izzy's heart stopped again. She turned back to see what the group of zombies where doing. She could only pray that they would not notice anything.

A new group of zombies had joined with the first ones. At this point there were forty bodies standing no more than ten feet away from them, and the mob was becoming more agitated and rowdy. Zombies stamped their feet, let out low moans and screams and began to shamble back and forth in the road. Izzy elbowed her brother and motioned him to move further into the field. She held Mallory's hand tightly in hers and began inching backwards, all the while watching the walking dead in the road.

An older male zombie wearing a plaid coat and a knit cap, but no pants, had joined the first one. His legs were shredded to the bone and he trailed long strips of skin behind him. He began taking great gulps of air while moaning; then turned quickly to face Izzy.

Lifting his arm, he pointed directly at her as the female zombie sniffed the air and turning towards Izzy, pointing to her as well. The rest of the moaning undead stirred into animation and in unison, turned to face the cornfield.

Immediately a number of the younger zombies began to moan and wail as the whole group started a surprisingly rapid shuffle en masse into the cornfield and Izzy's group.

She knew they'd been found. The ghouls had seen the cornstalks move thanks to Jim and Stella or they had somehow smelled them.

"Run!" Mallory screamed as Izzy and Sam stood up

Izzy kept a tight grip on Mallory as Sam followed behind. Izzy knew she was at a disadvantage because she couldn't run very quickly and the cornstalks proved to be a constant obstacle as she tried to dash across the cornrows. Izzy also knew that she was still bleeding and this may have been how the zombies were able to find them so easily; the scent of blood carrying on the wind.

Truth was, she would never know how the ghouls had discovered them, and it didn't matter anyway.

All these thoughts rattled in her head as the five of them broke across the cornrows, aware of zombies following close behind.

Izzy looked up and saw the sky turning crimson, marking the end of night and the beginning of a new day.

"Red sky in morning, shepherd take warning," she whispered to herself. It sent a chill down her spine.

Mallory gripped Izzy's hand tighter as they raced along faster and faster.

Izzy turned to Sam. "Where's Stella and Jim?" her voice was ragged and labored. It was then that they heard a scream behind them. Izzy looked over her shoulder, seeing nothing but cornstalks and shadows. Coming from a distance behind them, she heard stalks of corn being pushed over and trod on.

Izzy stopped running.

Mallory broke free of Izzy's grip while still running forward at the same time Sam bumped into the back of his sister, nearly knocking her over.

"What're you doing? We have to keep going," Sam gasped.

"Where the hell are Stella and Jim?" Izzy repeated.

Another scream sounded from behind them and Sam's face fell. His expression said it couldn't be anyone else but Stella.

"We have to go!" Sam yelled, his face covered in sweat, his hair a tangled mess from crawling around in the corn stalks.

"Stay with Mallory and get to the other side of this cornfield," Izzy told him. "I have to find Stella. If something's happened to her, we have to find Jim and make sure he can get out of here with us."

"Izzy, you're in no shape to go look for them. What're you going to do if you run into those things? Reason with them?"

She actually smiled, her face calming. "Sam, nothing is going to happen to me in this cornfield. Believe me when I tell you this. Now, go!"

As Izzy watched Mallory and Sam disappear into the stalks of corn, she wondered if she would ever see them again. She then turned around and started moving slowly back toward the road. As she walked, she was listening for the telltale shuffle and moan of the undead; looking side-to-side and behind her.

Navigating through the field proved daunting, it was disconcerting not knowing what lay before her until she penetrated through the rows. At one point, she was five feet away from a zombie with only the stalks of corn sheltering her from its view. The stench of the dead was also a giveaway. Izzy quickly found that she could use her sense of smell as well as sight to evade them.

She was almost back at the road when she saw Jim bent low to the ground, holding something with both hands. Izzy's heart pounded at the sight of her friend. As she drew closer, she heard his soft sobbing and saw him bent over the body of his wife.

Stella's neck had been bitten nearly in half with ligaments barely holding her head on her shoulders. A pillow of crimson encircled her head and her face was the color of lead.

Izzy put her hand on Jim's shoulder and he looked up with a forlorn expression. Izzy had a feeling that even if she had been a zombie, Jim still wouldn't have moved, perhaps now wanting to die and join his wife.

"It's you. I was hoping it was one of them," he sobbed, proving her assumption true. He pressed Stella's dead hand tighter to his cheek.

"Leave me alone, Izzy. I want to die."

"How did it happen, Jim?" Izzy gripped his shoulder a little tighter as they both stared down at Stella's body.

"Stella was pullin' me back. I guess I was in a kind of haze. I never seen a zombie up close like that let alone dozens of 'em. I didn't know what was happening, then you guys popped up like jack rabbits and yelled *run*. Me, and Stella, that's all we had to hear and we got up and took off."

Jim was crying now, the effort of remembering causing his emotions to break to the surface again. Izzy's grip tightened on his shoulder and Jim continued.

"We was crashin' through the corn, not knowing which way to turn. We must have gotten turned around. We came through those stalks and ran right into one of 'em. It grabbed Stella and..."

"It's all right, Jim. I'm so sorry. Let's get out of here. You have to leave. She'd want you to come with me, you know that."

"No, Izzy, I don't know how I can go on. Stella was everything to me. I can't see how I can go on without her."

At that moment, Stella's eyes flew open and she let out a ragged, foul exhalation of trapped breath. Jim jumped out from under his wife and stood upright next to Izzy. His expression was one of utmost surprise and horror.

"Oh my God, she's one of them! Let's get the hell out of here, Iz. Right now."

* * *

The sky was now a dark crimson as Jim and Izzy ran through the field, sometimes stopping to let a zombie shuffle by, other times overtaking and outrunning the undead until they were through to the other side of the field.

Izzy looked up again then turned to Jim, saying, "Red sky in morning, shepherd take warning."

Jim actually laughed a little, still glad to be alive though he was distraught over Stella.

"It's a little late for that now, don't you think, Izzy?" he asked.

She could see how sad his eyes were even though he wore a slight smile.

A half hour later, they came out of the corn and happened upon a small cabin that lay at the edge of an adjacent field. They were both exhausted and decided to rest for a few short hours before figuring out what they needed to do next.

Mallory and Sam were out there somewhere, and they needed to try and find them.

As far as they knew, the zombies had been outdistanced, and for now they were as safe as they could be in a dead world.

* * *

When Izzy woke, it was dark. The room she was in didn't have any windows, just a single door. She looked around her but didn't know where Jim might be.

It was then that she became aware of the smell. It was like a thousand garbage heaps, rotting flesh, and dead dogs rolled up into one. Her heart quickened and her breathing became ragged and shallow.

Soon after, she heard the shuffling outside, not of one, but of dozens upon dozens of feet surrounding the cabin in force. Seconds hurtled forward as a soft, scratching at the door became a thud, and then many thuds until she knew that at any moment the door would explode open and her life, and that of her unborn baby, would be over.

In those remaining seconds, she wished for a quick and painless death, a way out of the building, a better life for herself and the rest of humanity.

There were many more wishes, but she was never able to formulate them. As the door suddenly shattered open, there was Sam, Jim and Stella, all three staring right at her with dead, glazed eyes, snapping their jaws and leading a massive mob of the undead into the cabin.

In Izzy's last moments on Earth, she thanked God that Mallory wasn't with them, that she had somehow escaped, and she wondered how much it was going to hurt when the ghouls began to tear her apart.

Just as the zombies surrounded and closed in on her, she felt her baby kick for the first time, and she smiled.

RED-NECKS, WHITE AND BLUE

Tommy's fingers and palms were wet with nervous sweat, making the pistol, an M9 semiautomatic Beretta, slippery in his right hand.

Of all the times for this to happen.

Back before dead folks got up and started eating people, the condition had been one of occasional social embarrassment. Like that one time, just a few months ago, when he'd taken Peggy Sue Miller to their junior year graduation dance. From nowhere, the disgusted grimace Peggy Sue made when she took his hand popped into his head.

Wrong time to be thinking about that shit.

Completely wrong. Back then all he had to contend with were the insecurities the sweaty hands dilemma brought to the fore. Now the condition was potentially fatal.

All around him, guns were going off. The field was being sown with seed size flecks of zombie brains. The shooters were men for the most part, though there were a handful of women, and even a couple of boys, one fifteen, the other thirteen. Some of the men wore army fatigues, some quilted shirts and hunting caps, some were cops in uniform, others just people in their day to day civvies.

Most of the zombies were spaced far enough apart or were distant enough that the men could take their time, crack a beer if they wanted, gather in a group, joke around some.

"Holy shit, Billy. Over by the old car, it's your ex, Debbie. She really dead? Yeah, she's gotta be. Too bad, man."

"Where? That fuckin' bitch gave me a dose of crabs so big the bastards must've been mutant. I shit you not: they were huge. Could've had a sign next to my pubes that said: **Welcome to Sea World.**"

Several yuks, beer swigs and one rifle shot later, Billy grinned at his buddies, "Guess she's double dead, dead Debbie now."

Occasionally one of the zombies got closer than it ought to, like the one that appeared from behind the broken down tractor, the one now slowly but steadily making its way toward the closest available food source. Specifically, the teenager with the clammy hands.

Tommy wiped his left hand on the thigh of his jeans, switched the pistol over to it, then dried his other hand on his sweater. He returned the gun to his right hand. Aimed. Readied to fire.

The zombie took a stumbling lurch in Tommy's direction.

Twelve feet and closing... Eleven...

Tommy had a clean shot. Had no reason not to fire.

Come on, man. Take the shot. Take it and move on to the next.

Whenever one got up close like this, Tommy invariably froze. Twenty feet away, hell, fifteen feet, and he was fine. Didn't hesitate. Not for so much as a second. And if there was a group of them that needed to be put down, he could keep blasting away like there was no tomorrow, no matter how close their proximity. But when he was one on one he stalled; the kill taking on a special kind of intimacy.

Shoot her.

It wasn't fear that made him freeze. It was the long look he'd taken at her face. Now he'd acknowledged her former existence, he'd begun seeing her less as the mindless dead thing she was and more as the person she used to be. That was why he'd gotten nervous and sweaty palmed. Why he couldn't finish the job.

The only visible wounds were to the woman's throat and left arm. Her throat had been ripped open. He could see the torn carotid artery, the remnants of muscle and cartilage and tissue glistening inside the wet darkness, the protruding muscular tubes of the woman's severed trachea and esophagus. The only other damage was a missing chunk of bicep. The area around the bite looked blackened and swollen from infection. Aside from the grayish-blue pallor of her skin, there were no physical signs of decomposition, meaning the woman had been dead a few days at most. That she looked so alive, despite her wounds, was part of the reason he'd hesitated. Why he'd allowed her to cross the threshold of his comfort zone. That and the fact she had a killer body and was wearing the sort of barely there red lingerie he'd only seen before in his older sister's underwear catalogs.

His sister Jean, that was. Poor Jean.

As his mind started to pull toward the memory he mentally blocked it.

The creature took another step closer. Tommy had never seen a woman so scantily clad and clearly dressed for sex. Not in the flesh anyway, dead or otherwise.

He could even see the promise of a dark triangle of hair behind her wafer thin panties. And oh sweet Lord, what a set of hooters. The jiggling of them inside the red bra had an almost hypnotic effect. His gaze moved to the garter belts and stockings she wore. The stockings were shredded, caked with mud. A whispery groan from her lips blindsided him, taking on a sexual connotation inside his teenage brain.

Christ; was he getting turned on? Turned on by a zombie with her throat ripped out, just because she had big tits and wore sexy undies and moaned like one of the gals in his Pa's porno movies?

No way. That's just plain wrong. I need to lose my virginity. Like, yesterday.

The woman's grimy hands reached out for him. She was close enough now that Tommy could see twigs caught in her honey blond hair; see insects crawling through the loose curls.

He looked into her eyes. All he saw looking back was dull blankness. Nothing remained of who she'd been. The woman was brain dead. Nothing but motorized instinct.

Tommy's finger squeezed back on the trigger. But before he could pull it all the way, a shadow fell on him from behind, followed by a voice.

"I feel your pain, kid," said the voice, a man's. "Damn shame to see a piece that fine go to waste."

Tommy didn't need to look to see who the voice belonged to. Bob Tucker. Of all the redneck assholes Tommy had met in his life (and hailing from a town that put the *back* in woods, that number was far from few), Tucker almost effortlessly took the crown.

"Leave be, Tucker," Tommy said. "I got this."

"Got this?" Tucker sneered. "Son, I been walking up on you from way over yonder, and in all that time you ain't had shit. Got this, my ass. Now, step aside, boy, this here's work for a man."

With that Tucker shoved Tommy hard, knocking him down to the mud. He unslung his rifle and aimed for the zombie woman, now just seven feet away.

"A man? Is that what you call yourself, Bob Tucker?"

Oh, Jesus, Tommy thought. It was Annie Burton, Tommy's grandmother.

Annie waded over, galoshes on her feet, sweatpants on her legs, a hooded glossy pink windbreaker covering her upper body and head and a 12 gauge shotgun slung over her shoulder. "Pushing around a kid a hundred pounds lighter than you? Some man."

The zombie with the hot bod actually stopped moving and stood in place, the expression on her face one Tommy could almost mistake for slow dawning curiosity. Of course that couldn't be. Not unless one of those trace memories had yet to fully evaporate.

Tucker turned at Annie's approach, free hand raised palm out, a gesture intended to pacify the scrunch-faced old woman. "Now take it easy. Just trying to lend a helping hand is all."

Annie gave him a disapproving grunt. "Well, you can start by helping my grandson up off the ground."

"Sure," Tucker said, extending a hand to Tommy. "Be my plea..."

"Bobbie, look out!" Annie yelled.

Whatever made the zombie woman falter had passed, and the creature stumbled the last few feet at what could almost have been considered a trot. Tucker turned just as the zombie made her move for his outstretched hand. She would have got him, too, if not for the speed of Grandma Burton's reflexes. She swung the shotgun down, set the stock against her shoulder, and took a firm grip on it with both hands. Tensing her leg muscles, she aimed for the zombie's head.

The recoil from the blast knocked Annie back a pace before she regained her footing.

When the three inch slug hit the zombie, it punched a hole in the center of her forehead and sent a high, arcing spray of brains, blood and bone out the back. The woman rocked back and forth then dropped forward onto her knees.

From where she lay on the ground, Tommy could see right through the hole in the front of her head. The slug, upon exiting, had obliterated everything from the crown to the base of the cranium, affording him a momentary view through her head of the woods at the edge of the field. The woman fell face first into a puddle, one deep enough that her head went almost entirely under. Muddy rainwater bubbled up out of the hole in the back of her head.

"Well, butter my butt and call me a biscuit," Tucker said, looking from the zombie to his hand to Annie. "You just saved my life, Mrs. Burton."

Annie gave a noncommittal grunt, broke open the shotgun and removed the casing of the spent slug, replacing it with a fresh one from the pocket of her windbreaker. "I believe you were about to help my grandson up out of the dirt."

Tucker nodded thoughtfully. He extended his hand, an expression that was intended to convey apology on his face. Tommy ignored the offering, preferring to get to his feet unaided.

"I guess these times can bring out the worst in a person," Tucker said. "Sorry I was such an asshole."

"Hey," Tommy said. "No need to apologize. I mean, you were born that way. Not much you can do to change it."

The earnest expression of regret on Tucker's face soured, curdled into a sneer. "On account of what your grandmother just did, I'm gonna let that pass. But be warned. Next time you insult me, boy, I ain't gonna be feeling so Christian."

Looking into the fat man's eyes, Tommy found himself on the receiving end of a hatred so intense he could barely manage not to back down and avert his gaze. Even though Tommy's pulse quickened, he was able to keep the fear from climbing up out of his gut, to keep his eyes flat and his face expressionless, and say in a monotone reply, "I'm just pissing in my pants."

A snort of laughter came hissing out of Tucker's nose. Grinning, the fat redneck leaned in close, whispered, "Take my advice, boy. Keep your distance."

Tommy didn't break eye contact, no matter how much he wanted to be free of the crazed expression of dark intent in the other man's eyes. Tucker turned, boots clomping across the muddy field, seeking out zombies to kill. Pickings were slim. The dead were dead for good and the field all but cleared.

"You know," his grandmother said, when she stood beside him. "You could've avoided that."

Tommy looked at her. "Yeah. But if I'd taken his hand and kept my mouth shut and accepted his apology, he might've got the idea some sort of alliance had formed between us. Maybe even think to take me under his wing, try to mentor me in an apprenticeship in assholedom. Then I would've had to kill him for sure. Probably sooner than later."

"Be careful, son," Annie said. "These are lawless times. Making enemies in times like these could end up costing you your life."

"I'm old enough to make my own decisions, Grandma,"

"Why sure you are," Annie said. "And who knows, maybe one of these days you'll decide it's time you washed your face."

From her pocket she produced a handkerchief. She wet one corner with her tongue, made to dab at the flecks of mud on Tommy's cheek, got one and wiped it off.

"Grandma, cut it out," he complained, pulling away. "Someone's going to see."

Ignoring Tommy's protests, Grandma Burton came at him with grim determination. The look in her eyes told him she meant to do her duty as his grandmother, meant to wipe away those mud specks if it was the last thing she ever accomplished.

A group of nearby national guardsmen were drinking Iron City beer and having their photograph taken with a dead zombie they'd hooked in the mouth like a fish, the tallest of them hoisting him up off the ground. They looked his way to see the cause of the commotion.

Tommy knew he was just moments away from becoming the laughing stock of the entire encampment, the depths of humiliation he'd suffer from here on out unfathomable.

Just as his grandma was about to deliver a dainty dab of one wetted corner of handkerchief, her walkie-talkie squealed, and a man's voice asked, "Annie, that you and your Coleen's boy I see standing over there in the field?"

Praise Jesus, Tommy thought, relieved to see Annie stash the handkerchief in the cuff of her windbreaker and unhook the walkie-talkie clipped to her sweatpants at the waist.

"Annie here," she said into the radio. "Yeah, that's us in the field. That you, Mack? What's your twenty?"

"Over to your right," came the reply. "See me standing atop this hill?"

They looked to the right where a man dressed in a black woolen cap, black duffel coat, jeans and boots was waving his arm in the air.

Annie pressed the call button. "Okay. We see ya. You can quit waving now."

The man, who wore his beard full and down past his neck to better weather the Pennsylvania winters, dropped his left arm and raised the walkie-talkie to his mouth with the other.

"Young Tommy got his knife with him?"

Annie relayed the question with her eyes and Tommy nodded.

"Affirmative," Annie said. "What's shaking, Mack? You finally decide to let me shave that nasty looking thing you call a beard?"

Mack laughed and said, "Annie you've been waiting to get your hands on this thing for years. And when the day comes, I promise to give you first crack at it. Deal?"

"Deal," Annie said into the walkie-talkie, then asked, "So, what do you need the knife for?"

"Hell of a thing..." Mack replied. "Come take a look. You won't believe it unless you see it."

*   *   *

Looking down into the adjacent meadow from the top of the hill, Tommy saw nothing unusual, that is, nothing he hadn't seen a dozen times by now.

Spread across the meadow were nine zombies, each drawn to a lone figure. At first glance the figure appeared to be a scarecrow. The zombies made their shambling, shuffling, lurching, staggering, stumbling, falling over and taking their sweet time to get up again, way, toward it.

Then the scarecrow moved and Tommy saw it was a man. The man moved again and Tommy saw it was two men, positioned back to back, a mop handle keeping their arms in Christ-like postures, neither able to escape the other. Rope had been tied around their torsos, running from their waists to chests. Countless wrappings of twine around their coat sleeves kept the wooden handle in place, and their outstretched arms were fixed at shoulder height.

The man managed a few faltering steps to the right and the side on view offered a look at both men in profile. As the second became visible, Tommy saw that in the traditional sense of the word, only one of the two was really alive.

The zombie's head was turned to one side, stretched as far as the neck would allow; slavering at the mouth, teeth ceaselessly chomping down. His teeth were mere inches away from the lobe of the other man's ear, near but not near enough, and all he got each time for his troubles was a mouthful of air.

A dead woman with rollers in her hair, wearing a powder blue housecoat over a billowing nightgown caked with mud, came at the man, arms raised and hands grasping.

"Shoot her," Annie urged. "Shoot her, Mack. Shoot her in the head."

Mack, who until now had kept his rifle pointed toward the ground, raised it to his shoulder and sighted his target. He wet his index finger with his tongue, held it in the air.

"What are you doing?" Annie asked. "There isn't any wind. Shoot her."

Mack readjustment his aim.

Down in the meadow, the man bent forward, raising the feet of the zombie at his back slightly off the ground. He did a little shuffling two step, turning himself away from the dead woman so the zombie he was tied to faced her instead. The dead woman stopped in her tracks. She stood there looking at the thing that had somehow replaced her intended meal. Her head cocked slightly to one side, putting Tommy in mind of a dog he'd owned as a boy, one who'd adopted a similar pose when he encountered something that vexed him. Then the dead woman, evidently baffled by the switcheroo tactic, looked a few seconds longer at the twisted necked zombie (who was still clacking his teeth and going after the earlobe) then lowered her arms and turned around and shuffled off in the opposite direction.

"Poor bastard," Mack said, lowering the rifle. "No telling how long he's been down there, fending them off like that."

"I'm surprised at you, Mack Watkins," Annie said. "Allowing that man to suffer in such a way, and you with the means to come to his aid."

Tommy knew his grandma referred to the Winchester the rugged outdoorsy looking Watkins held in his hands. But Tommy knew something else, something his grandmother in all likelihood did not. Mack might appear the part, what with the big beard and hunter's clothes and leathery look to what little of his face could be seen, but the sad fact was Mack Watkins couldn't shoot worth a shit. In fact, Mack's poor marksmanship had turned him into something of a social pariah among the rest of the men. Tommy had overheard some of them back at base camp one night, making jokes about it behind Mack's back, and others making them right when he was close enough to hear. Some of them didn't stop at making jokes either, opining that Mack was a walking liability. The general consensus was that the last person you wanted to entrust your life to going into battle was a man who couldn't shoot straight. All of which probably accounted for Mack's solitary position on the hill, while the others down in the field had been busy stamping zombie death warrants with bullets through their foreheads.

"Well," Mack said. "At first I didn't cotton on to what I was seeing. Soon as I did, I radioed you for the knife."

Annie's grunt conveyed her opinion about the paltriness of Mack's explanation.

Another of the zombies in the meadow had caught scent of the trussed up man and was making its way toward him.

"You want to know the truth?" Mack asked, looking at Tommy, his flinty eyes narrowing. "I saw young Thomas here choke down there in the field. Figured he might benefit from a little target practice."

Tommy was about to call the guy out over this latest line of bull, but couldn't get the words in his head to come out of his mouth. Damn his Ma and Pa...well, God rest their souls, his Pa dead six years ago thanks to an overindulgent taste for tobacco, his Ma, like his sister, lost to the epidemic. But damn them for raising him to respect his elders and not talk back.

Now Grandma Annie was nodding in agreement!

"Well, you're not wrong there," she said. "Choke he did. And it wasn't the first time neither. He needs to get it in his head that these folks are dead; that killing them is a kindness. Truth is, I'm starting to wonder if maybe the boy might be lily-livered."

What? Lily-livered! No.

Mack was the one who couldn't shoot straight. Who was the laughing stock of the men. Not him. If anyone was lily-livered - whatever the hell that meant - it was Mack, not him.

"Well, son?" Mack asked. Looking into Mack's eyes, Tommy saw that the other man knew that he knew but still wouldn't come out and admit he was a lousy shot.

"Give me that thing," Tommy said, snatching the Winchester out of his hands.

Tommy raised the rifle to his shoulder, looked through the sights.

Annie said, "A jar of my homemade apple jam says he doesn't get all nine in a row."

"Thanks a lot, Grandma," Tommy said.

"Just trying to keep it real, son," she said.

"Hmmm," Mack said, considering. "All right, you're on. Versus a jug of my shine."

The two spat into their hands and shook.

Tommy lowered the rifle and looked at them. "Grandma, aren't you forgetting your house and everything in it burnt to the ground? And Mack, aren't you forgetting that when we left Orchards Town, the entire place was overrun with those things?"

"True enough," Annie said. "Guess you'll just have to take my word I'm good for it, Mack."

"Same here," Mack said.

"Okay let 'em have it," Annie said. "And remember, aim for..."

"Yeah, I know, Grandma."

"Mind that you do," she said. "Bullets don't come easy these days, son."

Tommy raised the rifle and started shooting. From where they stood, the holes in the center of the zombies' foreheads the bullets made were beyond sight. But one by one they fell and that told Annie and Mack all they needed to know. When Tommy had dropped five of them, Mack reloaded the rifle. Tommy polished off another three, leaving only the housecoat zombie woman with rollers in her hair.

"Looks like you're about to lose this bet, Annie," Mack said, hurriedly unzipping the pack at his feet to retrieve his binoculars. "Go on, Tom. You can do it."

Maybe it was just the pressure of making the last of the nine shots, or maybe he was thrown off by Mack abbreviating his name the same way his Pa used to before hammering home his final coffin nail, and maybe the wind picked up. Whatever the answer, just as Mack glassed the meadow to get a better look at the last of the zombies, Tommy lost his aim.

Mack saw it as though he were standing right next to the zombie. The bullet drove through the nostrils, shattering bone. The fleshy tip of her nose went spinning up into the air and blood streamed down her face. Regardless of her injuries, the zombie tilted her head back and her eyes followed the flesh projectile as it ascended through the air.

Gravity staked its claim and the bit of nose came tumbling back down. The zombie stretched her mouth wide, caught the dime-sized piece of flesh in her mouth. She clamped her teeth together and stood there chewing. Blood continued to gush out of her ruined nose, painting a crimson goatee onto her chin along with the wattle beneath it. After a few chews, some type of realization stirred in her mud-dull eyes. She opened her mouth and pushed the piece of dead flesh out with her tongue and it dropped to land in the grass.

Tommy's next shot turned one of those muddy brown eyes into a splash of red. The dead woman toppled like a felled tree, her face landing in a cluster of dandelions. The tiny white flowers in the composite head separated from their stalks and danced delicately through the air all around her.

The pride radiating out of Annie's beaming face might at another time have been better put to use at Tommy's graduation ceremony. But of course, Tommy had never graduated. He'd still had a year of high school to finish when the epidemic yanked him out early.

"Not bad at all, eh, Mack?" Annie asked.

Mack stroked his beard thoughtfully, looking down at the meadow.

"Couldn't have done better myself, Annie."

Yeah right, Tommy thought, looking at him. "Come on," he said. "There's still one left."

Starting down the hill, he stopped and came back, realizing his on-going predicament of killing the undead up close and personal could be avoided.

"Here you go, Mr. Watkins," Tommy said, placing the pistol in Mack's hand.

"Me?" Mack asked, looking at the gun doubtfully.

Tommy grinned. "Sure. I wouldn't want to steal all the glory."

* * *

"Keep your head forward," Mack called.

"Oh, God!" cried the trussed up man. "Help me! Get me away from this thing."

The redneck with the blue-gray face was still twisting its head, doing his damnedest to get a bite of live feed.

Mack, who was just six feet away, aimed the pistol. "Tuck your chin into your neck and lean forward so I can get a clear shot at its head."

Christ, Tommy thought. *He's gonna blow this guy's head off for sure.*

Mack took a deep breath and let it out slowly through his mouth. He worked out a crick in his neck, readjusted his aim.

Annie clucked her tongue three times and said, "Would you just shoot the damn thing already, so we can get back to camp and get a bite to eat? I'm famished."

"Could we have a little quiet, please?" Mack said without looking around. "You're breaking my concentration."

"For the love of Pete," Annie muttered and pulled the drawstring of her windcheater's hood so it covered her mouth and nose. She walked to the man-zombie combo and swung the shotgun up above the man's head (which was doing a fair impression of a turtle into the neckline of his sweater by now), placed the barrels against the back of the zombie's head and fired both triggers.

At such close range the effects of the shotgun slugs were decisive. The blast decimated the zombie's head, blowing it off the neck, sending chunks of brain and skull flying through the air. Twenty feet away, the pieces showered down, painting the blades of grass red.

The stuff that sputtered out of the corpse's neck cavity looked more like oil than blood. This was no gushing geyser. Just a few thick spurts that came in stops and starts, making Tommy think the blood inside the zombie must have already begun to congeal.

Despite the treacle thickness of the zombie's blood, the back of the man's head didn't escape a dousing. With every fresh splash his whimpering became louder.

"Get it off me," he pleaded; his face a twisted grimace. "Get it off!"

Tommy got right to work with his knife. He sawed through the twine binding the man's arms to the zombie's, careful not to get any of the blood on him that was still sputtering out of the open neck. Once the mop handle dropped to the ground the headless zombie slumped forward. Next, Tommy cut through the rope wrapped around their torsos. As the rope fell away, the decapitated zombie dropped to the ground.

"Thank you," the man sobbed. "Thank you."

He came at Annie with arms outstretched, the ordeal he'd survived evidently summoning some need for human contact. The blood that had splashed the back of his head trickled down past his ears.

Annie held up her hands, warding him off. "Maybe when we're better acquainted," she said.

"Better wash that blood off," Mack said, reaching into his pack and removing a bottle of water. "Any of it gets in your eyes or mouth and you might turn into one of them."

A resurgence of terror dawned on the man's relaxed features, his facial muscles pulling taut.

"You think so?"

"You want to find out?" Mack asked.

"Give me that," Annie said, snatching the water from Mack's hand. "Today's your lucky day, mister. Just so happens I'm packing some of the good stuff."

Perplexed, the man just stared at her.

From a zippered side pocket of her windcheater, Annie retrieved her stash, and when she opened her palm, the man understood. In her hand was a travel sized bottle of Head and Shoulders.

While Annie wet the man's hair and got him lathered up, Mack searched his bag for a T-shirt he was willing to part with. He settled on one not only too small for him but also so ripely scented from being worn repeatedly without being washed that he was more than happy to part with it. He'd never been much of a one for doing his laundry. Even less so since the dead came back to life.

"Keep your eyes and mouth closed as tight as you can," Annie said. The man did as he was told while she rinsed the soap off.

Mack gave him the t-shirt to dry himself. He rubbed the top of his head a few times then the t-shirt fell out of his hand and the man broke down and sobbed.

Tommy put a hand on his shoulder. "You're going to be okay. It's over now."

Sobbing, the man shook his head. "They took them...my wife and daughter...please, you have to help me. They've got my wife...my little girl..."

"Who?" Tommy asked.

"Bikers," the man said. "We were heading north in our car. They ran us off the road. I tried to fight them off, killed two of 'em, but there were so many. They tied me to that thing and took my family."

"Not just bikers," Annie said. "Raiders. They're all over these parts. And if they took them they're as good as dead."

Neither Mack nor Tommy contradicted her.

"You got a name?" Annie asked him.

"Paulson," he replied but only she heard him. With hands shaking, he reached into his back pocket, pulled out his wallet, and removed a photograph. "This is them," Paulson said, holding the photograph out to them. The photo was of a mother and daughter, both looking very much alike. The older woman was laughing and the girl in the picture was fifteen or sixteen years old; her smile radiating out at them. "That's my little girl, Lisa. Please…"

"You can ask around back at the camp," Annie said. "Maybe you'll find some men willing to help you. But I wouldn't get my hopes up. Not unless you've got something valuable to barter with."

The man nodded rapidly. "There's our car," he gabbled. "The ones who took them, they shot out one of the tires. It's probably still sitting by the side of the road."

Annie sighed. "Car with a flat tire ain't worth a damn these days, mister."

"There's a spare," the man said. "The car's brand new. We just got it six months ago. These men can have it. It's theirs."

Annie shook her head, turned away, and started back up the hill. Mack gathered his pack and rifle, then followed.

"Come on," Tommy said. "Maybe you'll find someone who can at least show you where they are."

A glimmer of hope appeared in the man's eyes. "You know where they are?"

Tommy nodded. "Raiders got an encampment about fifteen miles outside Johnstown. It's a place deep in the woods from what I hear."

"Then I can go there," the man said. "Go there and find a way to get them back. Maybe even trade with them. There's money hidden in the car. Hidden real good. They searched it but I'll bet they never found it. They'll trade for money, right?"

"Who knows," Tommy said.

"Sure they will," the man said. "Sure they will."

These days money was less valuable than toilet roll. You could wipe your ass on one and not the other. After guns and food, that made asswipe one hot commodity. The higher the ply, the greater the value. But Tommy said nothing, thinking it better to leave the man's dream alive than destroy it.

"Name's Tom Burton," Tommy said, sticking out his hand.

The man shook it. "Paulson. Robert."

*   *   *

As soon as they reached the top of the hill, they knew something was wrong. Everyone still in the field was running for the vehicles they'd arrived in. Those who'd already reached the road scrambled into their trucks, vans and cars, slammed the doors shut and peeled out.

"What is it?" Tommy asked. "What's happening?"

His question was answered by a panicked voice that came in hitching breaths from Mack's and Annie's radios. "They're (static) here! You...gotta...get...back (static) they're... (static) all... (static) over us."

Tommy realized they must have been calling for help while he, Annie and Mack were down in the meadow, the hill preventing them from receiving the signal. Mack raised his binoculars, honed in on the farmhouse where they'd set up camp.

What he saw made him flinch.

"Mack," Annie said. "Tell me they're okay. He was exaggerating, right?"

Mack lowered the binoculars, looked at Annie and shook his head.

Tommy took the binoculars from him, needing to see for himself.

The women and children, the injured and those too frail to fight, were being eaten alive by the living dead. There were fifty or so zombies in all, spread out across the camp. Blood gushed out of their mouths, their teeth opening their victims flesh.

If the men had kept their heads, some of the people back at camp could have evaded their attackers; outrun them; escaped. But total panic reigned.

The old folks didn't stand a chance. Tommy saw one old man using a walker to try to escape a zombie. The ghoul moved at a speed just fast enough to catch up to its slow prey. The old man tried to bat the zombie away but he lost his balance, knocking the walker over. They fell to the ground together. The old man was unable to get his bearings; defenseless as the zombie sank its teeth into his withered hand. Tommy saw another figure, an old woman, turning the wheels of her chair with her hands. She narrowly avoided a zombie lurching toward her. And would have made good her escape, if not for a bump in the path that sent the wheelchair toppling sideways. The old woman tried desperately to crawl away. The zombie fell on her, bit into her face. Zombies didn't discriminate, didn't care if the skin was wrinkled and aged. Flesh was flesh. The wheelchair's upward facing wheel, yet to finish spinning, got splashed with blood. Tommy saw it drip from the slowing spokes.

Most of the children just stood there crying. The monster was out of the closet. It was going to get them and eat them.

And it did.

That left the women. Maybe if they'd been from a different time, or a different place, or had been raised with a different set of beliefs, they would have stood a chance. But for all the so-called progress of the times that served as a set-up for a glut of last year's sitcoms, these were women reared on a diet of small town tradition. And small town tradition dictated that the men made the money and went out with their buddies to hunt (if they were so inclined and most of them were), and the women cooked and cleaned and kept their husbands happy (no matter how much they reeked of beer), and any surplus energy leftover they dedicated to raising the kids. It wasn't written in stone. It wasn't always this way (hence the handful of women out in the field), but it was the small town way (in their small towns, at least), and until dead people started biting live people, they were happy to abide by it.

So the women were goners, one and all. Not just because the little target practice they'd had left them totally unprepared to accurately shoot the handguns they'd been provided, and not because they saw the slow moving strangers as anything other than dead, but mostly because of the kids. The kids went down quick, died quick and came back quick. Then they got up and moved around slowly. Their mommies ran to them regardless. Ran to them and scooped them into their arms, and were greeted by their freshly undead offspring with a silent, flesh ripping kiss.

By the time the first of the vehicles arrived back there, only a scattered handful of people were alive to save. The men piled out of the rear of the truck, which looked like an army troop transporter, with its green paint and camouflaged awning (though the closest thing to an official army presence was the National Guard). Cops, men in fatigues, hunters and civilians in plainclothes moved forward into the fray, weapons raised. Tears ran freely down the faces of those who recognized their kinfolk, either dead and lumbering toward them, or still on the ground being eaten alive.

There was only one thing to do.

Tommy saw the rest of the vehicles arrive; saw the weary looks on the faces of those joining with the others. As one group they proceeded with the mass extermination, moving forward, dropping the living dead to the ground.

Advance. Fire. Repeat. Advance. Fire. Repeat.

Gone were the cheers and camaraderie. Gone the sport of it all. Their own had fallen. Risen. Fallen again. Tommy had never had to kill one of his own. Had escaped his home with his grandma in her battered VW Beetle, his mother and sister, arms outstretched, tripping down the porch steps as they came after them. At night he still saw their faces in his dreams, saw their idiotic, open mouthed waxy gray-hued faces, distant when the dreams began with his feet unable to move; close enough he could smell the rot on their breath when he woke, shaking and drenched in sweat. Tommy knew that compared to these men he was lucky. Asleep or awake, for them there would be no escaping this nightmare.

"Tommy," Annie said. "What's happening? Let me see."

Tommy held up a hand. "Just a second, Grandma."

Through the binoculars, he saw the last of the zombies fall. Some of the men were pointing toward the woods, talking to the others, their anger plain to see. Moving the binoculars to the tree line, Tommy saw two more zombies come stumbling out of the woods; woods that ran several miles deep. He adjusted his view and found the farmhouse. Now one of the cops was pointing at some of the men grouped together. And Tommy understood what had happened.

"Those assholes didn't check the woods," he whispered.

He focused in on the group of men. It was Bob Tucker and his buddies. It had been their turn to sweep the woods behind the farmhouse earlier that morning. Either they'd ignored their assignment, or were so hung-over they forgot all about it.

What followed was so sudden; it was over before Tommy could believe it was happening.

A man Tommy recognized as Greg Youngs cradled a child with a bullet hole to the head (the boy, Tommy remembered was Greg's son, Eddie). Greg laid the body gently to the ground, got up and walked to Tucker. With shaking hands he drew his gun and shot him in the chest. As Tucker staggered away, looking disbelievingly at the hole in his shirt, one of his gang returned fire. The bullet hit Greg in the shoulder, causing the gun to fall from his hand.

But Greg didn't have to concern himself with being shot a second time. First a few and then twice as many again and soon every man, woman and even the two boys, were firing on Tucker and his gang. Their limbs jerked every which way; bullets riddling them with holes. Even after they were dead and lying face down in the dirt, the shots kept coming. It was like their killers regretted allowing them such easy deaths.

Tommy lowered the binoculars and passed them back to Mack.

He started down the hill, not for the field but toward the meadow.

"Tommy," Annie called. "Where're you going?"

"Not back there," Tommy called. "Not now, not ever."

"What's gotten into him?" Annie asked. "What did he see?"

Looking through the binoculars, Mack muttered profanities. He lowered them and looked at Annie, explained what Tommy had just witnessed.

"The boy's right," Mack said. "There's nothing there worth returning for now. Everything that just happened will drive those people apart. You think they'll be able to look each other in the eye once the guilt kicks in? My guess is by nightfall they'll have already started to disband."

"Then what are we to do?" Annie asked.

The man, Paulson, stepped in front of Tommy. "Wait a second," he said.

"What?"

"I have a place. It's in the mountains. A hundred miles from the nearest town."

"Look around," Tommy said, his arm sweeping to indicate their surroundings. "You see any towns? The closest is sixty miles away. Those things still got here. It made no difference."

"If they reached it," Paulson said. "Not that I think they would, not for a very long time, but if they did, there's a bunker, built back in the sixties. Fully stocked. The six of us could survive down there for months."

Annie and Mack, who'd been listening, approached.

"The six of us?" Mack asked.

"Look," Paulson said. "You know what I want. Help me and I'll do the same for you."

Annie grunted noncommittally. "What makes you think we'd even be interested?"

"We were at the shopping mall when one of those things came lumbering into the food court and took a chunk out of some guy eating his Reuben sandwich." Paulson's gaze drifted away from them as the memory played. "It was the first any of us had seen. Two days later the whole of Monroeville was overrun. We barely escaped with our lives." His eyes met Annie's. "This thing isn't going to pass any time soon. The further away from civilization you are, the better your chances. You ask me why you'd be interested. No offense intended, ma'am, but I think you'd be fools not to be."

"None taken," Annie said. "Like I said before, your family's good as dead. And we'd be good as dead if we went in after them."

"Be that as it may," Paulson said. "I won't leave without them."

Tommy could see Mack weighing their chances in his mind. For a guy who couldn't shoot straight he figured Mack must have been thinking their chances were pretty slim. But Tommy didn't have to decide for Mack, or his grandmother; only for himself. And after watching the men he'd looked to for guidance these last few days gun down Tucker and his gang, he felt a need to prove the ideals he'd been raised to believe in were more than mere words. It occurred to him that beliefs were easy to embrace when they were left untested. If he turned his back on Paulson, on the abducted mother and daughter, then wasn't he the same as those he'd seen massacre a handful of men, just for making a mistake? Driven by hatred, they'd taken life and snuffed it out. He knew they would justify their actions, would have to, to live with what they'd done.

But what reason did he have, other than self-preservation, to condemn Paulson's family to death when there was a chance, however slim, he might be able to help save them?

No reason whatsoever.

"I'm in," Tommy said.

Mack looked at Tommy like he thought he was the biggest idiot that ever lived.

"Me, too," Mack said.

"The hell you are, Thomas Burton," Annie said. "In case you'd forgotten, you're not yet eighteen, and as your only living relative that makes me your legal guardian." To Paulson she said. "Sorry, mister, but you'll have to find somebody else."

"Grandma," Tommy said. "I'm going to do this. You won't talk me out of it, so you might as well save your breath."

"Fine," she said. "But don't expect me to commit suicide along with you."

Tommy put an arm around her. "We can drop you at one of the rescue stations we heard about on the radio. Soon as we've got his family we'll come get you."

"Sure," Annie said, never looking more frail, never more defeated. "A rescue station sounds just fine."

* * *

Paulson led them across the meadow and through a copse of woods. On the road near the car, his wife lay dead in a pool of blood, the blade of a kitchen knife sticking out of her chest.

Annie found a blanket on the backseat of the car and covered her over, but even then Paulson couldn't look away from the shape of her body beneath it; couldn't stem the flow of tears.

"Why did they have to kill her?" Paulson asked. "She was defenseless. No threat to them."

Nobody had any answers for him.

In the road were two dead raiders, both killed by gunshots to the chest.

"Looks like he put up quite a fight before gettin' away," Tommy said.

"Poor bastard," Mack said, looking from the bodies to the figure the blanket lay draped over.

The dead raiders were dressed in motorcycle leathers, one with a leather hat and waistcoat under his jacket.

"Maybe we can use their clothes," Tommy suggested.

Mack saw what he was thinking and nodded. "Good idea,"

The two of them busied themselves with changing the flat tire, which was not so much flat as shredded by the blast of a bullet.

"I'm sorry for your loss," Annie said.

Paulson didn't reply but just stood there and wept.

She placed a hand on his shoulder, knowing it would offer little comfort, but also that any kind of comfort was better than none.

"I lost my daughter, Tommy's Mom, along with my grand-daughter. He's all I got left. I guess if he was taken, the same way as your girl was, I'd crawl through broken glass if there was a chance to save him."

Annie watched her grandson loosen the lug nuts on the wheel and nod to Mack to turn the jack.

"This place in the mountains," she said. "It really exists?"

Paulson looked her in the eye. "Of course."

Tommy got the lug nuts off the rest of the way, worked the wheel off the spindles.

Quietly, Annie said, "Then I guess I'll be coming along for the ride." A moment later she was her blustery old self, marching over to Tommy and Mack.

"Get that wheel on good and tight," she ordered. "If I'm driving us to our certain deaths, I want to be sure we get there safe."

"You're driving?" Tommy said. "But I thought..."

She jerked a thumb over her shoulder at Paulson. "He's in no shape to do it, you got no license and Mack's so blind since he lost his glasses he's liable to put us in a ditch. Don't leave me a lot of choices, does it now?"

"Lost your glasses?" Tommy said to Mack. "So that's why..."

Mack nodded sadly. "Goddamn zombie clawed 'em off my face and snapped 'em in half three weeks back."

"No, Grandma," Tommy protested. "It's too dangerous, you can't..."

"No arguments," Annie said. "My mind's made up. Don't try to sway me, boy."

Tommy knew his grandmother well enough to put forth no further protests.

"Wait," Paulson said. "Before we go, I need to bury my wife."

Tommy looked to Mack and Annie and both nodded.

"You don't have to do it alone, we'll help," Tommy said.

"Thank you," Paulson replied, and as the birds chirped in the trees, the four of them got to work.

*   *   *

Driving toward Johnstown, they saw other groups of people banded together; thinking there was safety in numbers. Thinking that because they were armed and out in the open, they were amply prepared to fend off the zombies should any attack. Tommy could understand their rationale. The walking dead they saw were few and far between, a handful in a field here; there one by itself ambling along a wood-lined stretch of road. The enemy lacked all but the most rudimentary of intelligence. It moved at a speed only those citified folks, who equated roughing it as an occasional power outage, could think was any kind of serious threat.

Like those they'd left behind, the gatherings they encountered were comprised of hunters and outdoorsmen, National guardsmen and cops. These were people who'd fought for their country in the war. The look Tommy and the others saw in their eyes as they passed, showed absolute confidence in their abilities

We got no reason to worry, those looks said. *No reason to run and hide. When the shit goes down you better believe we're gonna be ready.*

Tommy wanted to yell at them, tell them what fools they were. Tell them their macho bullshit was going to get them and their families killed; that he'd seen it first hand. But there was no point. He knew they'd only jeer and pelt the car with empty beer cans, maybe send them packing with a bullet or two.

A few miles outside Johnstown, they saw a Harley with a sidecar, the man seated within holding a machine gun across his chest.

Mack had taken the black leather waistcoat off of one of the dead bikers back at Paulson's car. Annie had acquired a pair of sunglasses along with the leather jacket she'd found and the leather motorcycle cap. In her get-up she looked just crazy enough to be the genuine article. Tommy claimed the other leather jacket, leaving Paulson without any kind of disguise. He was middle-aged and bald down to his ears and would stick out like a sore thumb amongst a gang of bikers. Once they arrived at the encampment, Tommy thought it better he stay behind. Even if he went unrecognized by those who'd attacked him on the road, their chances of pulling this off would get a lot slimmer with him in tow. Nobody needed to say it out loud for it to be known.

The leather clad bikers looked back, saw Tommy and company carried weapons of their own and pulled over, leaving them no choice but to pass.

A mile or so down the road, the Harley came rumbling up from behind and pulled out into the oncoming lane, intending to overtake the car.

"Get down low in your seat," Mack said to Paulson and he did as he'd been told.

Mack looked out the window, nodded to the bikers as they passed. With his beard, waistcoat and rifle, he must have passed muster.

When they got in line with the front of the car, the bikers looked in at Tommy and Annie.

Tommy's hand tightened on the pistol in his lap.

Mack leaned forward from the backseat. "Take it easy."

Annie turned and looked at the two raiders checking her out.

She threw them the devil's horns hand gesture, just like she'd seen the kids do in a bar when the juke played some of that raucous head banging music.

"Christ, Grandma," Tommy moaned. "Cut it out."

Ignoring Tommy, Annie stuck out her tongue and wagged it at the bikers.

Incredulous, the two bikers looked at her, then at each other, then back at her and burst out laughing.

The mustached raider riding the Harley gave her an okay with his thumb and forefinger and winked, while the younger one with the machine gun blew her a kiss. They drove on, passing them by.

Some minutes later, the Harley ahead came to a fork and took the road that led down toward a sizable number of untended forage pastures, the alfalfa running high and wild, with woods to the far left. When they arrived at the fork, Annie turned the wheel to the right, taking them up the road that led to higher woodland terrain.

"You're going the wrong way," Paulson said, leaning forward.

"Please," Annie said. "Credit me with some intelligence."

Paulson looked to the other men for support but neither said a word. Tommy turned his attention back to the road down below that they ran parallel to while Mack removed his binoculars from his pack.

"Used to be a time," Annie said, navigating a bend in the road. "We had us a genuine commune of hippies living out this way. In a region where nothing much happens out of the ordinary, them hippies were quite the attraction. Fella that let them stay on his land, fella by the name of Fry, didn't think it was right, all them folk driving out here to gawk at the hippies living in his field. So he had an area cleared within those woods you seen down there, over yonder. Even laid out the cash for a generator. For a good long time Fry's hippies, as folk were wont to call them, lived in peace and seclusion. That was until they decided it was time to move on; all of 'em heading out to other places. For years now, Fry's hippie commune's sat empty, abandoned along with them young folks' ideals. But if there's an encampment of these bikers, or raiders, or whatever, I'd lay my last dollar down and bet that it's the old commune site where they're located."

The road leveled out, running alongside the tops of the trees occupying the embankment separating the upper road from the one below. Annie stopped the car and they all climbed out, Mack using his binoculars.

Even with the naked eye, Tommy could see an object moving along the other road beneath them and knew it had to be the two raiders riding the Harley and sidecar.

"They're slowing down," Mack said. "They just turned into an opening in the fence. There's a dirt path that leads through the hay to the woods."

Annie nodded. "There ya go. They're heading right for Fry's old hippie commune. Got to be."

Mack directed the binoculars ahead of the Harley and sidecar, to where the dirt path met the tree line. What he saw made no sense to him. Four armed bikers guarded what looked to Mack like an iron ramp used for forklifts to drive onto the backs of trucks when loading or unloading pallets. Now the loading ramp spanned what looked like a trench, serving as a bridge.

The woods on Fry's land had been cut back long ago. This resulted in the formation of a rough circle of sorts, with the woods surrounded on all sides by large open pastures. Grasping the purpose of the trench, Mack thought it likely traveled the tree line's entire length. Certainly it ran in either direction to the tree line's inward curve. Anything beyond the curve was out of sight.

"The main route into the place is under guard," Mack said. "We'll have to go in further along, where we can't be seen."

He opened his mouth to tell them about the trench, then decided against it. No point spooking them when soon enough they'd get a close up look for themselves.

*　*　*

Two miles past where the Harley turned, they stopped the car and set off across the pasture, pushing through the high alfalfa for the woods.

"Stay alert," Mack said. "If there's zombies in here with us, they could be on us before we knew it."

All of them heeded Mack's advice; listening for sounds of movement.

What Tommy took at first glance to be farming equipment were in fact earth movers, three in all, with mounds of earth between them. Looking the length of the trees to where they curved away, he saw further excavated mounds of earth.

Tommy's suspicions about the purpose of the earth movers and the mounds of dirt were confirmed when they arrived at the trench.

"Well, knock me down and steal my teeth," Annie said. "That's just about the craziest thing I ever saw in my life."

"They must have been prepping this place for months," Mack said. "Since this all first started."

The trench ran approximately twenty feet deep and between seven and eight across. With a good run up, Tommy felt pretty certain he could make it. The others, particularly his grandmother, he had his doubts about.

And if one of them failed and fell into the trench?

Even if they survived the drop, they would be dead within a matter of minutes. Only the zombie who'd broken its neck from the fall and lay flopping about uselessly at the bottom of the trench could be evaded. The rest, six directly below them and countless others all the way along on either side, would move in and devour anyone who fell short of making it across.

The zombies below them all had their arms raised and appeared almost as though they were waiting to be rescued from the trench. But Tommy knew the truth. They didn't want to be pulled out, they wanted to pull one of the four of them down inside with them.

Others were moving along the trench now, closing in from farther away.

"Maybe we should try for the bridge," Mack suggested. "See if we can take out those guards."

"Ah, phooey," Annie said. "It's an easy jump. What are ya, pussy?"

"Maybe Mack's right, Grandma," Tommy said. "This is too risky."

"Maybe he is," she said, walking back the way they'd come. She laid the shotgun on the ground. "And maybe he ain't."

She turned suddenly, mimicked spitting into both palms and rubbed them together, then came running full speed toward the trench. At the edge her legs lifted into the air. Silently she sailed over the trench, the zombies down below reaching up for her, heads following her trajectory, and down she came, landing safely on the other side.

"You did it, Grandma," Tommy said, awestruck.

"Well of course I did," Annie grinned, readjusting her leather biker's cap. "I might be old, but I'm not *that* old."

Tommy tossed the weapons across then Mack threw Annie his pack. Tommy went over next, followed by Mack.

Paulson stood on the other side, looking down at the living dead inside the trench. Their number had swelled on account of all the commotion, and now at least twenty were directly below, their grasping hands clutching at air, their throats issuing guttural moans.

"Don't think about it," Annie advised. "Like they say in the ads, just do it."

"I can't..." Paulson whimpered.

"Mister," Annie said. "It's you we're here for. Either you jump or we're coming back over and we can call the whole thing off."

"I showed you her picture," Paulson reasoned. "You know what she looks like. And you know I can't go inside that place. I'll be recognized. Once that happens we'll be finished."

"Why of all the lily-livered..."

Tommy put a hand on his grandmother's shoulder, stopping her mid-sentence.

"Let him stay here, Grandma," Tommy said.

"We need him to point her out to us," Annie argued. "If they took one girl you can bet your ass they took others. We'll never know which one's his for sure."

Tommy shook his head. "If he doesn't think he can make it, then..."

"No, wait. Your grandmother's right, Tom," Paulson said. "I have to do this."

From his pocket, Paulson withdrew the photograph he'd shown them of his daughter. He walked backwards, taking ten paces away from the trench. He kissed the photograph and looked at the portrait of the girl fondly, then he lowered his head and ran, arms pumping.

But he miscalculated and took off from the edge of the trench way too soon.

Because of this, his feet landed on the opposite side of the trench right on the edge. If one of his new friends had been able to snatch his hands or grab a hold of his clothing and pull him the rest of the way, Paulson might have made it. But instead, finding no purchase beneath his feet, his arms performed a wild wind-milling action, his feet going up and out from under him. Paulson dropped down into the trench, back-slamming the zombies waiting below.

Several of the animated dead were knocked to the ground, and Paulson lay there a moment amongst them, blinking up at Tommy, Annie, and Mack watching from above. Then the dead leaned in and claimed him. Paulson tried to scream, but one of the zombies stopped him with a kiss that ripped off his lips and most of his tongue. Issuing a gurgling wail, Paulson thrashed as their teeth sank into his arms, neck and face.

Chunks of bloody flesh filled their mouths, blood gushing from the wounds. His clothes were torn away, his shirt ripped open. Two zombies unwittingly worked side-by-side chewing into the soft fat of Paulson's paunch.

Tommy raised the rifle and aimed for Paulson's head.

"No," Mack said, a hand to the barrel forcing Tommy to lower the weapon. "One shot and we'll have those raiders all over us."

"He's right, son." Annie said.

Tommy knew they spoke the truth. He could only stand there and watch helplessly as the feeding frenzy continued down below. When he saw their dirt caked fingers unraveling Paulson's intes-tines, saw the innards burst between their teeth like they were biting into sausages, Tommy could watch no longer.

He staggered away into the woods.

Annie and Mack hurried to catch up to him.

"Tommy, it's over," Annie said. "It's almost dark. We should go back."

"Go if you want." Tommy said, his feet kicking up leaves. "But I'm going in there to get the girl."

"Tommy," Annie reasoned. "Think this over. Any agreement we made just died with Paulson. The place in the mountains, he didn't even tell us where it is. We have to think about ourselves now."

"She's right, Tom," Mack said. "If there's nothing to gain, what's the point?"

The look of disbelief on his face made it clear he thought they had to be from a different planet.

"If you really need a reason then I'll give you one," Tommy said. "If we rescue the girl, the agreement stands. This place, she'll know where it is."

Annie couldn't argue with his reasoning. She sighed. Nodded. "Okay," she said. "Let's get her and get the hell out of here."

* * *

Guided by floodlights visible throughout most of their trek through the woods, the whoops and cheers of the bikers, and the sounds of Thin Lizzy blasting from the outdoor sound system, Tommy, Annie and Mack entered the raiders' camp.

Soon they merged with the milieu and were absorbed into the microcosm without anyone so much as batting an eye.

They were certainly of no interest to Freewheelin' Frank, who, much to his surprise and delight, had acquired a degree of celebrity of late. Frank was giving the crowd just what they wanted; and boy did they love him for it. The idea of a trench to protect them from the zombies had been Taso's, but it was Frank's background in construction and knowledge of where they could steal the earth movers, that turned a moment of drunken inspiration into a reality. When he won Taso's respect and was promoted through the ranks to their leader's inner circle, Frank didn't think life could get any better. Then, shitfaced again, Taso had another of those eureka moments, proposing to Frank the idea of mounting a presentation of nightly games.

"We'll have guys on choppers with lances like they did in medieval times," Taso said, his eyes lit by the amphetamines and whiskey coursing through his blood. "Only instead of fighting each other, we'll have a zombie as the opponent, and the objective to impale the zombie through the head."

And they had it.

"We'll strap a zombie down and have a bike take off from a ramp and land on the zombie's head."

And they had it.

"We'll kidnap some people, arm them with an ax, and put them in a ring with a bunch of zombies, and if they win they get to live another day. We'll have…" Taso took a swig from the bottle. "We'll have a whole bunch of crazy shit."

And a whole bunch of crazy shit they had.

"Key to it all has gotta be safety," Taso went on. "We got too much of a good thing goin' here to have us a zombie outbreak pop up. That's why I'm coming to you with this, Frank. 'Cause I know you're the man who can get it done."

Frank took to his role as the camp's safety officer like a duck to water. If the zombie was just for killing, he had some of the boys chop its hands off and knock its teeth out with mallets. If it was for fighting the people they abducted, Frank used catch poles to hold the zombies down, while one of his team squirted a tube of Super glue into its mouth, then used a steel toe-capped boot to keep its jaws closed until the glue sealed the thing's lips together. When it was fight time, they used the catch poles to put them in the arena and reopened their mouths with a slice of a knife before turning them loose for battle. When Frank started inventing ideas for games of his own, he wasn't sure if Taso would berate him for getting ideas above his station. But the boss man loved them all. Loved every twisted idea Frank came up with, the sicker the better. And he loved Frank, too. Treated him like a brother. Even shared with him his personal stockpile of grade-A pussy.

And so here he was sitting inside the cab, working the levers that controlled the wrecking ball, the crowd cheering him on while Taso raised a bottle, saluting him all the while Frank grinned out at them, basking in their adulation.

Up on the scaffold that overlooked the arena, Taso sat in his leather Lazy Boy, too consumed by anticipation of a death foretold to notice the three strangers moving through the crowd below. He watched the wrecking ball move through the air on its chain, watched the witless cretin that used to be a human being and now had neither hands nor teeth, stare dumbly at the people on the other side of the fence. They shook their fists and yelled obscenities at the ghoul, who, at the sight of so much live flesh in such abundance, only stood there drooling, ignorant of its impending doom.

Taso leaned forward in his chair, his eyes following the ball as it swung toward the hapless idiot that didn't have the sense to get out of the way. The ball hit the zombie square in the chest, caved in its ribcage and sent it flying through the air.

The onlookers went wild, hooting and hollering with delight.

The dead thing, which was relatively fresh and still resembled the store clerk it used to be, down to the name badge **Paul**, lay on its back looking up, entirely unaware that its chest had collapsed, that the sharp protrusions of its blood slicked ribs were visible.

The wrecking ball swung into position over its head.

Inside the cab, Frank worked the levers. The ball dropped; its weight flattening the clerk's head so effortlessly that when the ball thudded into the ground, everything from the chest up was no longer visible.

Again the crowd roared their approval.

Frank worked the levers, raised the ball, and there were groans of delighted disgust from the spectators, all of them leaning forward against the mesh fence surrounding the arena to get a better look. Most of the zombie's flattened head adhered to the bottom of the wrecking ball as it lifted up off the ground. Then the back part, the mush that had been its skull, brains and eyes, fell off with a wet plop, leaving only scraps of the face and some hair clinging to the base of the ball.

Taso had to hand it to Frank. The man never ran out of new ways to snuff a zombie. But was the man becoming too popular? Was he any kind of threat to his position as leader of the raiders?

Taso didn't want to think about it; not now. Not when he was having so much fun watching the zombie killings. Instead, he directed his attention toward a recent acquisition; one that in the few hours since taking her he'd come to prize above all others.

She was down below, in the bar area, the hottest piece of ass he'd ever seen; and just sixteen. And to top it all off, the girl was pure fucking evil.

"You should have seen the look on my Mom's face," said Lisa Paulson, knocking back a shot of bourbon and taking a drag on her cigarette, regaling two hairy faced raiders. "When I stuck the knife in her chest. Fucking priceless."

"You're one cold bitch, Lisa," mused one of the men.

"Yeah," Lisa said, not noticing the three new people who sat at the bar and eavesdropped on her story. "Well, maybe if she'd done something about that creep putting his hands on me all these years, I might have thought twice about sticking her. I've only got one regret and that's letting Taso tie dear old Dad to that thing and send him off into the woods, instead of letting him see me off my Mom, and then letting me do him, too." She grinned dementedly. "At my leisure, of course."

Lisa, who had arranged the roadside attack two days prior, by contacting Taso on the CB radio from Joe Shelby's van, felt eyes upon her and spun around.

The old woman, who was in her sixties, looked away, as did the man with the beard. Only the boy, a kid around Lisa's age, kept his eyes on her.

"You got a problem, dick wipe?" Lisa sneered.

Tommy looked at the girl a moment longer; the girl who barely resembled the one in the photograph her father had shown him. Now she was made up with heavy make up and had cut her hair messily with a knife. Tommy shook his head and looked away from her.

"That's what I thought," Lisa said, downed another shot, then nodded to the two hairy guys who joined her as she went on her wobbly way through the bar crowd, heading back toward the scaffold Taso occupied.

The three of them turned and watched Lisa awkwardly swing herself onto the scaffold, flashing legs wrapped in fishnets and topped off with a tight leather mini she wore without underwear, leaving nothing to the imagination. One of Taso's men on the scaffold hauled her the rest of the way up and she plopped into Taso's lap, planted a sloppy kiss on his bearded face and earned herself an ass slap by way of reward. Taso pointed to a zombie in the arena who was being chain sawed to pieces by a fat man in a leather thong, and Lisa slapped her knee, guffawed and wet Taso's beard with another slobbery kiss.

Annie looked at Tommy. "Nice girl we risked life and limb to rescue."

"Leave it, Grandma," Tommy said. "You heard what he did to her."

Annie clucked her tongue. "Yep, a real class act, that one is."

"Just drop it, Grandma."

Annie faced forward, gestured for the barkeep, who was polishing a pair of oval shaped eye glasses on his shirt. He stood beneath a hand painted sign that read: **The rule of lead. You get bit you get dead.**

"Gimme a cold one," Annie said. "After the day I had I'm ready for it. Set these two fellas up as well."

"What about him?" the barkeep asked, grinning. "He got ID?" When none of them laughed, his smile dropped away. "That'll be three bullets. Paid in advance."

Annie sighed and reached into the pocket of her leather jacket. Onto the counter she deposited two shotgun slugs. "Keep the change," Annie said and pushed the slugs toward him.

The barkeep reached into a cooler, set three bottles of IC beer on the counter. It wasn't a real bar counter, just a collection of kitchen islands with Formica tops that had been bolted together.

Annie took a long swallow of her beer and Mack and Tommy did likewise.

"And now!" a tinny voice announced over the PA. "Witness a zombie being hoisted into the air and having all its limbs and head torn off simultaneously!"

The bar emptied out fast, with practically everyone inside jockeying for a good position over at the fenced in arena.

"This is some classy joint you fellas brought me to," Annie said. She took another long pull on her beer. "Real classy."

Annie was about to polish the bottle off and order another when a hand fell on her arm, the fingers digging deep through the leather and into her skin.

"What the fuck," a man's voice said, "are you doing wearing Chico's jacket?"

Annie turned and found a red-eyed, bearded biker baring his teeth at her. There were three more bikers behind him, all of them armed.

"You must be mistaken," Annie said. "Had this jacket almost as long as I've had gray in my hair."

"Fuck you have," growled the biker. "That jacket belonged to Chico. We left him wearing it where he fell. You wanna know how I know this? Before we joined up with Taso, me and Chico rode with a chapter out of Pittsburgh. Club by the name of The Pagans. My old lady Gail, God rest her, stitched that patch onto the back of the jacket you're wearing. I was there when she did it. Most people don't notice, but Gail ran out of black thread and had to finish the job with blue. So don't give me any shit about that being your jacket. It's Chico's and you stole it off his dead body. Admit it, you old bitch."

Tommy saw where the thread changed color as he took a cursory glance at the patch, which depicted the Norse fire-giant Surtr sitting on the sun, wielding a sword, plus the word 'Pagan' in red, white and blue.

He waited for the inevitable, and didn't have to wait long.

"Hey, now wait a minute," said one of the armed goons, stepping forward, inspecting Tommy's jacket. There were no patches on the back of his, just a grinning skull on one of the sleeves.

"Look at this, Rabbit," the goon said. "The kid's got on Rollo's jacket."

Rabbit, who'd earned his nickname because he liked to get hopped up on speed and fuck like the aforementioned furry animal, leaned across Annie's shoulder and studied the design.

"Looks like we got two thieves in our midst," Rabbit said, taking no interest in Mack, who, despite being seated alongside Annie and Tommy, wore only a black leather waistcoat with no identifiable features.

"What are you two?" Rabbit asked, his disgust taking the form of a sneer. "A pair of fucking parasites? They used to have a name for your kind. They used to call you ghouls. But I got a new name for you now." Rabbit pulled a .44 from the waist of his pants and aimed it at them. "Dead meat."

*　　*　　*

Annie and Tommy stumbled toward the arena, Rabbit and the other armed bikers kicking them in the seat of their pants and shoving them along. They were led to a latched gate and told to wait. Rabbit went over to Taso's scaffold, climbed up onto the platform, leaned in close to Taso and spoke in his ear, his finger jabbing toward Annie and Tommy, who had not only been stripped of their weapons but also the leather jackets that had condemned them to certain death.

"I'm sorry, Grandma," Tommy said. "If it wasn't for me..."

"Hush, now," Annie said. "You did a noble thing today, Tommy. You were willing to risk your life to help that man. Not for reward, but because he needed your help. Of course, as it turned out he was probably one of them pedophiles and his girl a heartless, psychotic bitch. But you didn't know that. If only your Mom and Dad could have seen you. You done them proud today, son."

"Thanks, Grandma," Tommy said, and they shared the beginnings of a hug before a biker at their rear used his recently acquired shotgun to separate them.

They parted in time to see the climax of the event out in the arena. Two trucks were revving their engines, a zombie's arm and leg attached by rope to the hitching post of each. Above, a crane operated by Freewheelin' Frank hoisted a length of rope into the air that was tied tight around the middle of the zombie's head. Inside the crane's cab, Frank honked the horn.

The people pressed up against the fence and those up on the scaffolds counted down.

"*Five...*" They bellowed. "*Four... Three... Two... One... Rip that fucking zombie a new one!*"

The drivers of both trucks floored the gas as Frank worked the crane. The zombie's head, arms and legs were ripped from its torso, geysers of blood blasting out from all five openings.

A cheer passed through the crowd, the volume of its frenzy and excitement eclipsing all that preceded it. The spectators' hands beat against the fence and bottles were raised in salute.

Out in the arena, the trucks dragged the body parts behind them through the dirt, leaving behind a red smear. Inside the decapitated head (which was still swinging on the rope attached to the crane) the zombie's eyes roved like it was at a tennis match, left to right, left to right, left to right.

Taso got up from his Lazy Boy, a sideways swiping hand commanding the crowd to fall silent. Slowly the cheers, whistles and applause diminished, the trucks came to a halt and cut their engines, and the only sound was the groan of the twisting hangman's rope tied to the crane.

Rabbit arrived back at the prisoners' side and opened the latched gate. Tommy and Annie were jostled into the arena, the barrels of guns urging them on until they stood in its center. Rabbit and his cohorts withdrew, leaving grandmother and grandson standing alone with hundreds of faces pressed to the fence looking in at them. Tommy saw two areas that were like cattle pens, both with zombies inside. One pen contained the handless, toothless variety, the other the kind with their mouths super glued shut.

"Today," Taso bellowed, "two of our finest soldiers fell in battle. And before their bodies were cold, two grave robbers stripped them of their coat of arms!" Taso had to wait for the boos and catcalls to fall quiet before continuing. "These grave robbers thought they could come here and pass themselves off as members of our clan. Thought they'd just come waltzing in and put their feet up and help themselves to all that we worked so hard to build."

A thunderous rumble of boos and hisses assailed Tommy and Annie from every direction.

"Grave robbers?" Annie muttered. "They left 'em lying in the middle of the road."

Another sweep of the hand earned Taso the crowd's attention.

"Now I'm not a greedy man. Share and share alike, that's always been my way. But when someone comes here thinking they can take what they want without showing me the common courtesy of asking me to share? Well, that's a direct insult; an insult to me and an insult to all of you, too. Well, now we're gonna show these two dirty lowlife scumbag motherfuckering freeloading leeches the price paid by those who dare to disrespect us."

The uproar was deafeningly loud.

Frank, who was just now climbing down from the crane, looked at Taso to see how many zombies he wanted released into the arena. Taso held up a hand, indicating five. Frank nodded and jogged away. But then Taso held up another hand.

Five more.

Then another and another and another hand until he reached twenty five in all; their entire inventory. That meant going out to the trench tomorrow and hauling some fresh ones out of it. But it would be worth it. These two had offended them all with their dirty tricks and nothing would satisfy the amassed raiders short of a full scale massacre.

Frank was about to go get an ax each for the old woman and kid to fight with when Taso held up a finger. He then shook it from side to side and mouthed the words, "no weapons."

Frank nodded, grinning widely. The two grave robbers were going to be executed...zombie style, and the crowd was going to love every second of it. Frank ran over to one of the pens, told the zombie wrangler standing at its gate Taso's orders. The man, who was bald, wore his goatee long, and whose massively developed arms and chest were covered in tats, opened the gate, allowing the first of the super glued zombies out into the arena.

The wrangler, who wore chemical handling rubber gloves, grabbed the first zombie around the throat from behind and used the hunting knife in his other hand to slice open the super glued lips. He gave the zombie a kick in the ass which sent it sprawling in the dirt, then returned to the pen to repeat the process.

Annie and Tommy backed toward each other while the zombies set free of their state of imprisonment moved across the arena toward them. The crowd cheered and rattled the fence, baying for their blood.

Up on the scaffold, Taso sat on the edge of his Lazy Boy throne, the girl Tommy and Annie had come to rescue curled up in his lap like a cat, both their eyes lit with anticipation.

"Looks like we're done for, son," Annie said.

Tommy didn't reply.

All twenty five zombies were released now; all slowly shambling across the arena in their direction. They could evade them easily but with nowhere to escape to, it was only a matter of time before the zombies tasted their flesh. Tommy was about to tell his grandma he loved her and apologize again for getting them into this.

But before he could speak, an explosion went off; its effects changing everything.

*　　*　　*

Ten minutes earlier.

Mack watched the raiders lead Annie and Tommy away from the bar, his rifle propped against the bar counter beside him, useless even if he were able to aim straight. They were outnumbered. Any move he made to save Tommy and Annie would only result in condemning himself to death along with them.

Other than the barkeep, the bar area was entirely empty.

As he racked his brain on what to do, he got an idea, and although he didn't much rate the chances of seeing it successfully transition to fruition, he figured what the hell, any idea was better than none at all.

"Say," Mack called to the barkeep, who was standing on tip-toe and looking out at the arena, getting the best view available to him of the zombie about to be torn limb from limb.

"What's that?" the barkeep asked, without turning his head.

"Those are some nice glasses you got on," Mack said. He set his rifle on the counter. "Would you be willing to trade?"

The man came over, looked at the rifle, took his glasses off and wiped them on his shirtfront. "Can't," he said. "I'd be half-blind without them. But I got lots of stuff back here to trade."

"Nah, not interested," Mack said. "Just the glasses is all I want."

"Sorry," the barkeep said. "No can do."

"Wrong answer," Mack said as he reached up and grabbed the back of the man's head and slammed it forward against the counter. The man dropped away to fall behind the counter. Mack hoped he'd only knocked him unconscious and hadn't caused the guy any serious damage. He seemed a decent enough type, for a raider.

On the other side of the bar, next to the unconscious man, Mack found the barkeep's glasses on the ground.

Thankfully, the lenses were still intact so he put them on. They were slightly weaker than his prescription, but not by much. And then Mack saw the weapons stashed in boxes beneath the counter and realized he was interested after all.

It appeared the days of needing nothing back there except a baseball bat were long gone.

*   *   *

Higher than Taso's scaffold, and located to the right of the bar, was a platform built to contain the main floodlight used to illuminate the arena. Mack climbed up and disabled the guard with a head blow from the butt of his rifle. Nobody saw a thing. All eyes were on the arena, on Annie, Tommy and the zombies advancing on them.

Mack returned to ground level and collected the gear from behind the bar that had helped him form his plan. With the strap of his rifle, along with his recent acquisition slung through his arm and over his shoulder, Mack climbed the scaffold a second time. Once he was back on the platform, he scanned the area below. He set his rifle beside him.

Zombies were moving in on Tommy and Annie from all sides and Mack knew he couldn't delay another second. He raised the shoulder launched RPG, sighted Taso's scaffold, said a short and silent prayer in his head, and fired.

*   *   *

The HE (High Explosive) warhead detonated upon impact. Pipes, couplers, boards, a section of torn and twisted fence, and the raider's upper echelon, all rained down into the arena. Most of the bikers' top dogs were blown to pieces and dead before the chunks hit the ground but a few were still alive. The wounds they'd sustained, lacerations that had sliced open their chests and bellies and spilled their innards across the dirt, drew the zombies' attention away from Tommy and Annie.

As the dead moved in to feed, the injured raiders could only lie there and scream.

Along with the downpour of debris came Taso and Lisa, who were still both seated in his Lazy Boy. Though Taso was now missing a leg and Lisa three fingers off one of her hands (the one she'd been using to massage Taso's inner thigh when the explosion ripped off his lower limb and the aforementioned digits), the Lazy Boy, being a model designed not only for comfort but also endurance, survived the blast and subsequent drop with surprising resilience. Chief among its injuries was an area of charred fabric, a chunk of stuffing ripped from the cushioned headrest, and the uncoiling of several springs, two of which tore through the seat and resettled in Taso's lower back, effectively pinning him to the chair.

The propulsion of steel springs through Taso's lower vertebrae wiped from his mind the pain and shock of losing his leg, raising the pitch of his screams an additional three octaves. To say he sounded like an opera singer gargling razorblades would be an understatement.

Mack didn't bother taking any of the grenades out of the gym bag (which was how he'd found the stockpile stashed under the bar counter). He just reached in and pulled the pin on one and then hurled the bag down into the crowd of bikers pressed closest to the fence.

The explosion took out close to fifty people and ripped a large part of the fence to shreds. The zombies below in the arena didn't know which way to turn; so widespread was the distribution of body parts. There were raiders' guts, heads, arms, legs, torsos and everything else a zombie might put on a wish list (had it such capabilities) of things it wanted most in the world.

Mack raised his rifle, lined up the zombie wrangler in his sights and made a fountain of his head. Freewheelin' Frank he shot in the groin, which he knew was pretty low, but this was about survival not playing nice.

Mack's woman, Wendy, had run off with a trucker four years ago, and the memory of coming home early one day and catching them going at it hell for leather in their matrimonial bed had forever burned like a fever inside his mind. Frank sort of looked like the guy. And since this was in all likelihood the last opportunity he'd get at achieving any kind of closure, Mack figured he might as well get what sense of satisfaction he could so he left Frank doubled over in the dirt, blood pissing out of the hole the bullet had torn in his Levi's, turning the crotch of the denim dark.

Across the arena, Tommy and Annie saw Mack silhouetted against the floodlight. They were not alone in locating the assassin in their midst. Guns were drawn and aimed. Bullets flew, one on them shattering the floodlight; another dropping Mack to his knees. He returned fire, dropping raiders, every shot sure of its target and ringing true.

"Let's go," Annie said.

"What about Mack?" Tommy asked.

Annie shook her head.

Tommy wanted to disagree but knew it would be a lie. There was not a gun in the camp aimed anywhere other than Mack's scaffold. Nobody could have that much lead directed at them and walk away from it.

If anybody had decided to help Taso and his girl before avenging them, and had thought to put down the zombies in the arena, they might have survived. But everyone was too busy firing on the scaffold, even though the man lying face down up there had to be dead by now. As it was, when the zombies shuffled toward him, Taso could only sit there, unable to pull himself free of the springs embedded deep in his spine, his terrified wails only helping to gain the attention of more of the walking dead.

Lisa saw the dead moving in and scrambled out of Taso's lap, all the while clutching her injured hand as she fell to her knees. Through the dust cloud caused by the collapsed scaffold, she saw two figures walking in her direction.

Behind her, Taso's screams reached a crescendo as teeth tore pieces from his tattooed arms, tore the meat right down to the bone, and dirt-caked fingers raked at his face, digging into his eyeballs and yanking out his tongue.

When Tommy saw Lisa, he knew that if he'd had a gun he would have shot her point blank without a moment's hesitation. So instead he drew his fist back, and for a moment he almost followed through.

Annie didn't try to stop him.

Tommy could have knocked her out, let the dead have her, and lived without her death ever bothering his conscience.

"Well?" Lisa asked, looking up at him. "What're you waiting for? Do it."

"Let's just shake hands and call it a day," Tommy said.

Lisa looked at the bones protruding through her shattered knuckles, at the places where three of her fingers should have been.

Her head dropped as she quietly wept, and Tommy was satisfied enough with what he saw to lower his fist and walk away.

*　　*　　*

One of the Harley's parked in a row of them still had the keys in the ignition. Tommy, who'd ridden a dirt bike back on the farm, thought he could handle it. Behind them in the arena, the raiders were shooting the zombies and putting bullets through the brains of their fallen own before they had the chance to return. Tommy kick-started the bike and Annie climbed on the back, wrapping her arms around his waist. They pulled out of the camp and headed along the dirt road that led away, back to the main road.

"I'd feel a lot safer if I had a weapon," Annie called over the sound of the hog's roaring engine. "We still gotta get past that trench and if we want to keep these wheels that means making it past them guards. And they're all armed."

"Grandma," Tommy called back to her. "We'll cross that bridge when we come to it."

Annie was about to jab him in the ribs for making such a feeble joke, but after the day they'd had she figured he'd probably lose control of the bike, so she thought better of it.

She held on tight and looked at the darkened trail ahead, hoping their luck would hold out long enough to make it safely through the night.

ABOUT THE WRITERS

Anthony Giangregorio is the author and editor of more than 25 novels, almost all of them about zombies. His work has appeared in *Dead Science* by Coscomentertainment, *Dead Worlds: Undead Stories Volumes* 1, 2 , 3, and 4, and an upcoming anthology (Zombology) by Library of the Living Dead Press and their werewolf anthology titled *War Wolves*. He also has stories in *End of Days: An Apocalyptic* Anthology Volumes 1 and 2

Check out his website at www.undeadpress.com

John Goodrich finds inspiration by listening to nocturnal, buzzing whispers that emanate from the Vermont's Green Mountains. His stories have been published in *Arkham Tales* and *Cthulhu Unbound*, and more are slated to appear in *Tales out of Miskatonic University* and *Cthulhu 2012*. To find out more, or just read some free fiction, visit his website at www.qusoor.com.

Jennifer Hudock is an author, poet, editor and podcaster from northeast Pennsylvania. She holds a BA in Creative Writing from Bloomsburg University and is an editor for the online literary arts journal, *eMuse Zine*. To learn more about her and her ongoing literary endeavors, visit her personal website: http://jenniferhudock.com

Kelly M. Hudson grew up in the wilds of Kentucky and currently resides in California. He has a deep and abiding love for all things horror and rock n' roll. If you wish to contact Kelly or find links to other stories he's had published, please visit www.kellymhudson.com for further details. Kelly thanks you for reading his dumb old story and wishes you and yours a very happy day!

Scott Michael Kessman currently resides in Long Island, New York, where he lives happily with his beautiful wife and two annoying cats. He has written numerous short fantasy and horror short stories, and his first fantasy novel, *"The Tales of Tanglewood: The Lon Dubh Whistle"* was published in 2007. The second novel in the *Tanglewood* series is now complete and will be published shortly. Both novels can be previewed at www.talesoftanglewood.com

Lance Looper is a copywriter in Austin, Texas and spends his days writing about the marvels of modern technology for his corporate overlords. His nights are spent with his wife Donna and their two loving but schizophrenic boxers. Contact Lance at lancelooper@yahoo.com.

Rick Moore, originally from Leicestershire, England, moved to the US ten years ago and now lives in Phoenix, AZ. Rick's fiction has appeared in numerous zines and anthologies, including *The Undead: Flesh Feast, History Is Dead, The Beast Within, Cthulhu Unbound, Harvest Hill, Dark Animus,* the 2009 Stoker nominated *Horror Library 3* and *Bound For Evil* (his inclusion in which still regularly sends Moore into a geekified frenzy of frothing at the mouth fanboy excitement as the collection also contains fiction by two of his childhood heroes, H.P. Lovecraft and Ramsey Campbell). To earn his daily crust, Rick works for the Arizona State Hospital as a Mental Health Specialist. Visit him online at http://www.myspace.com/zombieinfection

G.R. Mosca was born in Birmingham, England, is a graduate of Bard College and currently resides in Thomasville, Pennsylvania. He and his companion Annalisa are currently zombie-proofing their civil war era house and keeping an eye on the surrounding cornfields for any suspicious activity.

C.H. Potter was born and raised in the hills of Western New York. His work has also appeared *The Copperfield Review* and *Dead Worlds: Undead Stories Volume 1.*

Michael Presutti has been writing since the age of 19. He lives in Worcester county Massachusetts. His book *LAST WORDS* that was released in November 2008 has been receiving excellent reviews. The sequel *SHADOWS AND ASHES* will soon be finished. He is also working on a book of short stories.

Alison Seay writes as many different people. Once in a blue moon she writes as herself. This story is one of those instances.
Visit her at alisonseay.wordpress.com

Michael Simon resides in eastern Canada where he practices medicine in his spare time to support his writing habit. Published works have appeared in *Apex: Science Fiction and Horror, Andromeda Spaceways Inflight Magazine, The Sword Review, Ragged Edge, Drabble, Mindflights and Art* and *Prose*. He has been shortlisted for the AEON Award and Writers of the Future and has contributed to several anthologies including *Travel a Time Historic, Tall Tales* and *Short Stories and The Unknown*. Nonfiction articles have appeared in *Stitches Magazine, The Physician's Chronicle, Physician's Review, The Medical Post* and *Hockey Net*. Recent publications include a travel article in *Canadian Doctors Magazine* and horror stories in *Dead Worlds: Undead Stories Volumes 1 & 2*. *The Patron* will appear in the *Sunpenny Publishing Anthology* later this year.

Joe Tonzelli is a writer of short stories and screenplays. He currently resides just outside of Philadelphia and works as an editorial coordinator for a publishing company in Sewell, NJ.

DEAD MOURNING: A ZOMBIE HORROR STORY

by Anthony Giangregorio

Carl Jenkins was having a run of bad luck. Fresh out of jail, his probation tenuous, he'd lost every job he'd taken since being released. So now was his last chance, only one more job to prevent him from going back to prison. Assigned to work in a funeral home, he accidentally loses a shipment of embalming fluid. With nothing to lose, he substitutes it with a batch of chemicals from a nearby factory.

The results don't go as planned, though. While his screw-up goes unnoticed, his machinations revive the cadavers in the funeral home, unleashing an evil on the world that it has not seen before. Not wanting to become a snack for the rampaging dead, he flees the city, joining up with other survivors. An old, dilapidated zoo becomes their haven, while the dead wait outside the walls, hungry and patient.

But Carl is optimistic, after all, he's still alive, right? Perhaps his luck has changed and help will arrive to save them all?

Unfortunately, unknown to him and the other survivors, a serial killer has fallen into their group, trapped inside the zoo with them.

With the undead army clamoring outside the walls and a murderer within, it'll be a miracle if any of them live to see the next sunrise.

On second thought, maybe Carl would've been better off if he'd just gone back to jail.

DEAD TALES: SHORT STORIES TO DIE FOR

By Anthony Giangregorio

In a world much like our own, terrorists unleash a deadly disease that turns people into flesh-eating ghouls.

A camping trip goes horribly wrong when forces of evil seek to dominate mankind.

After losing his life, a man returns reincarnated again and again; his soul inhabiting the bodies of animals.

In the Colorado Mountains, a woman runs for her life, stalked by a sadistic killer.

In a world where the Patriot Act has come to fruition, a man struggles to survive, despite eroding liberties.

Not able to accept his wife's death, a widower will cross into the dream realm to find her again, despite the dark forces that hold her in thrall.

These and other short stories will captivate and thrill you.

These are short stories to die for.

THE NEXT EXCITING ADVENTURE IN THE DEADWATER SERIES!
DEAD SALVATION
BOOK 9
by Anthony Giangregorio

Henry Watson and his band of warrior survivalists roam what is left of a ravaged America, searching for something better.

HANGMAN'S NOOSE

After one of the group is hurt, the need for transportation is solved by a roving cannie convoy. Attacking the camp, the companions save a man who invites them back to his home.

Cement City it's called and at first the group is welcomed with thanks for saving one of their own. But when a bar fight goes wrong, the companions find themselves awaiting the hangman's noose.

Their only salvation is a suicide mission into a raider camp to save captured townspeople.

Though the odds are long, it's a chance, and Henry knows in the land of the walking dead, sometimes a chance is all you can hope for.

In the world of the dead, life is a struggle, where the only victor is death.

RANDY AND WALTER: PORTRAIT OF TWO KILLERS
by Tristan Slaughter

Randy Barcer lived his life the way he wanted to, joyfully slaughtering innocent women and children.

But sometimes he did much worse to them and those that died would be considered the lucky ones.

That is until he met Walter Brenemen, and he soon found out that this man who claimed to be his brother, was far more dangerous than Randy could ever hope to be.

"I'll give you the name of a woman and tell you where to find her. Then we'll see which one of us can get to her first. If you win, I'll leave you be. But if I win...well, I guess we'll just have to wait and see."

With those words, Walter changed Randy's life forever.

It was a simple game.

Whoever kills the most, wins; with a small town caught in the middle.

Forget what you know or think you know about horror. Let go of everything you've ever been taught about serial killers. Step into the world of Tristan Slaughter and discover what it is that makes a killer.

This is not your typical slasher novel.

This is:

Randy and Walter: Portrait of Two Killers.

You will never look at a man the same way again.

Welcome to a world of despair, desire, cruelty, punishment, pure evil and most of all...Death.

REVOLUTION OF THE DEAD
by Anthony Giangregorio
THE DEAD SHALL RISE AGAIN!

Five years ago, a deadly plague wiped out 97% of the world's population, America suffering tragically. Bodies were everywhere, far too many to bury or burn. But then, through a miracle of medical science, a way is found to reanimate the dead.

With the manpower of the United States depleted, and the remaining survivors not wanting to give up their internet and fast food restaurants, the undead are conscripted as slave labor.

Now they cut the grass, pick up the trash, and walk the dogs of the surviving humans.

But whether alive or dead, no race wants to be controlled, and sooner or later the dead will fight back, wanting the freedom they enjoyed in life.

The revolution has begun!

And when it's over, the dead will rule the land, and the remaining humans will become the slaves...or worse.

KINGDOM OF THE DEAD
by Anthony Giangregorio
THE DEAD HAVE RISEN!

In the dead city of Pittsburgh, two small enclaves struggle to survive, eking out an existence of hand to mouth.

But instead of working together, both groups battle for the last remaining fuel and supplies of a city filled with the living dead.

Six months after the initial outbreak, a lone helicopter arrives bearing two more survivors and a newborn baby. One enclave welcomes them, while the other schemes to steal their helicopter and escape the decaying city.

With no police, fire, or social services existing, the two will battle for dominance in the steel city of the walking dead. But when the dust settles, the question is: will the remaining humans be the winners, or the losers?

When the dead walk, the line between Heaven and Hell is so twisted and bent there is no line at all.

RISE OF THE DEAD
by Anthony Giangregorio
DEATH IS ONLY THE BEGINNING!

In less than forty-eight hours, more than half the globe was infected.

In another forty-eight, the rest would be enveloped.

The reason?

A science experiment gone horribly wrong which enabled the dead to walk, their flesh rotting on their bones even as they seek human prey.

Jeremy was an ordinary nineteen year old slacker. He partied too much and had done poorly in high school. After a night of drinking and drugs, he awoke to find the world a very different place from the one he'd left the night before.

The dead were walking and feeding on the living, and as Jeremy stepped out into a world gone mad, the dead spotting him alone and unarmed in the middle of the street, he had to wonder if he would live long enough to see his twentieth birthday.

DEADFREEZE
by Anthony Giangregorio

THIS IS WHAT HELL WOULD BE LIKE IF IT FROZE OVER!
When an experimental serum for hypothermia goes horribly wrong, a small research station in the middle of Antarctica becomes overrun with an army of the frozen dead.

Now a small group of survivors must battle the arctic weather and a horde of frozen zombies as they make their way across the frozen plains of Antarctica to a neighboring research station.

What they don't realize is that they are being hunted by an entity whose sole reason for existing is vengeance; and it will find them wherever they run.

DEAD WORLDS: Undead Stories
A Zombie Anthology Volume 1
Edited by Anthony Giangregorio

Welcome to the world of the dead, where the laws of nature have been twisted, reality changed.

The Dead Walk!

Filled with established and promising new authors for the next generation of corpses, this anthology will leave you gasping for air as you go from one terror-filled story to another.

Like the decomposing meat of a freshly rotting carcass, this book will leave you breathless.

Don't say we didn't warn you.

VISIONS OF THE DEAD
A ZOMBIE STORY
by Anthony & Joseph Giangregorio

Jake Roberts felt like he was the luckiest man alive.

He had a great family, a beautiful girlfriend, who was soon to be his wife, and a job, that might not have been the best, but it paid the bills.

At least until the dead began to walk.

Now Jake is fighting to survive in a dead world while searching for his lost love, Melissa, knowing she's out there somewhere.

But the past isn't dead, and as he struggles for an uncertain future, the past threatens to consume him.

With the present a constant battle between the living and the dead, Jake finds himself slipping in and out of the past, the visions of how it all happened haunting him.

But Jake knows Melissa is out there somewhere and he'll find her or die trying. In a world of the living dead, you can never escape your past.

**DEAD WORLDS: Undead Stories
A Zombie Anthology Volume 2**
Edited by Anthony Giangregorio

Welcome to a world where the dead walk and want nothing more than to feast on the living.

The stories contained in this, the second volume of the Dead Worlds series, are filled with action, gore, and buckets and buckets of blood; plus a heaping side of entrails for those with a little extra hunger.

The stories contained within this volume are scribed by both the desiccated cadavers of seasoned veterans to the genre as well as fresh-faced corpses, each printed here for the first time; and all of them ready to dig in and please the most discerning reader.

So slap on a bib and prepare to get bloody, because you're about to read the best zombie stories this side of Hell!

THE DARK
by Anthony Giangregorio
DARKNESS FALLS

The darkness came without warning.

First New York, then the rest of United States, and then the world became enveloped in a perpetual night without end.

With no sunlight, eventually the planet will wither and die, bringing on a new Ice Age. But that isn't problem for the human race, for humanity will be dead long before that happens.

There is something in the dark, creatures only seen in nightmares, and they are on the prowl. Evolution has changed and man is no longer the dominant species. When we are children, we're told not to fear the dark, that what we believe to exist in the shadows is false.

Unfortunately, that is no longer true.

SOULEATER
by Anthony Giangregorio

Twenty years ago, Jason Lawson witnessed the brutal death of his father by something only seen in nightmares, something so horrible he'd blocked it from his mind.

Now twenty years later the creature is back, this time for his son.

Jason won't let that happen.

He'll travel to the demon's world, struggling every second to rescue his son from its clutches.

But what he doesn't know is that the portal will only be open for a finite time and if he doesn't return with his son before it closes, then he'll be trapped in the demon's dimension forever.

FAMILY OF THE DEAD
A Zombie Anthology
by Anthony, Joseph and Domenic Giangregorio

Clawing their way out of the wet, dark earth, these tales of terror will fill you with the deep seated fear we all have of death and what comes next.

But if that wasn't bad enough to chill your soul, these undead tales are penned by an entire family of corpses. The zombie master himself, Anthony Giangregorio, leads his two young ghouls, his sons Domenic and Joseph Giangregorio, on a journey of terror inducing stories that will keep you up long into the night.

As you read these works of the undead, don't be alarmed by that bump outside the window.

After all, it's probably just a stray tree branch...or is it?

DARK PLACES
by Anthony Giangregorio

A cave-in inside the Boston subway unleashes something that should have stayed buried forever

Three boys sneak out to a haunted junkyard after dark and find more than they gambled on.

In a world where everyone over twelve has died from a mysterious illness, one young boy tries to carry on.

A mysterious man in black tries his hand at a game of chance at a local carnival, to interesting results.

God, Allah, and Buddha play a friendly game of poker with the fate of the Earth resting in the balance.

Ever have one of those days where everything that can go wrong, does? Well, so did Byron, and no one should have a day like this!

Thad had an imaginary friend named Charlie when he was a child. Charlie would make him do bad things. Now Thad is all grown up and guess who's coming for a visit?

These and other short stories, all filled with frozen moments of dread and wonder, will keep you captivated long into the night.

Just be sure to watch out when you turn off the light!

THE MONSTER UNDER THE BED
by Anthony Giangregorio

Rupert was just one of many monsters that inhabit the human world, scaring children before bed. Only Rupert wanted to play with the children he was forced to scare.

When Rupert meets Timmy, an instant friendship is born. Running away from his abusive step-father, Timmy leaves home, embarking on a journey that leads him to New York City.

On his way, Timmy will realize that the true monsters are other adults who are just waiting to take advantage of a small boy, all alone in the big city.

Can Rupert save him?

Or will Timmy just become another statistic.

The Lazarus Culture
by Pasquale J. Morrone

Secret Service Agent Christopher Kearns had no idea what he was up against. Assigned on a temporary basis to the Center for Disease Control, he only knew that somehow it was connected to the lives of those the agency protected...namely, the President of the United States. If there were possible terrorist activities in the making, he could only guess it was at a red alert basis.

When Kearns meets and befriends Doctor Marlene Peterson of the Breezy Point Medical Center in Maryland, he soon finds that science fiction can indeed become a reality. In a solitary room walked a man with no vital signs: dead. The explanation he received came from Doctor Lee Fret, a man assigned to the case from the CDC. Something was attached to the brain stem. Something alive that was quickly spreading rapidly through Maryland and other states.

Kearns and his ragtag army of agents and medical personnel soon find themselves in a world of meaningless slaughter and mayhem. The armies of the walking dead were far more than mere zombies. Some began to change into whatever it was they ate. The government had found a way to reanimate the dead by implanting a parasite found on the tongue of the Red Snapper to the human brain.

It looked good on paper, but it was a project straight from Hell.

The dead now walked, but it wasn't a mystery.

It was The Lazarus Culture.

END OF DAYS: AN APOCALYPTIC ANTHOLOGY
Edited by Anthony Giangregorio

Our world is a fragile place.

Meteors, famine, floods, nuclear war, solar flares, and hundreds of other calamities can plunge our small blue planet into turmoil in an instant.

What would you do if tomorrow the sun went super nova or the world was swallowed by water, submerging the world into the cold darkness of the ocean?

This anthology explores some of those scenarios and plunges you into total annihilation.

But remember, it's only a book, and tomorrow will come as it always does.

Or will it?

DEADFALL
by Anthony Giangregorio

It's Halloween in the small suburban town of Wakefield, Mass.
While parents take their children trick or treating and others throw costume parties, a swarm of meteorites enter the earth's atmosphere and crash to earth.

Inside are small parasitic worms, no larger than maggots.

The worms quickly infect the corpses at a local cemetery and so begins the rise of the undead.

The walking dead soon get the upper hand, with no one believing the truth.

That the dead now walk.

Will a small group of survivors live through the zombie apocalypse?

Or will they, too, succumb to the Deadfall.

ANOTHER EXCITING CHAPTER IN THE DEADWATER SERIES!

DEAD CITY
by Anthony Giangregorio
BOOK 3
NEW PERILS IN AN UNDEAD WORLD

After narrowly surviving an attack by a large pack of blood thirsty, wild dogs, Henry and his companions stumble upon an enclave that has made its home in an abandoned shopping mall.

Hoping for a respite from the perils of the walking dead, Henry and the others plan to settle down for the winter, safe in the company of fellow survivors of the zombie apocalypse.

But unknown to the group is the dark secret the enclave keeps, a secret that could threaten to destroy the companions and anyone else unfortunate enough to be caught in the trap.

In a dead world the only thing still living... is hope.

DEADTOWN: A DEADWATER STORY
BOOK 8
By Anthony Giangregorio

WORLD OF THE DEAD

The world is a very different place now. The dead walk the land and humans hide in small towns with walls of stone and debris for protection, constantly keeping the living dead at bay.

Social law is gone and right and wrong is defined by the size of your gun.

UNWELCOME VISITORS

Henry Watson and his band of warrior survivalists become guests in a fortified town in Michigan. But when the kidnapping of one of the companions goes bad and men die, the group finds themselves on the wrong side of the law, and a town out for blood.

Trapped in a hotel, surrounded on all sides, it will be up to Henry to save the day with a gamble that may not only take his life, but that of his friends as well.

In a dead world, when justice is not enough, there is always vengeance.

ANOTHER EXCITING CHAPTER IN THE DEADWATER SERIES!

DEADRAIN
BOOK 2
By Anthony Giangregorio
Welcome to the New America, population: 0

When a bacterial outbreak contaminates America's lower atmosphere, the resulting rain mutates into a deadly conduit for death.

Human's all over America are exposed and within a matter of days society has crumbled and the walking dead rule the land.

The America we know is gone, replaced by a new order; where the dead walk and humans are the prey.

Henry Watson and his small group of companions travel the country, searching for someplace better, someplace where the rain is safe.

In the New America the rules have changed; survive or perish.